Praise for the Welcome Back to Scumble River Mysteries

"Based on this delightful entry, this cozy series should have a long, bright future."

—*Publishers Weekly* for *Dead in the Water*

"It's a pleasure for Swanson's readers to welcome back her Scumble River characters, even though she throws them into danger from the first chapter to the last. A tornado, a corpse, and a kidnapping make life in Scumble River challenging for Skye Denison-Boyd as she awaits the birth of her first child, but fans of Swanson's series know she can handle it all. Swanson's strongly drawn characters and vivid descriptions make this welcome return of her Scumble River series a pleasure to read."

—Sheila Connolly, *New York Times* bestselling author of *Buried in a Bog*, for *Dead in the Water*

"Rejoice, Scumble River fans! Skye and Wally and the whole gang are back—and Denise Swanson proves once again that she is among the top writers of the genre. With more twists and turns than a tornado—a real tornado!—*Dead in the Water* is fast-paced and fun, with a smart, savvy protagonist, some truly sinister villains, a suspenseful plot, and a delightfully satisfying ending. I can't wait to visit Scumble River again!"

—Kate Carlisle, *New York Times* bestselling author, for *Dead in the Water*

"Denise Swanson is one of my favorite cozy mystery authors, and *Dead in the Water* is yet another hit from her. I love that Denise Swanson has remained true to the heart of the Scumble River characters and atmosphere in her reboot of the series. If you love quirky characters combined with a darned good cozy mystery, then don't hesitate to give *Dead in the Water* a try. You won't regret it!"

—*Fresh Fiction* for *Dead in the Water*

"The writing is flawless."

—*Cozy Review* for *Come Homicide or High Water*

"*Come Homicide or High Water* is a marvelous addition to this series. I can't wait for my next trip to Scumble River."

—*Escape with Dollycas* for *Come Homicide or High Water*

Praise for the Chef-to-Go Mysteries

"Once again, Denise Swanson demonstrates why her books are bestsellers. In *Tart of Darkness*, the first of her new Chef-to-Go Mystery series, Swanson delightfully delivers murder, intrigue, and romance as she introduces us to Dani Sloan and a lively cast of supporting characters. Fast-paced and fun—as is Swanson's style—*Tart of Darkness* is utterly unputdownable. I cannot wait to revisit Dani's B&B in the next installment of what's sure to be a long-lived, well-loved series."

—Julie Hyzy, *New York Times* bestselling author, for *Tart of Darkness*

"Denise Swanson's new Chef-to-Go Mystery series is off to a delicious start with *Tart of Darkness*. Readers will enjoy rooting for Dani and her young tenants as they work to solve the perplexing murder in this tasty tale, full of warmth and charm."

—Cleo Coyle, *New York Times* bestselling author of the Coffeehouse Mysteries, for *Tart of Darkness*

"Fans of Joanne Fluke and Diane Mott Davidson will enjoy the cooking frame, the sympathetic characters, and the small-town setting."

—*Booklist* for *Tart of Darkness*

"With each turn of the page, I became deeper ensconced into this mystery. Twist after twist truly kept me guessing."

—*Escape with Dollycas* for *Leave No Scone Unturned*

Also by Denise Swanson

Welcome Back to Scumble River
Dead in the Water
Die Me a River
Come Homicide or High Water

Chef-to-Go Mysteries
Tart of Darkness
Leave No Scone Unturned
Winner Cake All

BODY Over TROUBLED WATERS

DENISE SWANSON

Poisoned Pen
PRESS

Copyright © 2021 by Denise Swanson Stybr
Cover and internal design © 2021 by Sourcebooks
Cover illustration © Traci Deberko

Published by Poisoned Pen Press, an imprint of Sourcebooks
P.O. Box 4410, Naperville, Illinois 60567-4410
(630) 961-3900
sourcebooks.com

Library of Congress Cataloging-in-Publication Data

Names: Swanson, Denise, author.
Title: Body over troubled waters / Denise Swanson.
Description: Naperville, Illinois : Poisoned Pen Press, [2021] | Series:
   Welcome back to Scumble River ; book 4
Identifiers: LCCN 2020054457 (print) | LCCN
2020054458 (ebook) | (paperback) | (epub)
Classification: LCC PS3619.W36 B64 2021 (print) | LCC PS3619.W36 (ebook)
   | DDC 813/.6--dc23
LC record available at https://lccn.loc.gov/2020054457
LC ebook record available at https://lccn.loc.gov/2020054458

Printed and bound in Canada.
MBP 10 9 8 7 6 5 4 3 2 1

CHAPTER 1

First Time Ever I Saw Your Face

A S SCHOOL PSYCHOLOGIST SKYE DENISON-BOYD WAITED for the Scumble River school district superintendent's impromptu meeting to begin, she squirmed on the uncomfortable metal folding chair. With few exceptions, these types of seats seemed to be designed for individuals with much smaller derrières than hers. She'd always tended toward a rounder figure than was socially acceptable, but her recent pregnancy had certainly increased her already generous curves.

Closing her eyes, Skye took a deep cleansing breath in an attempt to regain the feeling of serenity she'd had when she arrived at school—before being summoned from her office. Immediately, the list of urgent psychological evaluations waiting for her attention danced in her head.

She worried her lower lip, wondering how far behind the superintendent's spur-of-the-moment summons would put her. This was so not how she'd planned to begin her week.

Glancing around Scumble River High's cavernous auditorium, Skye noted that the rest of the staff seemed equally unhappy to be have their Monday morning appropriated by Dr. Wraige's unscheduled gathering. The only employees

in the building who had been excused where those who had
hall monitoring duty. They would be informed about the big
announcement by their team leader.

Skye's best friend, Trixie Frayne, the high school librarian, sat with one shapely leg crossed over the other. Her foot
swung back and forth, a kitten-heeled magenta suede pump
dangling off her toes.

From the look on Trixie's face, Skye figured her friend
was either plotting her next book—her agent was trying to
sell the first one—or thinking about everything she had to do
before the students arrived and descended on the multimedia
center. When her nut-brown eyes widened and she dug into
her bag for a pencil, Skye decided it was the former.

On Skye's other side, Piper Townsend, the school psych
intern, sat as if at attention. Her feet, shod in sensible low-
heeled black pumps, were firmly planted on the floor, her
knee-length pleated skirt was tucked around her legs, and she
had a notepad open on her lap. Pen poised, ready to capture
whatever vital information the superintendent was about to
impart, Piper faced the stage nearly quivering in anticipation.

A screech from the PA system refocused Skye's attention,
and she turned her head in time to see district superintendent
Shamus Wraige striding across the stage. Homer Knapik,
the high school principal, walked the appropriate three paces
behind his boss.

Skye shivered. In order to save money on heating bills, the
building's boiler was turned down over the weekend. It took
several hours to bring the school's interior up to its normal
temperature on Mondays, and the auditorium was still chilly.

So why was Dr. Wraige's forehead damp and beads of
sweat running off his chin?

What in the world was he about to announce?

When the superintendent picked up the microphone,

Skye noticed that his hand trembled so badly the mic shook as if he were playing it like a tambourine, but when he spoke his voice was strong. "Beginning today, Scott Ricci will no longer be working at the high school."

A murmur from the audience rose and Skye looked at Trixie. Her friend shrugged. She clearly had no idea Scott had been fired either.

The superintendent continued, "I've finally convinced the board members that a community like ours really has no need for a glorified security guard in its schools." He chuckled. "It's not as if anyone here is going to pull a Columbine or a Sandy Hook. We don't have crazy people like that in our little town."

Appalled at both the administrator's cavalier attitude toward those tragedies and his appalling lack of understanding about when and where that type of violence occurred, Skye fought to keep her expression neutral. She really would have to send him a memo outlining the statistics surrounding those kinds of shootings.

Due to the choices he'd made in his personal life, the superintendent had never been Skye's favorite person, but at least, unlike Principal Knapik, Dr. Wraige had previously displayed a reasonable grasp of educational rules and regulations. In addition, he was savvy enough to realize that following those rules and regs helped keep the district from being sued or denied funding.

A desire that, sadly, was the superintendent's prime motivation, so he often acted with expediency rather than choosing what was best for the students. And in this case, his expediency could very well put everyone in the high school at risk.

A month or so ago, Skye and Dr. Wraige had come to an uneasy pact. She had handled a sticky situation and he had agreed to treat the position of school psychologist with the respect the profession deserved. This respect included adequate space in which to do the job and an increased budget for supplies and equipment.

Too bad Skye hadn't realized that she needed to negotiate continued employment for the support staff she relied on to make her job easier. Which position was next on the superintendent's list to be eliminated?

Forcing herself to remain calm, Skye reminded herself that anger never solved anything. In order to deal successfully with Dr. Wraige, she needed all the facts.

Concentrating, she heard Dr. Wraige continue, "By replacing our present safety officer with an attendance and residency investigator, we'll be able to ensure that our district receives all the funding that is due to us. In addition, we will make sure that the students benefiting from our wonderful school system actually live within our district boundaries. Those despicable individuals trying to scam the system by claiming residency for children who do not in fact reside with them will be thwarted."

Piper and Skye exchanged a troubled look. While Skye had been out on maternity leave, the school psych intern had been involved in a contested residency issue with Homer. Was this a response to that incident?

While the superintendent droned on about the increased funding that they would be able to secure with less truancy and how much money they would save by kicking out students who didn't live within the district limits, Skye worried about who would take up the slack left by the safety officer's departure.

Granted, Scott had only been at the school for the past year and a half. But he'd quickly filled a gap Skye hadn't even been aware existed.

In addition to keeping the students and faculty safe, Scott had helped with conflict mediation, worked with parents seeking information about substance abuse, and talked to kids who had problems. With him gone, Skye, Piper, and the high school's all-but-useless guidance counselor would have to shoulder those additional duties.

"We will be using the twenty-eight thousand dollars per year that we paid Officer Ricci to be here sixteen hours a week," Dr. Wraige's voice broke into Skye's thoughts, "as part of our new full-time attendance and residency investigator's salary."

"Where's the rest of the money coming from?" Someone in the audience—Skye was pretty sure it was the physical education teacher—shouted.

Her guess was validated when that same voice continued, "It better not be coming from our sports program or our stadium fund."

The superintendent briefly frowned at the interruption, but then pasted a fake smile on his face. "You all will be happy to hear that the money is available to us through a grant that I personally was able to secure for this new position." He held up his hands palms outward as if to placate them. "No programs or building improvements will be impacted financially in any way."

With the assurance that the cash wasn't coming from the teachers' line in the budget, the rumblings in the audience subsided and Skye mentally shook her head. Not that she blamed the rest of the faculty. They probably saw little reason for Scott's presence.

Most of the staff were unaware of the problems that the safety officer prevented. And it was hard for the majority of the faculty to imagine a sleepy little town in central Illinois, like Scumble River, ever having the kind of violence that the majority of them only saw on TV.

As Skye checked her watch, hoping she'd have time to

prepare for her first period evaluation before classes began, Dr. Wraige raised his voice and announced, "Now, I would like you all to welcome Tavish Wraige, our new attendance and residency investigator."

There was a polite spattering of applause as a thirtyish man wearing a stylish blue suit with a matching checked shirt and navy tie joined the superintendent at the podium. Both men were solidly built, but the younger one was several inches taller than the older one.

And while Dr. Wraige's hair had faded to rust and receded into a bushy Bozo-style half-moon around his head, Tavish's was a true red and his curls were clipped close to his scalp. Similar teak-brown eyes surveyed the audience.

Skye stared at the duo as she rubbed her chin. Wraige was an unusual surname and the resemblance was remarkable. Tavish may have a more muscular chest and broader shoulders, but he had to be a fairly close relative of the superintendent—maybe even his son.

Searching her memory, Skye realized that she knew very little about Dr. Wraige. He had been hired as the district superintendent during the twelve years that she had spent away from Scumble River—first as she attended college, then worked in the Peace Corps, and finally went to graduate school. By the time she'd moved back to town, he was firmly established in his role of head honcho.

Outside of school, she and the superintendent didn't travel in the same social circles. And the few times she'd interacted with him in his role as the district's chief administrator, their encounters had been strictly professional and blessedly brief.

Strangely, considering the inherently gossipy nature of a small town like Scumble River, she'd never heard much talk about him. The only piece of personal information she knew about him, she'd learned in her role as the local police's psych consultant. It was during a murder investigation and it centered on his unusual sex life, which included kinky goings-on with women other than his wife.

Skye closed her eyes and pushed the image away. She had tried hard to get the picture of Dr. Wraige dressed in leather, wielding a whip, out of her head and was very sorry it had popped back into her thoughts.

Back then, there had been no talk of Dr. Wraige having children. However, considering that the superintendent was in his late fifties, perhaps that was because none of his offspring lived in town. If he had sons or daughters, they would most likely be adults. Which coincided perfectly with the age of their new attendance and residency investigator.

Skye sat through the remainder of the meeting as Dr. Wraige extolled Tavish's extensive qualifications for the position, considering her next step.

Without any warning, Dr. Wraige stopped talking and hurried across the stage. His newest employee followed him. When they both disappeared behind the curtain, the audience took that, and the sound of the first bell, as permission to get to their classrooms, and surged out of the auditorium.

Making a snap decision, Skye told Piper and Trixie not to wait for her. Then, instead of following the crowd out into the corridor, she ran up the steps to the stage and hurried after the superintendent. He was doubtlessly heading for the theater's back exit. It opened to the school's rear hallway, which ended at the door to the parking lot.

If she didn't catch up with Dr. Wraige now, she'd have to make a formal appointment to talk to him later. The knowledge that any request for a meeting would most likely be met with delay after delay caused Skye to put on a burst of speed.

Jogging through the various cartons, theater props, and

other detritus that occupied the offstage area, her footsteps stuttered to an abrupt stop just before she reached the exit.

She could see the two men standing in the open door. Both wore disgruntled expressions.

Dr. Wraige had his hand on the younger guy's arm as he said, "Son, I pulled a lot of strings and promised a lot of favors to get you here. You need to hold on to this job because I won't rescue you again."

"Did I ask for your help?" Tavish retorted and walked away.

Skye waited a few seconds, then cleared her throat to get the superintendent's attention and said, "Dr. Wraige, may I speak to you for a moment?"

"Make it quick." Scowling, he swung toward her. Instantly his demeanor morphed into a bland smile and he replied, "Mrs. Denison-Boyd, are you finally back from your maternity leave?"

"I am." Skye returned his smile with the exact same degree of warmth as he'd given her, which is to say tepid. "For several weeks now."

"That must be why Homer hasn't been whining as much about having to deal with parents." Dr. Wraige moved toward her, stopping only inches short of invading her personal space. "What can I do for you?"

Skye had noticed that the superintendent often used his size to intimidate people, and while he had a good six inches in height on her, she was no lightweight. Refusing to step back, which she suspected he intended her to do, Skye instead moved slightly forward.

He involuntarily leaned away, and before he could recover, Skye said, "So Tavish is your son? I didn't realize you had children."

"My first wife and I had a son together. He stayed with

his mother after our divorce." Dr. Wraige adjusted his tie. "As of yet, the present Mrs. Wraige and I do not have any children together. But you never can tell. Nanette's biological clock is certainly still ticking." He winked. "At least for a little while longer."

"Oh, I see." Skye was a bit taken aback at his oversharing and didn't know where to go from there. "Right."

She was aware his wife was much younger, so, as he said, a second family was possible. Still, most men the superintendent's age were generally looking forward to being grandfathers, not parents of a newborn.

"Is that all you wanted to talk to me about?" Dr. Wraige tilted his head. "Because I need to use the restroom and then get back to my office."

"No," Skye quickly replied. "Sorry. I was just wondering what the duties of our new attendance and residency investigator will involve. You really didn't elaborate on them at the meeting."

"Like the title implies, he'll mostly be dealing with truancy and looking into students we suspect do not truly live in our district," Dr. Wraige answered.

"What about all the issues Scott Ricci handled?" Skye asked.

Dr. Wraige snickered and shook his head dismissively. "Surely you aren't worried that we're about to have a mass shooting event."

"Although that isn't my primary concern, an incident like that isn't as improbable as you seem to believe. In fact, I'll send you the latest report from the National Association of School Psychologists." Noting his uninterested expression, she added, "We live in a rural area where nearly every household has at least one gun and kids are taught to hunt at very young ages."

The superintendent frowned and crossed his arms. "I hope you aren't—"

She interrupted. "I'm not saying that's a bad thing. Obviously since I'm married to police officer and grew up on a farm, I'm not suggesting that guns are evil. What I am saying is that a troubled adolescent would have access to a vast array of weapons."

"Then you'll be glad to know Tavish was an MP in the army and is as qualified as Mr. Ricci to keep our school safe. In addition, as he is a full-time employee versus Mr. Ricci's part-time status, it is much more likely that he'll actually be on-site in case of an emergency." Dr. Wraige raised a rust-colored brow. "Anything else?"

"Yes." Skye was relieved to hear that the new guy had safety training, but she was still concerned about Scott's other duties. "What about handling conflict mediation among the students, working with parents seeking information and help with their child's substance abuse, and talking to kids who have problems?"

"Isn't all of that in your area of expertise?" Dr. Wraige smirked.

"It is," Skye agreed. "But there is only one of me and I'm split between three schools. You may recall we have never been able to hire a social worker that lasted very long, which means I end up taking on most of those responsibilities too."

"How about Ms. Townsend?" Dr. Wraige countered, then swayed as if he were dizzy. "And the guidance counselor?"

"Piper will be gone at the end of the May when her internship ends." Skye shrugged. "And sadly, the guidance counselor only handles scheduling. He claims to be too busy with his duties as football coach to be involved with anything else. Quite frankly, with all the great guidance counselors out there, I have to wonder why his behavior is tolerated."

Dr. Wraige made a noncommittal sound, then backed toward the still open door. "Look, I really need to use the restroom, so let's see how it goes. Maybe Ms. Townsend would be willing to take a position here after her internship is complete. I'll look into finding the funds to hire her or another psych."

"That would be great." Skye wasn't about to hold her breath, but she added, "Even a part-time person would be wonderful."

As he hurried away, he threw a dart over his shoulder. "It might be helpful if you talked to your godfather. As president of the school board, he'd be able to deliver the votes I'd need to add a position."

And there it was. The reminder that, like Tavish, Skye, too, owed her job to nepotism. She should have realized he would bring up the circumstances of her own employment.

Of course, no one had been fired so she could be hired. And in all the years that she'd been working for the districts, they'd had significant difficulty securing additional support personal.

Before Skye could come up with a pithy response to yell after the superintendent's retreating figure, the wall-mounted alert beacon next to the backstage exit began to flash and a loud siren stared to blare, "School lockdown in effect. Go into the nearest room, lock the doors, turn off the lights, and remain silent."

CHAPTER 2

Draw Back Your Bow

S ON OF A BISCUIT!" CHIEF OF POLICE WALLY BOYD SLAMMED down the telephone.

His wife, Skye, would have a fit when she found out that her godfather, Charlie Patukas, was under investigation by the state police. But that wasn't the worst of it. The woman Wally was truly afraid of was his mother-in-law. May would lose her ever-loving mind when she heard the news.

Speaking of which, he clicked his mouse and brought up the PD's work schedule.

Phew! May was working her normal afternoon shift. She wasn't due into the station until three thirty, and by then he'd make sure he was busy elsewhere.

Having his wife's mom employed as one of the department dispatchers was tricky at the best of times. But with the man who had been May's father figure for nearly half a century currently under arrest, Wally could only imagine what she might say or do or destroy in her quest to save him.

Wally leaned his head on the backrest of his chair and gazed at the ceiling. He probably should have given Skye a heads-up that the state police were looking into the allegedly illegal goings-on at the motel that Charlie owned. Then she could have prepared her mother for the possibility of his arrest.

Not that anything could have adequately prepared May, but she might have taken the news better from Skye and at least she'd be used to the idea by now.

Normally, as the Scumble River Police psychological consultant, Skye would have been read in on the sting taking place in their jurisdiction. However, because of her close ties to the suspect, the detective in charge had sworn Wally to secrecy.

In fact, he had been warned not to inform any of his staff. Scumble River was too small, and Charlie too influential, to risk a leak.

The state police probably only told Wally because they needed his help in concealing their investigation. They'd requested that he keep his officers' patrol routes away from the Up A Lazy River Motor Courts and direct any calls to the PD from the motel phones to a special number.

Squaring his shoulders, Wally flipped open the folder sitting in front of him on his desktop and reread the contents. According to the reports that he'd received from the state police, they'd received numerous complaints from people who had patronized Charlie's motel, alleging that criminal activities were being conducted at that establishment.

With Charlie running the motor court entirely on his own, as well as sitting on both the school board and the town council, Wally had prayed that Skye's godfather had been careless rather than criminal. He'd hoped that Charlie was just unaware of the goings-on behind the closed doors of the cottages and not an active participant.

That still might be the case. However, the lead investigator had just informed Wally that when the troopers had moved in and concluded their sting, Charlie had been among the individuals taken into custody for questioning.

Thankfully, according to the detective, Charlie had had the presence of mind to call a lawyer. Wally was grateful that he didn't have to figure out if it was ethical for him to do that for Skye's godfather or not. If he'd had to arrange for an attorney for Charlie, it would have gotten him in a bind with the state police, an entity he depended on for backup. Then again, if he did nothing, his wife and mother-in-law would have been angry.

Relieved that the matter had been taken out of his hands, Wally smiled as he pictured his sister-in-law, Loretta Steiner-Denison, racing toward the state police district headquarters to defend the family's longtime friend. The detective in charge of the case would never know what had hit her.

Until her marriage to Skye's brother, Vince, Loretta had been a hotshot defense attorney in Chicago. Although after she and Vince started a family, she'd opened a small law firm in Scumble River, and her skills were still razor-sharp.

Wally sighed, laced his hands behind his neck, and tilted his chair back to consider his next move. He did believe that Charlie was, if not completely innocent, at least not technically guilty. And now that Loretta knew about Charlie's predicament, it was only a matter of time until the rest of the family found out.

If Wally wanted a happy marriage and a good relationship with his in-laws, he'd better be the one to tell Skye so she could inform May.

Deeply absorbed in coming up with the best way to break the news, an urgent knock on his closed door made him jerk forward, and his chair came down with a *thud*. Before he could respond to the knock, Thea Jones, the dispatcher on duty, burst into the room.

Thea was a large woman in her early sixties wearing a slightly too snug uniform. A froth of brown curls liberally sprinkled with gray haloed her head was at odds with her no-nonsense attitude. This morning her usually ruddy complexion was ashen.

Wringing her hands, she rushed up to Wally's desk and announced, "The high school is on lockdown and no one inside is responding."

"What!" Wally jumped to his feet, instinctively checking to make sure his utility belt was around his waist and fully stocked.

Thea explained, "Ten minutes ago, the automatic notification system sent us a message. I tried to confirm, but when no one answered, I contacted Zelda."

Early Monday mornings were often a bit chaotic at the school, so Wally had assigned Zelda Martinez to patrol that area. She was there mostly to slow down cars driving on the street in front of the building, but also to keep the parents who were transporting their children from jumping the drop-off line and causing a riot.

Motioning Thea to follow him as he headed toward the stairs leading down to the main level of the police station, Wally urged her to continue her report.

Thea drew a shaky breath, then explained, "When Zelda arrived, she found the front office and foyer empty. She tried to contact someone via text, but no is replying to her messages."

"Right." Wally nodded as he continued his sprint down the narrow steps, then made a beeline for his vehicle. "She's following protocol, which dictates that she coordinates with a school official before proceeding any farther into the building."

"Exactly," Thea puffed as she ran after him, nearly slamming into his chest when he stopped and turned toward her. "She has requested instructions on how to proceed and backup to the location."

"Tell her to hang tight." Wally flung open the interior

door leading to the attached garage. "I'll be there in five. Check that she has on her vest and instruct her not to leave the lobby." He grabbed his own body armor from the rear of the Hummer, fastened it over his chest, then slid behind the wheel and shouted at Thea, "Call all our officers in and alert the county sheriff's department deputies that we may need them."

Tires squealed as he pealed out of the garage, shifted into drive, and sped toward the school. His heart was in his throat. Skye was scheduled to be in that building, and his wife and their twins were his whole world.

Wally had been drawn to Skye since she was sixteen, but at the time, he'd been twenty-two, way too old to do anything about his feelings. In the back of his mind, he'd thought that if the attraction was still there when she graduated from high school, he'd pursue the matter.

Sadly, she'd gone off to college before he got up his nerve to approach her father. Considering their age difference, he wanted to get the man's permission to date his daughter.

Wally had still intended to ask Skye out when she returned, but he never got the chance. Once she was gone, she rarely came back to Scumble River.

Although he'd hadn't forgotten the sweet, smart teenager who had enchanted him, when it became apparent that she'd left town for good, he'd tucked her memory away and settled for someone else. That had been the biggest mistake of his life.

He'd ended up trapped in an unhappy marriage to a woman he had never truly loved. His conscience wouldn't allow him to leave her because she seemed too emotionally fragile to handle a divorce.

Clearly, he'd been wrong since his wife had run away with another man.

Everyone had been so sympathetic, but Wally had been thrilled. He'd nearly danced for joy that he was now able to pursue the woman he'd always wanted.

Unfortunately, before his divorce was final and he could tell Skye how he felt about her, she had agreed to a committed relationship with Simon Reid.

Wally knew that Skye wasn't the type to date more than one man at a time so he'd kept away from her. But the minute that Reid screwed up and Skye dumped him, Wally made his move. He wasn't about to blow his second chance at love.

It had taken him a while to convince Skye that he was the right man for her, but he finally had and they'd been married for a little over a year now. It had been, and continued to be, the most blissful time of his life.

When Skye had told Wally she was pregnant, his heart had nearly burst with happiness. He'd never thought he'd be a father—his ex-wife had blamed him for their infertility—and to have Skye and their baby was all he'd ever wanted. All he'd ever dreamed of having.

When it turned out she was carrying twins, he was over the moon. His wife, daughter, and son were everything in the world to him.

All of those thoughts crowded his mind as Wally pressed down harder on the gas pedal. His fear that Skye was in danger made him arrive at the high school in record time. He skidded to a stop in front of the building, flung himself out of the Hummer, and tore up the sidewalk toward the entrance—which were the only set of doors that were supposed to be unlocked while students were in the building.

Martinez met him in the empty foyer and reported, "Everything is quiet. Still no responses to my repeated attempts to reach someone."

As always, Zelda Martinez was immaculately put together.

Her ebony hair was wound tightly in a bun at the back of her head. Her uniform was crisply pressed and her utility belt held everything required by the rules and regs.

Wally barely acknowledged her as he concentrated on texting Skye to ask her where she was and if she was safe.

When Martinez cleared her throat, without looking up from his cell, he said, "Staff is instructed to silence their phones during a lockdown, but they should be feeling the vibrations from your messages. Whose numbers do you have?"

"The principal, guidance counselor, and safety officer." Martinez held up a tablet. "I'm following the agreed-upon protocol."

"Right." Wally stared impatiently at his cell phone, willing Skye's gorgeous face to appear, indicating that she had answered his text. "I almost forgot you had that info available."

The tablets and onboard computers in the squad cars were a recent, and anonymous, donation. Wally suspected his father was behind the gift. Carson Boyd was a Texas oil billionaire, but since his grandchildren's birth, he'd been spending more time in Illinois than in his native Lone Star State. He'd even bought a house on the river not too far from Skye and Wally's recently built home.

"It's invaluable in this situation." Martinez ran her finger down the screen. "I heard the call for backup go out on the radio. Once they arrive, the next step is to go room to room clearing the building." She glanced up at Wally and quirked a raven brow. "Right?"

"Correct," Wally confirmed as his phone chirped.

His gaze flew to the screen and Skye's emerald-green eyes sparkled up at him. He touched a chestnut curl on the image and eagerly read her message.

I'm fine. The superintendent and I are secured backstage in the auditorium.

Wally hastily typed:

Thank goodness. Stay put until I come get you.

Skye responded immediately: What's going on?

Unknown. We're unable to reach Knapik, the guidance counselor or safety officer. Any idea where they are?

Safety officer was fired. Guidance counselor's office is in the gym and Homer is probably hiding under his desk.

Give the superintendent your phone.

Will do. He's been looking over my shoulder.

Wally waited a few seconds then typed:

As you've read principal and counselor unavailable and no sign as to why the lockdown alarm was activated. Any ideas?

None. Follow protocol.

Wally pressed his lips together while he considered his options. According to Skye, the guidance counselor was a buffoon, and Wally knew from his own experiences with Knapik that the man was a coward. As soon as the alarm sounded, he could very well have escaped outside via the secret door he had concealed behind some curtains.

Besides, even if Wally located either man, it was highly unlikely that they'd have any helpful knowledge. And clearly the superintendent was in no position to make decisions.

Deciding he was on his own, and not altogether upset about it, Wally stilled his breathing and listened carefully. The complete silence was reassuring. There hadn't been any shouting or the sound of gunfire, and that had to be a good sign.

Before he could issue an order to Martinez, Quirk and Anthony ran through the front door. Sergeant Roy Quirk was Wally's right-hand man at the PD. The ex–football player usually worked second shift, but he almost always responded to a call for backup.

Anthony Anserello had been a part-timer for a couple

of years, but as soon as he'd had the opportunity, Wally had hired him full-time. The slender young man was still a little green and needed to bulk up some, but he was eager to learn and had the makings of a fine officer.

Nodding at the two men, Wally took a deep breath and filled them in on the situation, then asked, "Everyone wearing their vests?" When Martinez, Quirk, and Anthony all nodded, Wally continued, "We'll clear the main office first. We are looking for potential threats and any victims."

"Arnold is in the squad car." Martinez motioned toward the parking lot. "Should I get him? We've been working on bomb detection."

The giant schnauzer was their newest officer. Mayor Leofanti had foisted the only partially trained police dog on Wally a couple of months ago and Martinez had volunteered to be his handler.

"Let's see what the circumstances are first." Wally didn't need a less-than-proficient animal running around in an unpredictable situation.

Wally assessed the surroundings. The main office consisted of an open central area behind a chest-high counter. Beyond that was a first aid room where the itinerant nurse worked, a bathroom, and the principal's large office was in the rear.

He checked behind the counter. The only place to hide was under the school secretary's desk and that space was empty.

Pointing to the closed door on his left, Wally ordered, "Quirk, you and Anthony have the first aid room. Be aware that it has an attached bathroom. Martinez and I will process the hall bathroom and the principal's office. Remember, innocents may be hiding or be in the hands of the perp. Weapons at the ready, but they're our absolute last choice."

Fanning out, they proceeded to clear the area. Quirk and Anthony reported that there was no one in the first aid room and Martinez and Wally found the hall and bathroom empty.

Finally, with Martinez at his heels, Wally moved on to the principal's office. The door was ajar, and as he reached for the knob, he heard voices.

Putting his finger to his lips, Wally peered into the gap. It was dark, but he could just make out the profile of a slight woman holding a gun. He squinted. Was that the school secretary, Opal Hill?

Judas Priest! What in the world was she doing with a pistol, and who did she have it aimed at?

He waved Martinez away, and they retreated to the main office. Once they were out of earshot, Wally informed his officers of his observations, then ordered Martinez to retrieve her spare vest from the squad car. If this was a hostage situation, he would need a mediator.

The county's hostage negotiator was forty-five minutes away at the sheriff's office. The situation couldn't wait that long.

Intellectually, Wally knew that his best option was Skye, but his chest tightened at the thought of putting her in danger. Still, as the police psych consultant, she had the required training for the circumstances and she was her own person. As much as he'd like to protect her, he couldn't make decisions for her.

Grudgingly, Wally told his officers to sit tight and, texting his wife as he walked, he headed toward the auditorium's backstage entrance.

Skye met him on the threshold, and after a brief hug, he asked if she was willing to help. Before he could list all the reasons that she should turn down his request, she grabbed his hand and started tugging him down the hallway.

Wally had been afraid Dr. Wraige would insist on accompanying them, but instead the superintendent sprinted past them and disappeared into the boys' bathroom.

Skye shook her head, then said, "I can't imagine what Opal would be doing holding someone at gunpoint unless that person is the threat."

Wally noticed that his wife's beautiful emerald-green eyes were clouded with concern and offered, "Opal could have been the one to trigger the lockdown. She might have, then contained that person in Homer's office until help arrived." He paused, then asked, "But where would she get the weapon?"

Although Wally certainly hoped his initial scenario was the case, the gun was a sticking point.

"If I had to guess, Homer had it in his desk." Skye shrugged. "He's spouted off about not needing a safety officer because he could protect the school himself. I thought he was full of hot air, but…"

"Okay." Wally nodded. "Let's pray that's the case and that Opal doesn't accidently shoot someone."

Once they reached the foyer, Wally instructed Martinez to fit Skye with the Kevlar vest she'd gotten from her squad car, then he and Skye approached the principal's office.

Standing to the side of the door, Skye shouted, "Opal, it's Skye and Wally. Are you okay?"

"Thank the Lord." Opal's voice was shaky. "I'm fine. I got the threat under control. Come on in."

Wally motioned for Skye to stay behind him and eased through the door. When Opal saw him, she stepped to the left and gingerly gave him the gun she'd been holding.

A teenage girl wearing a short pink satin dress with feathered wings stood with her hands up. At her feet was a bow and arrow. The bow was painted a sparkly red and had a piece of pink yarn as its string. The arrow had a glittery heart tip and silver streamers.

Wally tried to stop Skye as she stepped around him, but she shook him off, moved over to Opal, and asked, "Why is Bambi Doozier dressed as cupid, and why were you holding her at gunpoint?"

CHAPTER 3

Valentine's Girl

THERE WAS NO ONE AROUND AND WHEN SHE CAME IN WITH a weapon, I had no choice," Opal sobbed into Skye's shoulder. "I never believed that I could, but then I thought about all the innocent children in class, and I just did what Mr. Knapik taught me to do."

Students and teachers had been notified that the lockdown was over and everything was fine. Parents had been emailed or sent a text reassuring them that there never had been a threat, and classes had resumed.

Zelda was watching Bambi Doozier in the health room, while Anthony went into town to track down Homer. Opal reported the principal had come to the main office right after the superintendent had walked off the stage. He'd told her to hold down the fort while he made a donut run and left the building.

Evidently, Dr. Wraige's impromptu assembly had interfered with Homer's usual morning visit to Tales and Treats to pick up his breakfast pastries. Skye could sympathize with the principal's desire for the combination bookstore and café's tasty delicacies. She'd been too busy with the twins to eat before heading off to work, so right about now, she could use a long john.

Everyone else had been instructed to return to their normal Monday morning activities. That is, everyone but Skye, Opal, Dr. Wraige, and Wally, who were crowded into Skye's office.

She wasn't sure why Wally hadn't wanted them to use Homer's lair, but he'd insisted they leave it exactly as they found it. And because Scumble River High School had long ago turned their conference area into a special education classroom, the psych office was their only option.

Wally and Dr. Wraige were perched on two metal folding chairs facing Opal and Skye across the small trapezoid table she used for testing students. The men shifted awkwardly in their seats, bumping knees on the table legs and jabbing each other in the side with their elbows as they tried to get comfortable.

Skye ignored their grumbles and patted Opal's back as she murmured, "Wally and Dr. Wraige just need to ask you some questions so they know exactly what happened. No one blames you."

Dr. Wraige snorted his disagreement, but Skye shot him a silencing look over Opal's head as the secretary continued to cry in her arms. He rolled his eyes, then flung up his hands as if giving up.

Skye was thankful when Wally took over and said, "Opal, when Bambi Doozier entered the building this morning, was she alone?"

"Yes." Opal slowly straightened, accepted the tissue Skye handed her, and wiped her eyes. "The bell had already rung. She was a minute tardy."

"That isn't like Bambi," Skye informed Wally. "Her brother, Junior, and her cousin, Cletus, yes, but Bambi is a conscientious student."

"Did she say why she was late?" Wally had his memo pad out and was taking notes. "Did she have an excuse from her parents to explain it?"

"I didn't ask." Opal sniffed and blew her nose. "I saw that she was carrying a weapon and I told her to halt. Then I triggered the lockdown, ordered her into Mr. Knapik's office, retrieved the official school pistol from his desk drawer, and waited for the police to respond." She blinked at Wally and creased her forehead. "Wasn't that what you all taught us to do when we had the active shooter drill here last September?"

"Not the part about the principal's gun," Wally muttered. "We definitely didn't teach anyone that. Homer must have added that step himself."

"Well, yes." Opal tilted her head, reminding Skye of the tiny bluebird that often visited the feeders near their deck. "Mr. Knapik said the pistol was a secret. It was only for him and me to use."

Wally blew out a breath, frowned, then raised his eyebrows at Skye. He clearly was having a difficult time figuring out what to do about Opal's actions.

Skye gave him a slight nod of acknowledgment and asked, "Opal, didn't you notice that the bow and arrow Bambi was holding were a part of her costume? That they were basically toys?"

The secretary opened her mouth, then licked her lips and shrugged. "It's not my place to make that kind of decision."

"Still, you had to have realized the weapon really wasn't capable of harming anyone." Skye probed as she studied Opal, whose tired brown eyes were half-closed.

The sixty-something woman looked asleep on her feet. She had sole responsibility for her elderly mother. And while there was a home health aide who stayed with Mrs. Hill during the day, once Opal was through with work, she took on the role of caretaker.

"I…I…" Opal stuttered, then lifted her chin and said, "We have a zero tolerance policy. No weapons of any kind, including toys, are allowed in school."

"That is true," Skye assured Wally. She turned to Dr. Wraige and asked, "I can't recall if the rule specifically says anything about the correct response to a toy weapon. Do you remember?"

"Confiscation and detention." Dr. Wraige leaned forward and shook his finger in Opal's face. "There is nothing about hitting the lockdown alarm. Or waving a gun around for that matter. We could be sued by that girl's parents. Earl Doozier has already tried to bring one suit against us that on our behalf Mrs. Denison-Boyd was only narrowly able to avert. I'm sure he won't hesitate to do it again."

Skye shared a look with Wally. He had already been scowling, but the reminder of Earl's involvement deepened his frown. The Doozier family was a thorn in the side of both the school and the police department.

Heck! Probably the entire citizenry of Scumble River, as well as its neighboring towns, thought they were a nuisance. Not that anyone would dare say that to their face. Not if they valued their personal property.

Earl Doozier was the patriarch of the Red Raggers. The townspeople called this group of loosely related kinfolk by that derogatory term because they tied the strips of scarlet cloth around most of their possessions to claim them.

The clan was hard to wrap one's head around. They were the kind of folks that mothers warned their children not to rile and that teenagers dared each other to challenge. In short, they were the type of people that no one was willing to cross without being backed up by a heavily armored vehicles and several assault rifles.

No one purposely got on the wrong side of the Red Raggers or knowingly trespassed into their territory. In a nutshell, because they didn't live by the rules of society, everyone tiptoed around them.

Throughout her years working as the school district's psychologist, Skye had formed a special relationship with Earl Doozier. She helped him and his family with the school's bureaucracy, and in turn, Earl protected her from whatever he perceived as a threat. Sometimes it was a real danger and sometimes it was one that was only in his imagination.

Skye blinked back to the present and realized that Wally, Opal, and Dr. Wraige were staring at her expectantly and she narrowed her eyes. If she was smart, she'd refuse to take on the Earl situation. She had enough on her plate without adding him to it.

However, after a few seconds, Skye blew out a resigned breath and said, "Fine. What do you want me to do?"

Knowing how bad things could go if Earl was approached in the wrong way and got his feathers ruffled, she just couldn't walk away without helping. Not that she wasn't tempted, but the idea of the possible chaos overrode her desire to stay out of it.

Dr. Wraige straightened his tie. "Apologize for the school and explain that this was all a mistake. Assure him that Bambi isn't in any trouble and this won't go on her record." He tapped his nails on the tabletop. "Is there something we could offer him to compensate him and his family for the embarrassment?" Skye opened her mouth, but before she could speak, he shook his finger. "Something within reason, of course."

"Let me think." Skye was in a tough spot.

Approaching Earl was difficult because his wife, Glenda, hated Skye. She had somehow gotten it into her head that Earl was in love with Skye, and her jealousy knew no bounds.

No matter how often Earl told his wife that wasn't true or that Skye was too chunky for him, the Red Ragger queen ignored his assurances.

Skye had to handle this carefully or instead of Bambi in Opal's gunsights, Skye would end up in Glenda's—and she would be armed with a rifle, not a puny little pistol. This would only work if the school's compensation was something Glenda wanted.

But what?

"While Skye is figuring out how to save the district's butt yet again, I still have a few questions." Wally tapped his pen on his memo pad. "I understand that the school safety officer has been terminated. Will that position be filled by someone else?"

Skye hadn't had a chance to give Wally the lowdown, but Dr. Wraige quickly summed up what he'd told the staff at the meeting, ending with, "So we're actually expanding that role in our district."

Noticing that the superintendent didn't mention either Tavish's last name or the information that the man was Dr. Wraige's son, Skye made a mental note to let Wally in on that little fact.

"I'll need this Tavish's number. Has he started working yet?" Wally asked.

Dr. Wraige reeled off the digits, then said, "He's currently checking the residency of some students who claim to be living with their aunt but whom we suspect are just using her address so they can attend school in this district. Would you like me to call him in?"

"That won't be necessary." Wally shook his head. "But when he has a chance, ask him to stop by the station so I can meet him and we can coordinate." He paused, then added, "The sooner the better."

"Will do." Dr. Wraige nodded. "You and Tavish should get along well. He was an MP in the army, so you probably have a lot in common."

"Hmm," Wally answered noncommittally. "Any idea why neither Homer nor the guidance counselor responded to my officer's texts?"

"Homer changed his cell phone plan and probably forgot to update the manuals with his new number." Dr. Wraige shook his head. "I have no idea about the guidance counselor."

Opal raised her hand, and when Wally nodded at her, she said, "Mr. Pool's attending a conference in Chicago." She looked at the superintendent and asked, "Didn't you see the documentation that I sent over to you about his absence and expenses?"

"Karolyn probably just filed it away." Dr. Wraige shrugged. "If the principal approves it, I don't need to see every piece of paper."

Hmm. That was odd. Skye would have bet that the superintendent was a micromanager.

"So out of our three contacts, one was fired, one was not at work, and one never gave us his new number," Wally said calmly.

Skye wasn't fooled by his mild tone of voice. Her husband's handsome face was the color of her favorite merlot and his biceps were bulging as he squeezed his hands into fists. He was definitely angry.

"That's about the size of it." Dr. Wraige's expression was conciliatory. "We will certainly make sure these types of errors do not slip through the cracks again. I guarantee Tavish will be keeping the police department fully informed. I'll make sure that he has that as a priority."

"Good," Wally snapped, then took a deep breath and asked. "Any idea where we go from here?"

Dr. Wraige raised a brow. "I would think that would be your job to decide."

Skye shook her head. He just couldn't let Wally have the last word. Some people should use a glue stick instead of a ChapStick on their lips.

Attempting to prevent a clash, Skye hastily said, "I'd like to speak to Bambi to see if she's okay." Skye rolled her shoulders, trying to release the tension that had been there since the lockdown alert had sounded. "Being held at gunpoint would be disturbing for most people, but she is a Doozier, so…"

"So you're hoping she's had enough similar experiences to have not been too traumatized," Wally filled in when Skye trailed off.

"Exactly." Skye figured that growing up as Earl's daughter had to have toughened her or maybe even made her immune to threats. "I talked to Bambi a few minutes before we left the main office and she seemed fine. The only thing that was bothering her was missing a test in her math class." Skye checked her watch. "Now she's missed second, third, and most of fourth period as well."

Dr. Wraige pointed his finger at Skye. "Tell the girl not to worry and instruct all her teachers to give her an A for today."

"As you know, I am not an administrator and have no authority to order a teacher to do anything." Skye calmly met his gaze. "That would be Homer's job." She pursed her lips. "If he ever shows up."

"Believe me, Mr. Knapik and I will be having quite the chat when he returns." Dr. Wraige rose from his chair and looked at Wally. "You and your wife seem to have this under control, so I'll be going."

"Wait," Opal squeaked. "What about me? Am I fired or under arrest?"

Both men answered, "No," then Wally said, "I'm going

to let it pass this time, but never, and I do mean never, wave a gun around in school again." He paused for a second, then added, "Or anywhere else."

Skye was relieved that Wally had the discretion and kind-heartedness to overlook what Opal had done. The woman was only acting on orders from Homer. If anyone was going to be arrested it should be the principal, not his secretary. Skye glanced speculatively at her husband. Was there any chance he could charge Homer with a crime?

Dr. Wraige had his hand on the office's doorknob, but he seemed to think of something and whirled around, then marched back to where Wally was still sitting. "Any progress on the burglaries from my house?"

"What burglaries?" Skye asked before she could stop herself.

Wally hadn't mentioned anything about the superintendent being robbed. Of course, between their two full-time jobs and the twins, even with a live-in housekeeper, there wasn't much time for idle chitchat at night before they dropped into bed, exhausted.

Both men ignored her question and Wally directed his answer to the superintendent. "No. Your security company is taking its sweet time in sending us the recordings of your property."

"I'll call them again." Dr. Wraige frowned. "You'd think that after the thief was able to disconnect the alarm during the first break-in, they'd be bending over backward to help catch the guy."

"Yep," Wally agreed, then added, "But I suspect that something happened to interfere with the video this time too, and the company doesn't want to admit it. I'll be in touch with you if I actually I get the footage. I hope that I'm wrong about it being unavailable because it would give us the best chance of finding out who's stealing from you."

Dr. Wraige gave them all a curt nod, stalked back to the

door, flung it open, and disappeared down the hallway. Skye got up to close the door, but Trixie nearly knocked her over as she surged over the threshold.

"I was looking for Bambi Doozier and someone told me she tried to blow up the school, which can't be true. What in the devil kind of drugs are in the air around here today?" Trixie demanded.

A second later, she seemed to notice Opal and Wally. Trixie slapped her palm over her mouth and gave Skye a puzzled look.

After Skye explained what had really happened, Wally asked, "Why were you looking for Bambi? And who told you she tried to blow up the school?"

"She's one of my cupids." Trixie wandered over to Skye's desk and dug through the candy jar full of Jolly Ranchers sitting on it.

"Your cupids?" Wally echoed. "Why does the library need cupids?"

"Not the library, silly." Trixie unwrapped a watermelon candy and popped it into her mouth. "My service club. This week, we're raising money for the Stanley County Animal Shelter by delivering Valentine's Day greetings for five dollars each during the three lunch periods." She tilted her head. "I guess I should have specified not to wear the costume to school and just change into it before starting their cupid shift. That's what the other kids did."

"Well, heck. I forgot about that." Skye put her hands on her hips. "Now I feel even worse about this whole crud muffin of a mess."

"It tweren't your fault, Miz Skye." Earl Doozier stuck his head around the doorway, then slithered the rest of himself into the office and pointed a dirty finger at Opal. "She's the one who done it."

CHAPTER 4

Cupid's Chokehold

At least Earl was alone. Skye glanced heavenward and counted her blessings. He was a lot easier to manage without his entourage. His wife would have definitely added to whatever pandemonium was about to occur. Not to mention the violent propensity of his grandmother or maybe great-grandmother—Skye had never quite figured out the Dooziers' twisted genealogy, which was more like a topiary bush than a family tree.

Everyone in the now even more crowded office was silent, and before Skye could consider whether she really wanted to know or not, she asked, "Earl, how did you find out about Bambi and the lockdown so quickly?"

Wally and Opal had remained seated, and in fact, scooted their chairs as far away from Earl as possible. Trixie, who wasn't afraid of anything and always hoping for a good idea for her next book, had snatched a pen and a legal pad from Skye's desk and was jotting down notes.

"When the dang alarm thingy went off, Junior climbed outta the window and came got me." Earl's toothless grin was proud. "He ain't dumb enough to stick aroun' if somethin' bad's abouts to go down."

Skye wasn't at all surprised that Earl's son hadn't followed the rules, but she was curious how the Doozier patriarch had found out about his daughter's involvement.

"That explains how you knew about the alert," Skye said, "but what about Bambi?"

Before Earl could explain how he knew his daughter was a part of the brouhaha, a woman with a bleach job that had been done using a bottle of peroxide rather than a box of Clairol, a Kim Kardashian bust, and the personality of a Komodo dragon slammed open the door and barreled over the threshold. Skye and Trixie jumped out of her path, both taking refuge behind Skye's desk.

Earl's wife, Glenda, had arrived. She looked as if she'd just tumbled out of bed after a long, hard night of booze and bad decisions, which didn't augur well for any of their futures. Especially her poor husband's.

Ignoring everyone else, Glenda glowered at Earl and screeched, "What in the hell is goin' on? Junior woke me up lookin' for the keys to the tank and MeMa is loadin' all the guns, even the bazooka."

Earl, evidently having a death wish, snapped, "Confound it. I's told that boy we didn't need no wimmen involved. I said I'd handle it."

"Like yous handled the guy at the bar last night?" Glenda put her hands on her hips and narrowed her eyes. "Lucky for you, I had the SIG Sauer P238 in my purse or he woulda beat the twinkies out of you."

"But, honey pie," Earl whined, "I was a warmin' up. I coulda taken him if ya gave me the chance to get my muscles loosened—"

"Don't make me break a nail slappin' some sense in you," Glenda warned.

Skye gazed at the bloodred talons Glenda was using

to poke at her husband and cringed. Those claws could do some real damage. But at least her mood wasn't too bad or she'd have been holding her gun. A good indication that the Doozier queen was really angry was when she had a weapon in her hand.

"Ain't that sweet how concerned she is about me." Earl beamed. Skye wasn't shocked that he didn't seem to understand that his wife had insulted him or that there was a love-sick expression on his usual slack-jawed face as he said, "I won't let you or Bambi down. I's got a plan that could set us up for life."

Skye rolled her eyes. Earl always had a get-rich-quick scheme.

"Your last plan for our future nearly landed you in the hoosegow for murder." Glenda tapped the toe of a drunk-tank-pink high heel on the worn carpet. "I'm countin' to three and you better tell me exactly what's happen'." She shot a malevolent look at Skye. "Or is this all just a made-up reason to come and moon around her."

"But, sweet cheeks, you's knows that I love you more than Paula Deen loves butter." Earl clasped his hands to his heart. "Or likes you're the last package of toilet paper in the apocalypse."

"Well…" Glenda hesitated. "I jus' wished that every time you's goes missin', you didn't turn up wherever she's at." Glenda jerked her thumb at Skye. "What is she? Some sorta trouble magnet?"

"Hmm." Earl scratched his receding chin. "You's has a point there. Where Miz Skye goes, misfortune does seem to follow." He thought a few more seconds then nodded. "That's why she needs me to help her out, but you, my sugar dumplin', is the cheese in my nachos."

"You do love that jar of melty orange stuff." Glenda

batted her false eyelashes at her husband. "And I love you like a candle." She giggled and tapped his nose with the tip of her fingernail. "Because iffen you don't pay enough attention to me, I'll burn down your house."

While the lovebirds were cooing at each other, Skye murmured to Trixie, "Why don't you go get Bambi while I try to smooth things over?"

Bambi was the last of Earl and Glenda's brood—at least as far as Skye knew. She was a quiet girl, and one of the few Red Ragger offspring who hadn't been referred for any special education assistance, which meant she had more of a relationship with Trixie than Skye.

Once the school librarian had eased her way around the couple blocking the door and left, Skye glanced at Wally and Opal. Opal had slid so far down she was almost under the table, and Wally waved at Skye, indicating that she should continue to handle the situation.

Skye gave him a little nod, turned to the Dooziers, and said, "Earl, when Glenda arrived you were about to tell me how you found out that our lockdown involved Bambi. What's the scoop?"

"It's nothin' complicated." Earl dug his finger into his ear and mined for wax. "When that police lady was busy tinkling, Bambi used the office phone and called me. When my baby girl told me she thought she was in trouble, I's come a runnin'."

Tugging at the crotch of her skintight jeans, her low-cut tank top exposing a large expanse of chalk-white cleavage, Glenda looked daggers at Skye and said, "What have y'all done to my little angel?"

Skye was relieved that she was out of reach of Glenda's fingernails and said, "There was a slight error in judgment on the part of our school secretary." When Opal whimpered,

Skye quickly continued, "But Bambi is fine. She was never in any physical danger." Behind her back Skye crossed her fingers and hoped she wasn't lying. "The superintendent has authorized me to compensate your family for any embarrassment the school might have caused you or Bambi."

Earl looked from his wife to Skye and back. "We's had a lot of pain and sufferin', so we's goin' need a lot of compensation to get over it."

Glenda nodded her agreement, then squawked, "Making up for smearing my darlin' kitten's reputation won't come cheap. I'm talkin' a whole aisle at Walmart expensive."

Skye hadn't come up with anything she thought Glenda would go for, so she said, "Tell me what you want." She was hoping that the Red Ragger queen wouldn't ask for a new house or something equally outrageous.

"We's need to confer." Earl shot Glenda a crafty look. "Right, honeypot?"

"Right." Glenda gathered her faux fur jacket around herself, grabbed Earl's scrawny arm, and pulled him into the hallway, slamming the door after her.

As soon as the couple left, Wally stood, walked to the door, edged it open, and peered into the hallway. After a quick look, he motioned to Opal, and said, "This is your chance. The Dooziers are down by the fountain. Go in the other direction and make your way back to the office. You can help Anthony find Homer."

Opal nodded, jumped to her feet, and shot over the threshold. As soon as she was in the hall, she started running and didn't look back.

"You know she won't narc on Homer," Skye commented. "If he doesn't want to be found, she'll never tell us where he's hiding out."

"Even after he set her up to take a fall by telling her to use his gun to defend the school?" Wally's eyebrows rose into his hairline.

Skye shook her head. "It would take more than that to get her to snitch on him."

"Homer will have to face the music eventually." Wally perched on the edge of Skye's desk. "He has to show up sometime."

"He's probably somewhere nearby." Skye shrugged. "He's just making sure the superintendent is really gone before he announces his presence."

"Speaking of which." Wally crossed his arms. "How high did Wraige authorize you to go?"

"He never exactly said, but I'm guessing he'd pay a good sum to avoid having the Dooziers hire Loretta to sue him." Skye smiled. "Dr. Wraige is afraid of our sister-in-law. As well he should be."

Skye frowned and bit her lip. Something was bothering her. Suddenly it occurred to her what had been nagging at the back of her mind.

She snapped her fingers and asked, "Where's Homer's gun?"

"I confiscated it, bagged and tagged it, and gave it to Quirk to put into the evidence locker at the station." Wally gave her an odd look. "Did you think we'd just leave it sitting around?"

"No. Sorry. Evidently my hormones are still causing some blips in my thinking." Skye rubbed her eyes. "Dr. J says pregnancy brain can last up two years, so only eighteen more months to go."

Wally stood, walked around the desk, and hugged Skye. "You're doing fine. This morning's false alarm rattled all of us."

"Will Homer get the gun back?" Skye snuggled into

Wally's chest, determined to enjoy the warmth and the close-ness for a few seconds before she had to resume her professional duties.

"It depends." Wally stroked Skye's back as he explained. "Many states have laws prohibiting concealed carry in schools, but Illinois allows it. If Homer doesn't have a license, the gun is classified as contraband and we won't return it."

"Homer's an idiot, but he's got the self-preservation instincts of a skunk with fully loaded stink glands, so he probably does have a license," Skye muttered gloomily.

"Look on the bright side, we are allowed to keep evidence until the conclusion of the case." Wally winked at her. "Depending on our investigation and the decision on how to proceed, we may not wrap this thing up for weeks or months, or even years."

"But I thought you weren't going to press charges against Opal."

"I'm not. However, that doesn't mean we might not charge someone else."

"Ah." Skye nodded. "Especially if that someone presses you to return his gun."

"Exactly."

Skye chuckled, then realized it had been quite a while since Earl and Glenda had retired to the hallway to consult with each other.

With one last cuddle, she freed herself from her husband's embrace and walked over to the office door. Easing it open, she peeked outside.

It appeared that Earl was scouting the perimeter. Skye watched the skinny little man dressed in camo sweatpants and a torn T-shirt slide from locker to locker as he glided down the corridor. He almost looked like a ten-year-old boy playing cops and robbers, until you noticed the dense tattoos up and down his forearms and the basketball-shaped gut hanging over his trousers.

"What's he doing?" Wally joined Skye in watching Earl sneaking towards them.

Skye shrugged. "My best guess is that he's making sure that no enemies have snuck up on him while he was distracted by talking to Glenda." She closed the door and took a seat behind her desk.

"Sounds reasonable." Wally nodded. "Any idea why he's not wearing a coat? February in Illinois isn't exactly short sleeve weather."

"Earl told me he runs hot like his hero General Patton." Skye had long ago stopped trying to make sense of anything the Doozier patriarch did or didn't do.

"I never heard that about Patton." Wally frowned.

"Me neither." Skye shrugged. "Earl might have made up that detail or gotten it from a cartoon. Who knows with him?"

"Hmm," Wally grunted, then said, "I really need to find Homer. Do you want me to stick around or do you have this under control?"

"I've got it." Skye wasn't sure that she truly did, but there wasn't anything Wally could do to help. "When Trixie comes back with Bambi, I'll check that she's okay and send her to class with a note explaining that as per Dr. Wraige's instructions, she shouldn't be penalized for anything she missed. Then I'll negotiate with the Dooziers regarding the amount of the bribe they'll accept to forget all this ever happened. After that, we should be good."

Wally had his hand on the knob when the office door slammed open, and he had to jump out of the way as Earl and Glenda marched inside.

"You tell her, honeydew." Earl took off his dirty baseball cap, revealing muddy-brown hair that formed a ring around a bald spot the size of a cantaloupe. "You can explain what we's want better'n me."

Uncharacteristically, Glenda shuffled her stiletto-clad feet, sucked in a lungful of air, and finally blurted out, "We want to go to Beverly Hills for spring break. All of us, including Elvis and his wife, and Elvira, and Hap, and Cletus, and MeMa."

"So, ten people?" Skye asked, wondering what something like that would cost.

"Eleven," Earl piped up. "Sweet lips done forgot little Skeeter."

"Who's Skeeter?" Skye lasered the little man with a skeptical look. "I don't remember any of your kin named Skeeter."

"Elvis's boy." Earl shoved out his sunken chest. "T's a Pawpaw. He and Mavis had 'em round the same time as you's had your litter."

Skye glanced sideways at Wally. How had they missed that blessed event?

As if reading her mind, Earl explained, "Elvis got a good job managin' a Lock and Hole storage unit, and he done moved to the city."

"Chicago?"

"Laurel," Earl clarified. "He and the missus are livin' high on the hog. They's got one of them there storage units fixed up real nice."

"They're living in a storage unit? With a baby?" Skye asked Earl. "How?"

She'd had a hard enough time managing the twins in a luxury RV while their new house was being built. And her accommodations had had bathrooms, not to mention a washer, dryer, and complete kitchen.

"It has air conditioning and heat and electricity." Earl widened his bloodshot eyes and exclaimed, "The owner, Mr.

Drysdale, even rented them a Porta Potty and put it right out back."

"Okay, then." Skye had heard enough. "Eleven people for a week's vacation in Beverly Hills. May I ask why you chose that destination?"

Glenda's fish belly–white cheeks pinked up and she mumbled, "Cuz of the *Housewives*."

Skye was momentarily confused, then realized Glenda meant the reality TV program. "I see. Then you'll need airfare, accommodation, and food."

"We's want two rooms at a nice place. Something luxurious like that hotel where's they leave the light on for you," Earl demanded. "And we's want to eat good too. Restaurants where you sit down and they bring it to you."

"That's right." Glenda nodded. "And real china plates and steel forks. Nothin' plastic."

"Okay." Skye grabbed a pen and paper. "Anything else?"

"We need a rental van so's we can drive around and see everythin'." Her eyes gleamed with avarice. "And some spending money. A hundred dollars a day. I'm goin' buy me a fancy purse out there, just like Lisa's pink leopard one."

"Got it." Skye agreed quickly, before they changed their minds and upped their demands. It was a good thing that Glenda had no idea how much a designer handbag really cost. "I just need to clear it with the superintendent. Once he gives me the okay, I'm sure he'll want you to sign something."

Earl held out his hand to Skye. "You've got a deal." After she shook it, he said, "We's got to skeedadle." Over his shoulder, he added, "Call me when you have our tickets and stuff."

"Go ahead, baby. I'll catch up." Glenda waited until her husband left and said, "I thought I'd never get rid of him. Men's a lot like a curling iron." At Skye's puzzled expression, she explained, "They's always hot and they's always in your hair."

"So true." Skye glanced at Wally and giggled at his irate expression, then waited for the other shoe to drop.

"I want one other thing." Glenda narrowed her eyes. "And don't you go tellin' Earl."

"Okay." Skye hoped she could produce whatever the Doozier matriarch had in mind.

"I want to meet Calizone," Glenda demanded.

"You mean eat a calzone?"

"No! Is you an idiot?" Glenda stomped her foot, then dug into her enormous purse. She produced a torn-out magazine page that she thrust into Skye's hands. "Calizone is the greatest wrestler of all time and he's goin' be in LA during spring break. I want a ticket to his match and a backstage pass."

"Got it." Skye hustled Glenda out the door, then said to Wally, "How much do you think that all will cost?"

"Three thousand for the airfare. Fifteen hundred for the two motel rooms. Maybe that for the food. Five hundred for the van. And whatever wrestling tickets go for." Wally shrugged. "That makes what, seven thousand including their daily stipend. Pretty cheap, considering their daughter was held at gunpoint by a school employee."

Before Skye could respond, her office door thumped open and Shamus Wraige stomped inside. His gaze fell on Wally and he marched up to him.

He poked Wally in the chest and said, "This has got to stop."

"What has to stop?" Wally grabbed the superintendent's finger, and Skye winced as he held on to it, not quite bending it back, but the threat was implied. "You assaulting a police officer?"

"No, my possessions being stolen." Dr. Wraige's naturally ruddy complexion was lobster red. "My car is missing. My brand-new Black Label Lincoln Navigator with blue leather whitewashed wood interior is gone."

CHAPTER 5

Trouble in Paradise

LATER THAT AFTERNOON, SKYE BREATHED A SIGH OF RELIEF as she drove home after school. From start to finish, it had been a chaotic day. Even though the lockdown had been handled relatively quickly, both the staff and the students remained rattled until the dismissal bell rang that afternoon.

Skye and Piper had been called into numerous classrooms to reassure anxious students that there wasn't now and had never been a real threat. She suspected that her presence had been requested as much for the teacher as for the kids.

Pulling her Mercedes into the garage, Skye sat for a moment and deliberately shoved all thoughts of her workday aside. All she wanted to do for the rest of the evening was play with CJ and Eva, eat dinner with her husband, then cuddle with him on the couch.

The first hint that her night wasn't going to go as she'd hoped was the sound of babies screaming a duet when she walked into the laundry.

Skye hastily dumped her tote bag and purse on the bench, hung up her coat, and toed off her boots. The crying only got louder as she entered the kitchen.

Dorothy rocked Eva in one arm while she shook a rattle at CJ, who was sitting in his swing. Neither twin took any notice of her efforts and both their little faces were redder than a valentine heart.

Raising her voice above ruckus, Skye called out, "I'm home."

Dorothy took one look at her standing in the doorway and her shoulders slumped. "I'm so sorry. I don't know what's gotten into these two today. They've hardly napped and they've been fussy all afternoon."

"I take it they're dry and have been fed?" Skye asked, entering the room and picking up CJ.

She wasn't at all surprised when Dorothy nodded. The housekeeper had raised four of her own children, so Skye was sure the woman hadn't missed the obvious.

"At first, I thought it was teething, but none of the things that have been helping them seemed to work." Dorothy added, "And they don't have a fever or any sign of a cold or flu."

"Were their stools normal?" Skye couldn't believe she was discussing poop.

"Uh-huh," Dorothy continued, "I called their pediatrician and she said it didn't sound like an ear infection, so it was probably a growth spurt because babies are usually extra fussy when that happens."

"I remember reading about that." Skye bounced CJ who had quieted but was still whimpering. "When their bones, muscles, and tendons grow, it can be very painful. And they have seemed hungrier than usual, which would make sense because they'd need extra calories to get through the growth spurt."

"Yeah, the doc mentioned that it can mess up their sleep patterns." Dorothy paced the floor patting Eva's back.

Skye joined Dorothy in circling the kitchen. "Did the doctor have any suggestions?"

"Just to keep them on their regular schedule."

"So we should put them in their cribs for a nap now or their bedtime will be thrown off," Skye murmured.

"Right." Dorothy headed toward the nursery. "I was just waiting for you to get home since I know you like to see them before they go to sleep."

The two women deposited the still-sniffling twins in their cribs and grabbed the portable baby monitor. Skye followed Dorothy out of the room.

After she closed the door, Skye leaned against the wall in the hallway. It was tough hearing her babies in such distress.

Once Dorothy had gone upstairs, Skye hurried into the master bedroom to change. As she finished and walked back into the kitchen to start dinner, she was thankful that she could no longer detect any sounds from the nursery.

Sadly, a few seconds later she heard Eva whimper. Skye hesitated. Should she get Eva out of there so she didn't wake up her brother? Or should she wait to see if her daughter would go back to sleep?

When both babies started screaming again, Skye put her hands over her ears and prayed for strength. She'd try to be strong and let them cry themselves to sleep as the doctor had suggested, but she wasn't sure how long she'd last.

A half hour later, the babies had just fallen asleep when Wally arrived home. Skye cringed as he loudly shut the door between the garage and laundry room, then clomped down the hall.

As he entered the kitchen, Skye immediately whispered, "Be quiet."

"Why?" he whispered back.

Skye explained about the twins and returned to making supper. Wally kissed her cheek and went to change out of his uniform.

He reappeared a few minutes later wearing lounge pants and a sweatshirt. After a quick peek in the nursery, he set the table.

Finished, he grabbed a beer from the fridge and, keeping his voice low, asked, "Do you want Diet Coke or wine?"

"This day definitely calls for wine." Skye also spoke softly. "How was the rest of your shift?"

"Fine." Wally poured a glass of merlot and handed it to Skye. "But we didn't get to talk much after the lockdown, and there is something that I needed to tell you."

Skye's stomach clenched. "Oh?" What now?

"Maybe you should sit down." Wally's expression was apprehensive.

"Okay." Skye slid into a chair and took a gulp of wine, sure she was going to need it.

"Your Uncle Charlie has been arrested." He held up his hand before Skye could respond. "Loretta got him out on bail so he's not in jail, but he could be in big trouble."

As he explained the situation, Skye couldn't hold back her tears.

When he finished, she got herself under control, wiped her face with a tissue, cleared her throat, and said, "I'd better call Mom."

CHAPTER 6

Cupid Shot Us Both with One Arrow

WALLY STARED AT THE MESS IN FRONT OF HIM. MONDAY had sucked eggs and Tuesday was starting off even worse. He pulled Charlie's file toward him, groaning at the memory of Skye's reaction to the news her godfather had been caught up in the state police's sting. Even though Loretta had gotten him released, the threat of a conviction still dangled over his head.

Charlie claimed that he had no knowledge of the drug or weapons transactions that had gone on in the cottages of his motor court. Although Wally tended to believe him, that didn't mean the state police investigator felt the same way.

Wally was fairly certain that Skye's godfather had chosen to turn a blind eye to what was happening in his establishment. There was no other explanation. Charlie wasn't a stupid man, and the same people renting a couple of cabins the identical day every week had to have seemed fishy to him. Especially during the off-season, when there were no tourist or hunters or anglers around.

Certainly, the other owners of small motels up and down the I-55 corridor from Chicago to St. Louis had twigged to what was taking place. They'd been smart and reported the suspicious activity to the state police, making Charlie look even guiltier by his silence.

Normally, Wally would have kept his distance from an investigation involving another law enforcement agency, but Skye's tearful face, not to mention her mother's hysteria, had him looking through the paperwork for the investigator's number. He was fairly confident a call to the detective in charge of the case wouldn't be considered too much of an intrusion. After all, as the chief of police in the town where the sting had transpired, he was entitled to an update.

Wally was reaching for the phone when the intercom buzzed. Annoyed at the interruption, he punched the blinking red button for the mayor's private line.

"Yes?" Wally's tone conveyed his impatience.

"My office. Now." Hizzoner hung up before Wally could respond.

"Son of a nutcracker!" Wally cursed, wishing for the zillionth time he hadn't promised Skye that he'd stop swearing when the twins were born. "What in the devil does Dante want now?"

Cripes!

Just what he needed. Another of the mayor's inane demands.

Although Dante was May's brother, the relationship between him and the rest of the Leofanti family had never been overly cordial. It had deteriorated even further when Skye and Wally had exposed the mayor's scheme to save money by outsourcing the police department.

Hizzoner had planned to use those funds for the construction of a super incinerator, which he would use to burn neighboring communities' garbage. He'd then charge those towns a hefty fee and rake in the cash. He didn't care that the huge trucks and rancid smells would change Scumble River from a pleasant rural village to an unlivable nightmare.

This all had happened quite a while ago, but Dante held on to grudges as if they were his firstborn child, and he continued to delight in wasting the police department's time and resources. The mayor was willing to do almost anything to make Wally look bad, and this abrupt summons was probably something to further the man's game of revenge.

Holding on to his temper by a thread, Wally stood up and grabbed a legal pad. He straightened his shoulders and marched into the hallway.

The police station, city hall, and library were all housed in the same redbrick building they had occupied since it was built in the fifties. The city hall and PD shared the ground floor. The town's small library took up the back half of the second story while the chief's and mayor's office shared the remainder of the space.

A few years ago, Dante had ordered an opening cut in the wall between the city hall and the police department. While Wally wasn't fond of how easily Hizzoner could now stroll over anytime the urge hit him, he had to admit it was a hell of a lot simpler to walk through the archway rather than go downstairs, out the PD's door, enter the city hall, and climb the steps to the mayor's office. Especially on a day like this when the freezing wind was gusting hard enough to blow the mane off a lion.

A few seconds later, when Wally strolled into Dante's lair, he found Hizzoner appeasing someone on the phone.

"I promise you: your problem is my number one priority." Dante's voice vibrated with fake sincerity, and sweat beaded along his follicle-challenged hairline. "Yes, yes. He'll be there as soon as I fill him in on the situation. Just sit tight."

Wally took a seat and settled back to enjoy the show. One

of Scumble River's more prominent citizens must be raking the mayor over the coals. And while Hizzoner was more proficient at the sidestep shuffle then Fred Astaire, the sight of him dancing on the flames was always amusing.

"Shit," Dante said under his breath, then cleared his throat and soothed, "I'm very sorry that you're continuing to have these burglaries." The mayor glared at Wally. "We will definitely get your car back."

Well, crapola!

Although Wally maintained his bland expression, inwardly he cringed. That had to be Wraige complaining to the mayor about all the thefts.

"Yes. Right. Just let me hang up and get him going," Dante mollified. "I promise, he'll be there soon." Banging the handset into the holder, the mayor scowled at Wally. "That was Shamus Wraige."

"Did he have another break-in?" Wally asked, wondering why he'd called the mayor instead of 911. "What did they take this time?"

"Nothing." Dante's thin lips quirked. "But Dr. Wraige is sure someone just tried to get in again. He heard the back door rattle, and when he went to investigate, no one was there."

"And he called you instead of the police." Wally shook his head.

"Why would he call the cops?" Dante sneered. "You haven't caught the scumbag breaking into his house, and it's been going on for several weeks."

"We've done all we can." Wally crossed his legs. "We dusted for fingerprints—there weren't any that didn't belong to the family—the pawnshops within a hundred-mile radius have been notified to be on the lookout for the missing items, and the security company claims that someone put a piece of tape over the lens of their cameras and the recordings were compromised."

"How about the car?" Dante thrust out his chin. "What are you doing about that?"

"We've alerted the other law enforcement agencies." Wally shrugged. "There's not much hope. An expensive vehicle like that Navigator is either already sailing on a ship overseas or down to individual parts at a chop shop."

"I can't tell the superintendent of schools that BS." Dante shoved his chair back so hard it hit the wall behind him. "You need to do something."

"If you approve the budget for overtime reimbursement, I can have Martinez and Anthony do a grid search of the county." Wally knew that wouldn't fly, but it really was the only thing left to do.

Dante leaped out of his seat—quite an achievement for someone shaped like an egg—and screamed, "No more money! It already cost a fortune to specially equip a squad car so that dog of yours would be comfortable." Before Wally could protest that it was the mayor's idea to get a K-9 officer, Hizzoner extended a finger and shrieked, "Admit it! You're just dragging your feet on this to make me look bad."

"Not true." Wally shook his head. "But if you insist, I certainly can."

"Screw you!" Dante advanced on Wally flailing his arms like Humpty Dumpty about to fall off the wall. "You get over to Shamus Wraige's right now," the mayor screamed. "And do something to make him think your department isn't as worthless as it is!"

Wally stood, towering over Dante. "My department has a ninety-eight percent clearance rate." Wally barely stopped himself from punching Hizzoner. "Which you would know if you read the reports that you insist that I send you every month."

"You don't fool me!" Dante squawked. "You pad those statistics."

"Unlike you, I do not." Wally kept his voice calm, but just barely.

"Liar."

"If the nose fits." Wally stared at the mayor's long, pointy proboscis.

"What are you saying?" Hizzoner glared, but when Wally didn't answer, he deflated and muttered, "In any case, give me a call when you get Shamus to cool his jets. All we need is him badmouthing us to his cronies."

"Yes, sir." Wally gave a mocking salute and headed to the garage.

Once inside, he slid behind the wheel of the Hummer, secured his seat belt, and cranked the engine. He reversed out onto the parking lot and made a left on Basin Street.

Having been to the Wraige residence twice already in the past month, Wally was familiar with the route and he automatically steered the SUV toward the town's most exclusive neighborhood. Which ironically was a few miles past the McDonald's and near the water resource recovery facility.

As he drove south of town, Wally thought about the ruckus the residents of that subdivision had caused when they realized that their million-dollar-plus houses were not only within smelling distance of the sewage treatment plant, they also backed up to an old graveyard.

With all the two- or three-acre lots surrounded by a fairly thick band of trees, none of home buyers had noticed that there was an old cemetery on the other side of the woods. And evidently the developer had made sure that prospective buyers were only shown the property when the wind was blowing away from the water treatment facility.

There was nothing the new owners could do about the sewage plant, but they had fought long and hard to have the bodies in the old graveyard moved. When they had lost the fight, many had erected huge fences, as if they expected the corpses to rise from the ground and attack.

At the time, Wally had wondered why they'd never bothered to explore the area where they were building. It wasn't as if the tombstones had popped up overnight. Even though he and Skye were limited by already owning the acreage on which they were erecting their house, they had certainly considered every possibility when they'd selected the site for their new home.

Shaking his head, he turned onto Shamus Wraige's street. His place was on a cul-de-sac at the far edge of the development, which meant it had one of the largest yards but was also the closest to the graveyard. Wally wondered how the superintendent had taken that news.

Pulling the Hummer into the driveway, Wally noted that the area seemed deserted. The homes on either side were separated from the Wraige's house by lines of evergreens forming a natural barrier, as well as dense foliage that afforded even more privacy. In addition, there was a six-foot-tall wooden fence along the back.

Wally parked, exited the vehicle, and strode up the sidewalk. Ringing the doorbell, he examined the premises. On the two previous break-ins, the burglar had jimmied open the kitchen's sliding doors that led out onto the deck. Wally had recommended replacing them with sturdier French doors, but he doubted his suggestion had been heeded.

Several minutes went by and no one answered the bell. Wally frowned and knocked. Again, he waited three or four minutes, but there was still no response.

It was odd that after demanding that the mayor send the police right over, Wraige wasn't responding to either the bell or the knocks.

Wally pulled out his phone and dialed the superintendent's

cell phone. He was thankful that he'd put both that number and Wraige's landline in his contacts after yesterday's fiasco at the high school.

Normally, he'd have gotten that type of information from the dispatcher when she sent him out on the call. However, the superintendent had circumvented the system. A system that was in place for that very reason.

Wraige didn't answer either of his phones and eventually they went to voicemail. Wally left the same message on both, then sent a similar text.

After waiting another five minutes, during which he rang the bell and knocked repeatedly, Wally approached the front windows. The interior was in shadows, but there didn't appear to be anyone in the living room or dining room—all he could see through the glass.

He tried the front door and found it locked, then as he circled the house, he peered into each window in turn. It didn't look as if anyone was home. Had the superintendent grown impatient and left?

Reaching the backyard, Wally climbed the steps leading up to the deck and tried the sliders. He frowned when they slid right open.

Stepping inside, Wally cupped his hands around his mouth and yelled, "Dr. Wraige, are you here? It's Chief Boyd, responding to your attempted break-in call."

Nothing.

Wally stepped around the oak table, moved farther into the room, and tried again. "Dr. Wraige, it's Chief Boyd. I'm here to help you."

The same silence that greeted his first shout met his second.

The kitchen looked as if the family had had breakfast and left for work. There were dirty cereal bowls in the stainless steel sink, a discarded paper muffin cup crumpled on the granite counter, and a Mr. Coffee with an inch or so of brown liquid in the carafe. When Wally checked, the appliance was off. He felt the pot. It was cold.

Recalling the house's layout from his previous visits, Wally continued to call out the superintendent's name as he walked out of the kitchen into the combination living room–dining room.

There was no sign of Wraige. Hand on his weapon, Wally headed down a short corridor to his left. This held two bedrooms that shared a Jack and Jill bathroom. The last time he was here, the superintendent had informed Wally that his son was occupying one of the bedrooms and his wife's friend Colleen Vreesen was in the other.

According to Wraige, his son had recently moved to the area to start a new job. At the time, Wally hadn't known that the job was working for the school district, but Skye had given him the scoop last night.

Ms. Vreesen was staying with them because she was going through a messy divorce and had nowhere else to go. To repay her friend, she was working as the office manager at Mrs. Wraige's accounting firm. With tax season starting, the business could use the extra pair of hands.

Finding the guest wing vacant, Wally turned on his heels and approached the master suite. It was located on the opposite side of the house and he continued to call out as he walked.

In between shouts, he listened closely, but the place definitely had an empty feel to it. There was no sound of breathing or movement or anything else.

Wally made his way down the corridor, the polished hardwood floor echoing with his footsteps. The door to the master bedroom was ajar and after knocking and announcing himself, he pushed it fully open.

Peering around the room, it seemed untouched. The white-and-gold brocade spread on the king-size bed was smooth and a puffy quilt was neatly folded near the foot. There was a pile of artfully arranged pillows near the oversized tufted cream leather headboard.

From where he stood, Wally could see the entire bedroom. The space in front of the white-and-gold dresser and matching chest of drawers was empty. The two walk-in closets were full of clothes and shoes but otherwise unoccupied, as was the master bath. Unless Wraige was hiding under the bed, he wasn't there.

That left a small sitting room separated from the bedroom by closed louvered doors.

As Wally approached them, he heard a noise.

"Are you there, Dr. Wraige?" Wally tried the knob, which turned, but when he tried to open the door it refused to move. "It's Chief Boyd. Are you hurt?"

There was another sound, but Wally couldn't quite make it out. Worried that after talking to Dante, Wraige had had a heart attack and was unconscious and was unable to move or call out for help, Wally put his shoulder to the door and shoved.

Once the opening was large enough for him to squeeze through, Wally stepped inside. Facing him was a fireplace. A fancy love seat and chair faced the fireplace across a large, low table holding used coffee cups.

As Wally surveyed the scene, he heard a loud meow coming from behind the partially opened French door. He rolled his eyes and chuckled. He'd pushed his way into the room for a cat!

Laughing at himself, he moved around the door and stumbled to a stop.

The biggest Maine coon he'd ever seen was lying next to

Shamus Wraige. The man was sprawled in a pool of blood and there was an object sticking out of his neck.

Wally immediately called for an ambulance, then stepped closer and examined the prone figure. There was no pulse or sound of breathing, but he'd have to wait for the paramedics to arrive before the superintendent could officially be declared dead.

After closing up the cat in the bathroom, Wally inspected the scene. Near the body, there was a large metal statue that had toppled off its white marble stand. Squinting, Wally realized the statue was of cupid. The arrow that had been a part of the artwork had broken off, and that was what was buried in the superintendent's throat.

CHAPTER 7

Secret Valentine

FEELING A VIBRATION AGAINST HER HIP, SKYE'S GLANCE involuntarily jerked away from the student she was observing and down to where she was concealing a forbidden treasure. Technically, all cell phones were supposed to be turned off during school hours, and she was generally a by-the-book kind of gal, but having five-month-old twins being cared for at home by a housekeeper had motivated her to break the rules.

However, because she was in violation of the district's mandates, she couldn't just take the device out of her pants pocket and check to see who was trying to reach her. Only four people had the number to this cell phone—her housekeeper and nanny, Dorothy Snyder; her father-in-law, Carson Boyd; Wally; and Skye's mother, May.

Although May had sworn on her grandchildren's lives that she would only call in an emergency, she was unquestionably the one most likely to bother Skye at work. May's definition of a crisis and her daughter's description were as far apart as the current political parties' viewpoints.

When Skye's phone vibrated again, she stealthily slid it

from her pocket, and keeping it below the level of the student desk she was occupying, she swiped the screen with her thumb. Her husband's good-looking face appeared.

Anxiety sped up her pulse. Wally knew that she wouldn't be free to talk at this time. She always emailed her schedule to both him and Dorothy at the beginning of the week. He would only be calling her now if there was a problem—otherwise he'd wait until her lunch break.

Catching the teacher's eye, Skye nodded her thanks, rose to her feet, and slipped out of the classroom, then hurriedly walked toward her office. Once she was behind that closed door, she'd have the privacy to check her phone.

Although worried about the unexpected call from her husband, as Skye walked into her new office, she couldn't help but smile. Up until a couple of months ago, she'd been assigned to a space that had originally been a janitor's closet. It was windowless, with walls painted a disgusting rotten-egg yellow. And no matter what she'd tried, she'd never had been able to rid the room of the smell of ammonia.

It had contained a battered desk, a single metal folding chair, and a file cabinet that had probably been used to hold battle plans during World War II. She might have been able to find additional furniture, but just those three pieces had barely fit into the small room.

However, per the superintendent's agreement with her last December after she had successfully kept the district from being sued, Dr. Wraige had arranged for her to move into the junior high's old typing lab. With keyboarding as a part of the computer studies curriculum, that space had been sitting empty for several years.

The room had been used to store various pieces of broken furniture, boxes of old paperwork, and sports equipment that was long obsolete. When the original typewriters and other junk had been removed, Skye had ended up with a fairly spacious office, and the custodian reclaimed his storage area.

Settling into her new ergonomic chair—a budget for furnishings had also been part of the superintendent's agreement with her—Skye quickly checked her phone. There was a brief text from Wally asking her to call as soon as she was able to do so.

Something must have happened with Uncle Charlie!

Skye's heart launched itself into her throat and she could barely breathe. She had been none too happy with Wally last night when he'd explained her godfather's predicament. It wasn't that she blamed Wally for Charlie's arrest—well, maybe a little—but what upset her was that he hadn't told her about the sting going on in her town.

Wally's explanation that he was under orders from the state police didn't excuse him. He should have told her. He knew she could keep a secret.

It wasn't as if she would have rushed over to tell May. There was no possible chance on earth that Skye would voluntarily be the one to inform her mother that the man she thought of as a father was in trouble.

Skye wouldn't have warned Charlie, either. Well, maybe a teeny hint or suggestion that he pay more attention to whom he was renting his cabins. But she certainly wouldn't have blown the whistle on the sting.

Fingers trembling, Skye tapped the little receiver emblem and waited for Wally to answer. With each unanswered ring, her stomach fought to empty itself of the English muffin she'd had for breakfast.

After what seemed like forever, Wally's warm voice washed over her, soothing her fears. "Nothing's wrong with any of your family or friends. This concerns your role as the police psych consultant *and* as the district school psychologist."

"Thank goodness." Skye willed her breathing back to normal, picked up a pen, and said, "Okay, I'm ready to be professional. Go ahead."

"Shamus Wraige is dead." Wally paused as Skye gasped, then recapped his discovery and ended with, "It is highly likely that he was murdered."

"Wow!" Skye had not been expecting that. She would have guessed heart attack. "What makes you think it wasn't a natural death?"

"The arrow in his throat." Wally's tone was dry.

Skye thought he was kidding and quipped, "I hope you aren't accusing Bambi."

"Thank the police gods, there is no indication of any Doozier involvement." Wally sobered and explained the situation, then said, "The county forensic team is examining the scene and they believe he was pushed into the statue."

"Oh my. Couldn't he have stumbled?" It was difficult to believe that Dr. Wraige was dead.

Skye's mind flew to the students. Would they need crisis intervention? Probably not. Very few would have any real connection to the superintendent. When the announcement was made, she'd make it clear she and Piper were available to talk, but she'd be surprised if any of the kids took her up on the offer.

"The ME's preliminary examination leads her to conclude that he couldn't have harmed himself in this way by accident. As of yet, she hasn't given me the details as to why," Wally answered, then asked, "Would it be possible for you to meet me at Dr. Wraige's house?"

"Gosh. I don't know." Skye chewed her thumbnail as she mentally reviewed her to-do list. "I have a meeting in a few minutes, it will be over at twelve ten. I could probably come to the Wraige's then."

Neva Llewellyn was the junior high principal and she was extremely possessive regarding the assigned psych time at her building. There was no way she would excuse Skye from the weekly Pupil Personnel Services conference.

"Couldn't you have your intern cover it?" Wally urged.

"No. Piper has a parent interview," Skye said, flipping through her appointment book. "As it is, I'll have to get Homer to give me the afternoon off."

"Remind him that they owe you tons of flex time. If I recall correctly, that was the arrangement they made with you when you ended up working during your maternity leave." Wally's tone changed and he coaxed, "I'm about to send Quirk to find Wraige's wife and son and bring them here, and I think it would be best if you were with me to help break the news to them."

"Can you hold off for a bit?"

"I suppose." Wally didn't sound happy.

"Sorry, but that's the only solution that I can see working for both of us." Skye glanced at her watch, hurriedly gathered the various files and notes that she'd need for PPS, and got to her feet. Neva didn't tolerate tardiness. "I'm guessing that I shouldn't say anything about Dr. Wraige's death?"

"Right." Wally inhaled noisily. "Luckily, we didn't put anything out over the radio, which why I can put off sending Quirk to round up the family until you're available."

"Got it." Skye started toward the door, then paused and wrinkled her brow. Wally hadn't insisted she drop everything to consult with the police before. "Why do you want me there so badly? I've never met Mrs. Wraige and only saw the superintendent's son from a distance."

"Truthfully, I'm not sure." Wally sighed. "But my gut is telling me the motive for this murder is more up your alley than mine."

"Okay. I'll send you a text when my meeting is over. Love you. Bye."

After disconnecting, Skye stashed her phone back in her pants pocket, dashed out the door, and flew down the hall toward the art room.

As she entered, Skye sniffed, then wrinkled her nose to hold back a sneeze. The students must be doing oil paintings. The room smelled of linseed oil, and when she looked around, easels lined the walls.

The faded blue linoleum was decorated with brightly colored splashes that had escaped the young artists' brushes. And when the windows rattled with the gusts of wind and the cold air seeped around the frames, it rustled the rough charcoal drawings that were thumbtacked to the walls next to the student's work stations.

Per her habit, Neva occupied the teacher's desk while the other members of the Pupil Personal Services team sat at small tables for two arranged in an arc facing her. When Skye entered, no one was speaking and all eyes turned toward her as she slid into an empty chair.

Her tablemate was Violet Lawrence, the special education teacher. Ever since Wally's ex-wife, the former special ed teacher, had left town, they'd had a new one every school year. For some reason—perhaps the low salary, poor working conditions, or lack of respect—it was hard to keep good educators in Scumble River.

Violet had lasted two years, twice as long as most, and Skye wasn't sure why she stuck around. Perhaps it was because she'd been fresh out of college when she took the job and didn't realize there were higher paying, less demanding positions she could nab.

Whatever it was, Skye hoped Violet would remain with them.

Hmm!

Maybe she should try a little matchmaking. Getting Violet involved with a Scumble River guy might ensure the teacher's continued loyalty to the area.

Skye was impressed at how well the young woman managed her students. Her caseload consisted of kids with behavior disorders and learning disabilities. The majority of them were male and the petite teacher had her hands full with the testosterone-loaded class.

Luckily, Violet was a believer. A teacher who passionately believed that despite all the obstacles thrown her way, she would be able to have a positive impact on her students. Skye looked at her faith as a reminder to them all why they went to work every day.

As Skye settled into her seat and flipped open her legal pad, Neve gave her an annoyed look, then glanced around the occupied tables and said, "Now that we're *all* finally here, let's begin."

Skye checked the wall clock. *Shoot!* She was a minute late.

Neva nodded to Skye's tablemate and said, "Ms. Lawrence, please tell the team what you reported to me this morning."

In a soft voice, the teacher said, "Yesterday, just before the final bell, during the free time my class had earned, Tyson Howe was showing his friends a pocket watch." She cleared her throat. "It looked like family heirloom and I asked to see it."

Skye watched Neva's expression darken and wondered what was coming.

"It was heavy, which made me suspect it was solid gold, and it was beautifully monogrammed." Violet's face clouded. "I knew this young man's family weren't financially able to allow their child to bring expensive items to school that might get lost." Violet's cheeks reddened. "I, uh, wondered if his parents realized he had it and thought maybe he'd taken it from their house without their consent."

"Go on," Neva commanded.

"After the students were dismissed, I called Tyson's parents and spoke to his mother." Violet's periwinkle-blue eyes rounded in dismay. "She said that they didn't own such a watch and had no idea how their son had come into possession of the expensive antique."

"So the parents are aware and will deal with it?" Skye asked.

"Not exactly." Neva's mouth pursed. "This morning Mr. Howe telephoned me and informed me that their son assured them that Ms. Lawrence had misunderstood and that the watch actually belonged to their son's friend. They searched his room and backpack. They didn't find any watch, so they were inclined to believe him."

"But I didn't misunderstand." Violet crossed her arms. "In my classroom, he was definitely claiming ownership of the watch."

"Do you want me to talk to him?" Skye offered.

"I believe that would be best." Neva nodded. "We don't want to harm his relationship with Ms. Lawrence."

"And if he admits that it's his and that he obtained it by questionable means?" Skye kept her expression neutral. "Shall I contact the parents, or is that something you would want to do, Neva?"

The principal sat back in her chair and gazed at Skye. "Report to me, then once I have the facts, I'll decide how we should proceed."

"Of course." Skye nodded.

Neva could be prickly. She wasn't as difficult to work with as Homer, but she wasn't warm and fuzzy like the elementary school principal, either.

"I'd like you to get right on it." Twin lines formed between Neva's eyebrows and she stared at Skye. "I know your time with us is officially over at the conclusion of this meeting, but I'd like you to speak with this boy before you leave."

"Well." Skye stalled as she frantically tried to come up with an excuse. "The thing is, my husband phoned just before I came to this meeting and there's a bit of a personal emergency that he needs me to handle. Seeing as I have flex time accrued from coming in during my maternity leave, once I clear it with Homer, I'm hoping to take the afternoon off to deal with Wally's situation."

"I see." Neva's expression was sour. "I suppose our issue can wait until tomorrow."

"Thank you." Skye's stomach clenched. "Normally, I'd be happy to rearrange my schedule to talk to the young man right away."

"Fine." Neva pushed back her chair. "Ms. Lawrence, do not engage this young man until Skye has spoken to him. If he says anything regarding your call to his parents, avoid the subject as best you can."

"Yes, ma'am," Violet answered. "I doubt that he'll bring it up."

"Good." Neva nodded. "Now let's move on to item number two on our agenda."

Thirty minutes later, Neva stood to indicate the meeting was over and they were all dismissed. "Thank you, everyone. See you next week." She put her hand on Skye's arm stopping her attempt to slip out the door. "I need a word with you before you go."

Skye nodded, stepped back into the classroom, and waited.

Once everyone else had left, Neva shut the door and asked, "I don't wish to pry into your private life, but is there a problem with your babies?"

"No." Her pulse quickened.

Rats!

She had worked hard to gain the principal's trust and she wished she could tell her about the murder. "I can't explain right now, but I hope to be able to clarify the situation tomorrow."

"I would appreciate that." Neva's expression was troubled. "I know I can seem distant, but I consider you more than just an employee."

"Thank you." Skye swallowed a lump in her throat. "I'm happy to hear that."

"I depend on you. Probably more than I should," Neva admitted.

"In what way?" Skye was confused. "You've never asked me to do anything that I wouldn't consider my job."

"I appreciate that." Neva tilted her head. "But having you gone during your maternity leave, I realized that everyone turns to you for assistance."

"Which I'm happy to provide," Skye said.

"I'm sure you are." Neva shrugged her shoulders. "However, we really need to get you some help. In these trying times, three schools are just too much for one mental health professional to shoulder."

"I definitely wouldn't turn down some assistance." Skye beamed.

"Good." Neva nodded. "I've been impressed with Piper's performance. What would you think of offering her a job when her internship is completed?"

Skye stood stunned by Neva's words and spoke before she remembered that Dr. Wraige was dead. "I think that would be awesome. The superintendent also mentioned something of that sort, but I wasn't sure he was serious. Will he approve a second position and if he does, can he get it passed the board?"

"Dr. Wraige will do what I ask." Neva's smile was mysterious. "And he has the school board right where he wants them."

CHAPTER 8

Who Will Be My Valentine?

S KYE DASHED TO HER SUV, UNLOCKED THE DOOR, AND threw her purse and tote bag on the passenger seat. Sliding behind the wheel, she was already tugging her cell phone from her pocket and sending a message to Wally telling him she was finished with her meeting.

A few seconds later, she realized she had no idea where Dr. Wraige lived and followed up with a quick text asking for his address. Wally immediately responded with the superintendent's street name and house number.

Skye punched that information into her GPS and sent a prayer of thanks that after her Bel Air had been totaled in the tornado, Wally had surprised her with the wonderful new luxury vehicle. She had a terrible sense of direction and the Mercedes's navigation package was a lifesaver.

In fact, the system was so advanced, Skye was just waiting for the upper-crust British voice to start saying, "Your other left, madam," when she made a wrong turn.

Chuckling at her flight of fancy, Skye fastened her seat belt and drove out of the parking lot. She knew how to get to the elite subdivision but would have been lost without the GPS instructions once she passed the fancy stone entrance.

As she drove, Skye mulled over Neva's parting statements. Why would Dr. Wraige have agreed to do what the principal asked? And how had the superintendent gotten the school board right where he wanted them?

Bearing in mind that the man in question had just been killed, those were questions she definitely had to remember to share with Wally. There was a fair possibility that the answers might shed some light on the motivation behind Dr. Wraige's murder. Or could even point to the killer.

Approaching the housing development, Skye unmuted the GPS and followed the elegant voice's direction until she saw Wally's Hummer in the driveway of a whitewashed brick home. The adjacent cul-de-sac was filled with a squad car, a dark blue county crime scene van, and a white Ford Transit with *Medical Examiner* stenciled on it in gold.

It hadn't occurred to her when Wally mentioned that the ME was at the scene, but as Skye parked in the last open spot along the cul-de-sac's curb, she wondered why the medical examiner was there instead of Simon Reid, the county coroner. Then again, Simon was her ex-boyfriend and thus not one of her husband's favorite people. Had Wally found a way to cut him out of the loop?

Whatever.

Skye mentally shrugged. She didn't really care and had enough to worry about without adding Simon's absence to her list.

Besides, if Wally had bypassed him, it would make the situation a lot easier for her. Since her marriage, Simon always had a snarky remark about her husband or someone else Skye loved. At first, she cut him some slack because she knew he was hurt by their breakup. But it had been over a year now, and she was getting sick of it.

When she realized just how much weight had been lifted

from her shoulders by the knowledge that she wouldn't have to deal with Simon, Skye blew out a breath. She'd never allowed herself to think about how stressed she'd been by his spitefulness. Notifying the next of kin about the death of their loved one was bad enough without a snide ex around.

Grabbing her purse, Skye put the strap across her body, exited the car, and headed toward Wally, who was waiting for her in front of the large house. He motioned her over to him and Skye waved back, then hurried to join him on the sidewalk.

When Wally grabbed Skye's hand and started leading her away, Skye asked, "Where are we going?"

"The crime scene techs are still in the house and haven't released the scene yet," Wally explained. "But they should be finished any minute. In the meantime, while we're waiting for Quirk to return with Mrs. Wraige and her stepson, I'll bring you up to speed."

"Will Roy tell them that Dr. Wraige is dead?" Skye asked, pretty sure she knew the answer.

"No." Wally led Skye around to the back of the house and they climbed the steps up to the deck. "He'll just say there was another break-in."

"I see." Skye sighed. "Which means you'd like me to tell them."

Nodding, Wally cautioned, "But not until I give you the go-ahead."

Wally brushed the snow off a couple of patio chairs and dried them with a towel from the duffel bag he was carrying, then motioned Skye to take a seat. Once she was settled and he was sitting, she waited several minutes for him to speak. Finally, she cleared her throat to get him going.

Wally startled as if his thoughts had been somewhere else, then he took a deep breath and said, "I'm glad you were able to get away. Did Homer give you any trouble about leaving for the afternoon?"

"Not all." Skye chuckled. "Mostly because he was unavailable when I called. He'd gone out to lunch. So I just left a message with Opal and alerted Piper."

"Good." Wally leaned forward and gave her a quick kiss. "I'm glad you have someone to help you out. Too bad she's temporary."

"Actually"—Skye tapped his nose—"Neva just mentioned that the district might offer Piper a full-time job once her internship is over."

"Neva?" Wally's eyebrows shot into his hairline. "Why would she be the one to tell you that? Wouldn't that be something Wraige would announce? Or even more likely the school board would have to finalize?"

"Normally, yes." Skye explained her conversation with the junior high principal, then added. "She seemed sort of different today."

Wally wrinkled his brow. "Because she was making promises that she had no business making?"

"That." Skye pursed her lips. "But she also stated that we were more than colleagues."

"How odd." Wally's frown deepened. "You've always told me that she's extremely formal with her staff, right?" When Skye nodded, he continued. "And that she's really rigid about people staying in their lanes, which she definitely swerved out of when she told you about hiring Piper."

Before Skye could respond, a crime scene tech opened the kitchen's sliding glass door, pushed her jumpsuit hood back, removed her goggles, and said, "We're done here if you want to come inside, Chief." She glanced at Skye and added, "Oh, hi, Mrs. Boyd."

At first Skye didn't recognize the woman. She'd met quite

a few of the techs at various crime scenes and with them all usually dressed in identical protective gear, it was hard to identify them individually.

After a few seconds, Skye realized this was the tech who had processed her for evidence when their builder's wife was murdered and quickly said, "Hi!" She narrowed her eyes. "You know, I never did get my coat back after you took it from me at the other crime scene. How do I go about claiming it?"

"Oops!" The woman blushed. "It must have gotten misplaced. I'll find it and send it to the police station as soon as I get to the lab."

"Thanks." Skye had really liked that coat, and with the tornado taking must of her clothes, her wardrobe was still pretty meager.

"Unless there's something else, Chief, my partner and I will be taking off," the tech said twisting her dark brown ponytail. "We like to get everything secured in our evidence room ASAP."

"Not that I can think of right now." Wally tilted his head, considering. "Wait. Did you take the statue, including the base?"

"Yep. Cupid is in our van ready for his trip to Laurel." The tech's hazel eyes twinkled. "Maybe he can improve the love lives around our lab."

"If his last owner is any indication, you don't want this cupid's help," Wally said dryly. "Either you'll end up dead or in handcuffs."

"Oh. Yeah." The woman chuckled. "I almost forgot about the adult toys we found." She turned to leave, then just before she walked away, she added, "Oh. The ME has the body loaded in her Transit, but she wants a word with you."

"I'll be right in." Wally rose from his chair and offered Skye his hand. "Shall we?"

"Sure." Skye got up and followed him inside. "Where was Dr. Wraige?"

"In the master suite." Wally pointed to the left. "In the sitting area."

Wally started to say something else, but before he could speak, Doris Ann Norris, the medical examiner, strode into the kitchen. She was in her late fifties, wearing a pair of black slacks and a red turtleneck with a thigh-length black-and-red cardigan. A coordinating scarf looped around her neck and her ash-blond hair was styled in a smooth bob that stopped right below her chin.

Even the crumpled Tyvek coverall she held in her hands didn't mar her casual elegance. Although the PVC booties on her feet did make for an odd picture.

Smiling, she said, "Chief, Skye, good to see you both. Sorry it's under these circumstances." She chuckled. "I was hoping the next time we met, it would be over a nice dinner rather than a dead body."

Dr. Norris had only been on the job for a few months, but during their initial encounter, when Wally realized that she'd be alone over Thanksgiving, he'd invited her to join them for their family dinner. Soon after that, Doris Ann and Wally's father had become an item.

"Me too." Skye stepped forward and gave the ME a big hug. "So, what's the scoop?"

"I can't tell you too much yet," Doris Ann said. "But there was some powdery residue near his fly that might end up being helpful."

"Why is that?" Skye asked, not sure she really wanted to know.

"Because his time of death is roughly between eight and ten a.m."

"Actually." Wally flipped open his notepad. "The vic was

alive at eight thirty because that was when he called the mayor to complain that the police weren't doing enough about his burglaries and to say he'd heard someone rattle his back door, but no one was there when he went to check on it."

"Great." Doris Ann beamed. "Then you only have a ninety-minute window."

"What does his time of death have to do with the stuff on his pants?" Skye asked.

"Well." She looked at Skye as if to gauge her reaction. "I'm pretty sure the stuff, as you called it, is a powder-based makeup…"

"I see." Skye screwed up her face as she thought about the implications of Doris Ann's statement. "On his shirt or sleeve, he could have brushed up against the makeup on a dressing table or something."

"Right," the ME agreed. "But where it was located on his fly, it's more plausible that he was brushing against *someone* rather than something."

Wally glanced between Skye and Doris Ann, then said, "So what you're trying to tell me, Doc, is that he was probably getting intimate with someone, and she might very well be his killer." He shook his head. "Which means that his wife is a prime suspect."

Skye asked him, "You do remember what we learned about the superintendent's sex life when we investigated Palmer Wraige's murder?"

"Of course I do. That's why I mentioned the handcuffs to the crime scene tech." Wally took a breath, evidently processing the implications and cursed. "Shi-shizzle!" He corrected himself and Skye rewarded him with a smile for sticking to their no swearing agreement.

"What about his sex life?" Doris Ann asked, clearly intrigued.

Skye looked at Wally for permission to reveal the information and when he gave a slight nod, she said, "Dr. Wraige belonged to a BDSM club and had partners that weren't his wife."

"No shit!" Doris Ann's pupils dilated. "And he was superintendent of your school district? I would have never guessed in a million years that Scumble River was so liberal-minded."

Chuckling at the older woman's shocked expression, Skye said, "I doubt anyone, except the other members of his club, knew about his tastes."

Wally cleared his throat. "Since it wasn't pertinent to our previous case, we didn't reveal his proclivities, and I trust as a member of our investigative team, you'll keep it quiet as well."

"Absolutely," Doris Ann assured him. "But I am glad you mentioned it because I will take that information into consideration when I do the autopsy. There may be marks that might have to do with his consensual actions that I would have chalked up to his struggle with whoever pushed him into the cupid."

"Good enough," Wally answered. "I'll be looking for your report, when?"

"I'll have my prelim done by the end of business today," Doris Ann said, then added, "And I'll see you two at the Valentine's dance Saturday night. Bye!"

Once the ME was gone, Wally turned to Skye, "Quirk should be back any minute. In the meantime, shall we go look at the scene?"

"Sure." Skye winced inwardly, hoping there wasn't a lot of blood.

"Are you sure?" Wally asked, then searched Skye's face and added, "It's not too bad, but if you'd rather not, you can wait here."

"I'm fine." She fought to keep her expression neutral. "Let's go."

"Okay." Wally took Skye's hand and they walked down the hall into the shadowy bedroom, and then up to a pair of louvered doors.

As she followed Wally, Skye noted the furniture. French provincial wasn't her taste, too ornate, but she could tell that what the Wraiges had was authentic and worth tens of thousands of dollars. Exactly how much money was the superintendent's salary?

Before Skye could ponder the question of Dr. Wraige's wealth any further, Wally opened the louvered doors and she refocused. Studying the sitting room, she took in the cozy furniture arrangement by the fireplace, then scanned the rest of area.

Off to one side, on a white marble pedestal, stood a bronze statue of a nude woman. Opposite her was a space that Skye assumed had held the sculpture of cupid that Wally had mentioned to Doris Ann.

Moving closer to the empty spot, Skye almost stepped into an enormous pool of blood. She quickly averted her gaze and went around it.

Obviously, that was where the superintendent had been lying as he bled to death. The techs would have taken a sample but hadn't cleaned it up.

Skye hoped his family wouldn't have to see this. She reminded herself to tell them about the trauma and biohazard removal company that operated in their area. That business would also take care of the fingerprint powder and evidence-gathering chemicals that were left behind by the techs.

Lost in thought, Skye jumped when Wally touched her arm and asked, "Is there anything you've observed that might be a clue of some kind?"

Blinking, Skye tried to concentrate. She told herself this was sort of like the game she played with her counseling kids. What's not like the rest of the items? Or what's missing from the picture?

Determined to be professional, Skye began a search of the room. Taking a closer look, she saw that there were three beverage rings on the table in front of the love seat. Shouldn't there only be two?

Pointing the number out to Wally, she asked, "What do you make of that?"

Wally raise an eyebrow, then shrugged. "If we hadn't found out during our previous investigation that Mrs. Wraige wasn't a participant in her husband's BDSM sex life, I'd guess maybe ménage à trois."

"I take it the crime scene techs took the cups and will be testing them for DNA and fingerprints?" Skye asked.

"Yes, they mentioned bagging the mugs." Wally gestured toward the table. "They also recovered a paper muffin cup they found on the floor under there. It was similar to the one on the kitchen counter, so I had them grab that one too."

"Hmm." Skye tucked that info away.

She moved over to peer at the tall narrow bookcase on the wall opposite the statues. The glass doors were open and it was empty.

Wally stepped over to her and asked, "Do you see something?"

"From the imprints in the dust, it seems that whatever was in this cabinet was recently removed." Careful not to touch the surface of the glass doors, Skye pointed. "Look at the lock on the door."

"Okay."

"It doesn't appear as if it's been forced open." Skye wrinkled her forehead. "You might want to have the crime scene techs determine if it's been picked."

Wally scrutinized the shiny metal and shook his head. "I'll have them examine it, but there are no scratches."

"Which would mean whoever opened those doors had a key." Skye pursed her lips. "I wonder what was on those shelves. They remind me of a cabinet that my intern supervisor had in his office. It held his stamp collection." She rubbed her chin as she thought about what she knew about the superintendent, then confirmed, "Dr. Wraige has had several break-ins, right? Maybe someone stole whatever was here."

"I suppose that's possible," Wally murmured. "The thefts have all been of small but valuable items, like a painting or jewelry."

"My supervisor had a stamp that was worth over twenty thousand dollars."

"Wow!" Wally whistled. "What was the average price of his stamps?"

"Two or three hundred dollars." Skye crossed her arms. "But to a collector, it's not just the cash value, it's the feeling of owning an object that few others possess."

"If the superintendent was the collector rather than his wife, taking his collection would be hitting him where it really hurts," Wally mused.

"Exactly. And if Dr. Wraige caught the thief in the act, he'd have tried to stop him, which could have been when the burglar pushed him into Cupid."

CHAPTER 9

Blue Valentines

S KYE REACHED OVER AND GAVE HER HUSBAND'S HAND A
  sympathetic squeeze. They were sitting in the Wraiges'
kitchen waiting for the sergeant to show up with the deceased's
wife and adult son. Skye was using her time to answer various
texts and emails, but Wally had spent the past twenty minutes
pacing the length of the room, then back again, only recently
dropping into the chair next to hers.

"I can't imagine what's taking Quirk so long," Wally
grumbled.

"He'll be here soon." Skye had been at the crime scene a
good hour already, and although she was as restless as Wally,
she was better at hiding her impatience.

"It's not as if there's that many places they could be in
Scumble River." Wally tapped his nails on the tabletop.

"Maybe Mrs. Wraige or Tavish was out to lunch and
Roy couldn't find them," Skye offered before returning to
the message she was typing to Dorothy, thanking her for the
recording of Eva clapping her hands together. She also added
a message reassuring the housekeeper that CJ hadn't meant to
hit his twin when he tried to join her playing patty-cake. Once

Skye finished with her text, she showed Wally the video and said, "Look at our daughter."

Wally gazed at the small screen and crooned, "What a cutie pie." He watched the short clip, then jerked his head and asked, "Was that a car?"

Thrusting Skye's phone back into her hands, Wally strode out of the kitchen.

She stuffed her cell in her pocket, then rose and followed him to the foyer. Roy's cruiser was parked in the driveway and he was helping an attractive woman in her late thirties out of the passenger seat.

As a man exited from the rear of the cruiser, Skye recognized him as the superintendent's son. He had on an unbuttoned navy jacket over the same delft-blue suit he had worn at the meeting where he'd been introduced to the school staff the day before.

Ignoring his stepmother, Tavish walked quickly toward the front door and shoved it open. It swung inward toward Skye and she had to jump out of the way to avoid being smacked in the face.

"Watch it, buster!" Wally growled, snaking his arm around Skye's waist and pulling her out of the man's path. "Slow the heck down."

At Wally's command, Tavish stopped and looked around, then seemed to realize who had spoken, and straightened as he said, "Sorry, sir."

Before Wally could respond, Roy and Mrs. Wraige entered the house.

The woman marched up to Wally and demanded, "Why did you send for me? February through April are my busiest months. Shamus is perfectly able to handle reporting what-ever has been stolen this time."

"Ma'am," Wally said soothingly. "How about if we sit down and I'll explain?"

"I'd rather talk to my husband." Mrs. Wraige tightened the belt of her fashionable winter-white trench coat. "After Sergeant Quirk insisted that I accompany him back here, I called Shamus's cell, but he didn't answer."

"Mrs. Wraige." Skye glanced at Wally, and he nodded his permission. "I'm Skye Denison-Boyd." She held out her hand. "I don't believe we've met, but I'm the school district psychologist."

"Call me Nanette." She automatically accepted Skye's hand and shook it as she questioned, "Are you Loretta Steiner-Denison's sister-in-law?"

"Yes, I am." Skye held on to the woman's hand and guided her down the hallway toward the kitchen, then over her shoulder, she said to the men, "I really think it's best if we all sit down before we talk."

Nanette frowned but allowed herself to be seated at the table. Tavish took the place opposite his stepmother while Wally and Skye sat in the two remaining chairs. Out of the corner of her eye, Skye noticed Roy heading toward the master suite. She figured that Wally had assigned him to keep the crime scene secured in the event either of the family members tried to enter it.

"Did Loretta tell you that I'm also the police department's psych consultant?" When Nanette nodded, Skye continued, "That's why I'm here."

"Oh." Nanette glanced at Wally, her pretty blue eyes narrowed. "Why would you need a psychologist for a break-in? You didn't call her in for the previous ones."

"I promise to answer all your questions before we're finished." Wally took over the conversation. "But I need you to answer mine first."

Skye sat back, subtly indicating that Wally was now in charge.

"What's going on here, Chief?" Tavish spoke before his stepmother could reply.

"Again, if you'll both be patient, we'll get through this a lot faster."

"Fine." Nanette glared at her stepson, then smiled tightly at Wally. "Go ahead."

"What time did you two leave this morning?" Wally took out his memo pad.

"I left at seven ten, sir." Tavish squared his shoulders. "I report for duty at the high school at seven twenty, and it takes me ten minutes to drive there, park, and sign in at the office."

"And what time did you leave, ma'am?" Wally looked at Nanette.

"About seven forty-five," she answered. "My first client was scheduled for eight."

"Does your friend Colleen still live here?" Wally asked, and when Nanette nodded, he continued, "Did she also leave at that time?"

"No. She left a little earlier," Nanette explained. "She had an appointment in Chicago to discuss strategy with her divorce lawyer at eleven." She glanced at Skye and explained, "Colleen's husband is trying to get custody of their ten-year-old daughter, Rosemary, and Colleen's fighting him."

"Does the girl live here?" Wally hadn't seen any sign of a child.

"No. Currently, Rosemary is with her maternal grandparents. The judge thought it best that she lives with them until everything is settled between her parents. That way she can continue going to the same school she's always attended and Colleen and her soon-to-be ex can have supervised visits."

Supervised visits! Skye frowned. Something was fishy with that situation and she wondered what Nanette was leaving out of the story.

"Why isn't Colleen living with her parents too?" Wally asked, evidently on the same wavelength as Skye.

Nanette fidgeted with a strand of raven-black hair that had come loose from her bun. "While Rosemary's grandparents were happy to have their granddaughter live with them, they don't approve of Colleen and refused to let her stay there."

"Why don't they approve of her?" Wally probed.

Nanette seemed to realize she was saying too much. "I don't believe that's any of your business."

At this point, Skye could see from Wally's expression that he wanted to press Nanette for more information, but he knew he didn't have a good enough reason to do so without revealing the superintendent's murder.

"Okay," he conceded, then asked, "But why did Colleen leave so early for an eleven o'clock appointment?"

"She thought it might take longer than usual because of rush hour traffic and construction on I-55. She figured if she was early, she'd do some shopping. I expect her back late this afternoon."

"I see. How about your husband?" Wally asked. "Did he leave when you did?"

"Shamus wasn't going into his office until ten today," Nanette explained. "The board meeting went late last night and he didn't get home until midnight, so he'd only been awake for a short while when I left. Just enough time for us to have a cup of coffee together." She paused and frowned. "Haven't you talked to him? Who reported the break-in?"

"Just a few more questions and I'll clear up everything," Wally soothed. "What was in the locked cabinet in your sitting room?"

Tavish answered before his stepmother could speak. "My father kept his coin collection there. Those shelves were full of his albums. Was that what was stolen?"

"The cabinet is empty," Wally answered. "Who has the key to it?"

"Shamus keeps it in his office." Nanette shrugged. "But it's pretty flimsy and I've seen him pop it open with a paper clip a few times when he's forgotten to bring the key home with him."

"Is there any chance Dr. Wraige moved those albums somewhere else?"

"They were there this morning," Nanette answered. "I would have noticed if they were missing."

"Do you have a list of the coins?" Wally asked.

"No." Nanette stood, shrugged out of her coat, arranged it on the back of her chair, then resumed her seat. "Shamus keeps a record on his laptop."

"We'll need a copy of that list." Wally jotted down a note, then added, "Once we're through here, would you be able to get it for us?"

"You'll have to ask my father for the inventory." Tavish's hands had been resting loosely on the table, but now he clasped them together.

Skye, wondering what about that statement made him uncomfortable, asked in a mild tone of voice, "Is that because the computer is password protected or because it's not here in the house?"

"Both." Tavish's knuckles whitened. "He keeps it in his office. Since the break-ins, he's been keeping more and more of his personal belongings there."

"You can call him at work and ask him to bring a list when he comes home," Nanette offered, then her forehead wrinkled and she added, "Or did you say you tried him there and couldn't reach him?"

Ignoring her question, Wally turned to Tavish and asked, "Once you were at the school, did you leave the building again before Sergeant Quirk picked you up?"

"No, I had several residential discrepancies to follow up on and paperwork to complete," Tavish answered, then frowned. "Why do you ask?"

Just as he had ignored Nanette's question, Wally ignored her stepson's and asked, "Was anyone with you while you were doing that?"

"No. I'm currently using a desk in the basement and only the custodian comes down there," Tavish explained, then narrowed his eyes. "Do you suspect me of stealing my father's coin collection?"

"How long were you with your client, Mrs. Wraige?" Wally turned away from Tavish and focused his attention on Nanette, who Skye noted was nervously tapping her wedding ring on the tabletop.

"Uh." Nanette looked up as if she'd forgotten she wasn't alone. "Oh. She never showed up."

"Do you have any employees?" Skye asked.

"Just a part-time tax preparer, but she's home with the flu."

"Then you were alone all morning?" Wally asked.

Nanette's olive skin paled, and she swallowed. "This isn't about another burglary. Something bad has happened to Shamus, hasn't it?"

Wally and Skye exchanged looks. Neither family member had an alibi, and they weren't going to get much more information out of them. Wally gave Skye a slight nod. It was time for her to deliver the bad news.

"I'm afraid so." Skye took Nanette's hand, then gently explained, "The superintendent called the mayor to say he'd heard someone trying to get in, but that he had scared them away. As soon as Dante informed the police, Wally headed over here. When he arrived, your husband didn't answer the door or his phone. Wally investigated and discovered the sliding door was unlocked. He went inside to do a wellness check, and he found Dr. Wraige dead."

Tavish leaped to his feet. "What happened? Was it his heart?" Without waiting for an answer, he ran out of the kitchen.

Wally followed him and Skye heard Roy order, "Stop. Stay right there."

Interesting. It appeared that Tavish had headed right for the master suite, and Skye hadn't mentioned where Wally had found Dr. Wraige.

Of course, the superintendent's son had seen the living room–dining room from the foyer and been in the kitchen, so the only other places would have been Tavish's room or the guest room.

Skye turned her attention back to Nanette, who was sitting as if frozen in place with tears trickling down her cheeks. She silently offered the woman a tissue from the packet she kept in her pocket. One good thing about being a sinus sufferer is that she always had Kleenex tucked away somewhere readily available for a sneeze.

So far, Dr. Wraige's widow had displayed all the appropriate behavior, but Skye knew that killers often cried when informed their victims were dead. She wasn't sure if it was remorse or if they had just convinced themselves the murder never took place.

While she was waiting for the appropriate moment to offer Nanette a drink of water, Skye heard Wally in hallway say, "Let's sit in the living room. I'd like you to give me a list of anyone who might want your father dead."

She didn't hear Tavish's response, but he must have agreed because the men's voices became fainter. Wally was now separating family members so he and Skye could compare their stories later on.

Finally, Nanette sniffed loudly, then blinked away the remaining tears in her eyes. She drew in a deep breath and seemed to get ahold of herself.

After accepting another tissue from Skye and blowing her nose, she asked quietly, "How did Shamus die?"

"I'm not at liberty to share the details right now, but it appears that he was killed during a struggle," Skye said carefully.

"You mean it wasn't a natural death?" Nanette's gaze flew to Skye.

"We can't make any kind of definitive statement until the medical examiner completes the autopsy," Skye hedged. "Did your husband have a medical condition?"

"Just the usual for his age and stress level." Nanette made a face. "You know, high blood pressure, high cholesterol, and gout."

"I see." Skye nodded her head. "It's doubtful that any of those is the cause of death. But again, we'll have to wait for the ME's report."

"I want to see him." Nanette tried to rise to her feet, but Skye put a hand on her shoulder and pressed her back into her chair.

"I'm sorry, but your husband's body has already been removed by the medical examiner." Skye patted Nanette's arm and added, "You can go over to Laurel and see him there as soon as she finishes the autopsy."

"But…" Nanette looked around the kitchen as if she were lost. Focusing back on Skye she asked, "What do I do now? Should I call people?"

Skye felt sorry for the woman. She tried to imagine hearing the news that Wally was gone and shuddered. Quickly pushing away that horrific thought, she rummaged in her purse until she found the case where she kept the collection of business cards that she'd accumulated throughout the years.

Selecting two, she said, "Once we're finished here, give Mr. Reid a call at the funeral home. I'm sure he'll know what has to be done in these circumstances and can guide you. The other card is for a biohazard removal company that you can contact to clean up the scene once the house is released back to you."

"Finished here?" Nanette latched on to the first thing Skye had said and asked, "What else do you need from me?"

Skye knew she had to take notes for this next part. She wished she had brought in her tote bag, which contained a fresh legal pad, but digging through her purse again, she found a small pad of Post-Its and a pen.

Ready to proceed, she said, "Can you tell me anything about the recent spate of burglaries you and your husband have experienced?"

"Well." Nanette ran her fingers through her smooth black hair, messing up the neat bun on top of her head. "The only thing significant that I can think of is that the thief passed up a lot of valuable stuff and only took one item each time he broke in here."

"That is odd." Skye jotted down a quick note. "What was stolen?"

"The first time it was Shamus's jewelry box." Nanette held up her index finger. "The second time it was the leather case where he kept his Stefano Ricci neckties." She paused. "And you said this time it looked as if his coin collection is missing, right?"

"Right," Skye answered, thinking about the stolen items. "We'll have you and Tavish look through the house to see if anything else is gone, but that was the only obvious space I noticed that was empty."

"Okay." Nanette's voice cracked, then she startled. "I almost forgot. It wasn't taken in a break-in, but Shamus's Black Label Lincoln Navigator was stolen too."

"That's right." Skye stared into space for a few second, then snapped her fingers. "So the only items taken all belonged to Dr. Wraige?"

"You know, I guess that's true." Nanette screwed up her face. "I hadn't realized that before. But maybe it's because I keep my jewelry in my office safe, and I don't really collect anything or drive a fancy car."

"Hmm. Maybe." Skye nodded, then asked, "Did your husband have any enemies?"

"Of course not!" Nanette snapped. "He was a good man who worked hard for his community."

"Of course," Skye soothed, then took a deep breath. She hated to bring it up, but they were much more likely to get an honest answer now rather than later when Nanette was thinking more clearly. "How about someone from that social club he belonged to, the one in Laurel?"

"I don't know what you mean." Nanette looked down, refusing to meet Skye's gaze.

"Yes, you do. The BDSM club," Skye said gently. "We found out about it when Palmer Lynch was murdered, and I was told that although you didn't participate, you knew and accepted his activities there."

"Oh," Nanette gasped. "That closed down right after Palmer died." Her eyes widened. "Will what Shamus did there get out?"

"Not if it doesn't have anything to do with his death," Skye assured her, then searched her mind in order to phrase it as delicately as she could. "Once the Laurel club closed down, did your husband go elsewhere to uh…enjoy that kind of uh…release?"

"No." Nanette shook her head. "We came to a compromise that we both could live with, so he didn't have to seek outside stimulation."

"Okay." Skye wasn't sure she believed the woman, but she'd pushed it as far as Nanette could handle without making the woman close down completely. "Did Dr. Wraige have any additional children besides Tavish?"

"Not yet." Nanette's expression saddened. "But we were planning on starting a family soon. Tavish wasn't thrilled at the idea of an infant sibling," she said, then smiled meanly. "But there really wasn't anything he could do about it."

"Except maybe kill his dad," Skye murmured under her breath.

CHAPTER 10

I'd Do Anything for Love

HOW ABOUT HIS POSITION AS SUPERINTENDENT OF schools?" Wally probed. "Surely that could bring him into contact with people who might harbor hard feelings regarding some of his decisions or policies."

"My father didn't really talk about his work." Tavish shook his head. "The only part that we discussed were the duties included in my new job."

Wally and Tavish were in the Wraige's dining room. Once Skye had revealed that the superintendent was dead, Wally separated the two household members, leaving Skye in the kitchen to interview the victim's wife while he interrogated the man's son.

Like the rest of the house, this room was furnished with heavy French provincial pieces, and the men were seated across from each at an oak draw-leaf table. It wasn't Wally's taste, but he'd been exposed to enough valuable antiques growing up that he knew it was the real thing and probably darned expensive.

Wally rubbed a finger along the carved floral edge as he asked, "How about Scott Ricci, the guy he let go in order to hire you?"

"Nah." Tavish smiled. "My father gave him a glowing recommendation and helped him move into a better paying position in Normalton."

"So why didn't he get you that spot?" Wally picked up his pen and jotted that information in his notepad.

"I didn't have the school-based experience that Ricci had." Tavish's hands gripped each other tightly.

Wally noted that this was a frequent habit of the guy and wondered if it had anything to do with hanging on to his temper. "Still, giving another guy the superior job…" Wally murmured to see if he could prod the younger Wraige into losing his cool.

Instead, Tavish straightened his back and calmly explained, "I've only recently separated from the military. My father suggested I live here while adjusting to civilian life again. He said that taking a position with the school district would help me expand my résumé."

"I see." Wally's phone vibrated.

He held it in his lap and saw that he was getting a text from Skye. He kept his expression neutral as he read her message.

Looking up, Wally said, "Okay. One last thing. Why were you so against your father having a child with his current wife?"

"It was my opinion, sir, that neither of them would make good parents." Tavish met Wally's gaze without blinking. "Both Dad and Nanette are extremely career-driven people. They only wanted a baby because it would make them look better in the community, which would help my father get another contract from the board. He was afraid his age might be a concern when his next negotiations came up and was convinced having a child in preschool would make him seem younger."

"And Nanette?"

"Being a part of the 'Moms Club'"—Tavish used his fingers to indicate quotation marks—"would help her get more clients for her accounting firm."

"Or maybe they were ready to change their focus," Wally suggested to see how the younger man would react.

"Hardly," Tavish snorted. "Hell! Half the time they forgot they owned a cat. Snowflake wasn't affectionate enough for them and didn't show enough gratitude for her care. I was the one that usually ended up feeding her and cleaning her litter box." He frowned and leaped up from his chair. "Hey! Where is Snowflake?"

"We found a carrier in the garage and secured her in it." Wally motioned for Tavish to sit down. "Relax. She's fine."

"You left her in a cold garage?" Tavish seemed more upset about the cat's comfort than his father's death.

"No." Wally jerked his thumb over his shoulder. "We put the carrier in the hallway near your room."

Tavish nodded and resumed his seat. "Okay. That's good. Can I go check on her?"

Wally glanced at his notes. "When we're done." Was he missing anything important?

After asking Tavish a few more routine questions, Wally led Tavish back into the kitchen where the two women were sitting silently.

As Wally and Tavish walked into the room, Skye said, "We're finished in here. How about you?"

Before Wally could speak, Nanette asked, "What happens next?"

"The ME will notify you when she's ready to release your husband's remains," Wally began, "and unfortunately since this is a crime scene, I'll have to ask you to turn over your house keys and vacate the premise until we're sure we've gathered all the evidence. Skye will go with you while you get your things together and I'll accompany your stepson while he gathers his belongings. While you're at it, let me know if you notice anything missing."

Both Tavish and Nanette objected, but when Wally didn't react, they seemed to realize that their protests wouldn't change anything and acquiesced. Shooting him an annoyed glare, Nanette followed Skye out of the kitchen.

Wally trailed Tavish as he marched stiffly through the house toward his room.

After Tavish finished filling his large khaki duffel, he and Wally met the women at the front door and Nanette said, "I'll need to pack for Colleen too."

Wally nodded and Skye trailed Nanette down the hallway leading to the guest room. While Wally and Tavish waited, Tavish reached into the pet carrier and scratched the cat behind her ears. Snowflake purred contentedly.

When Skye and Nanette returned, Wally looked at the Wraiges and said, "We'll use the fingerprints you two and your guest gave us after the first burglary for elimination purposes from the ones that were found in the crime scene. And, as soon as Ms. Vreesen returns to town, she needs drop off her house key at the police station."

"I'll make sure she does that." Nanette nodded.

As they all walked outside toward their vehicles, Wally added, "I'll need to know where you all will be staying."

Nanette climbed into her car. "My office has a furnished two-bedroom apartment over it that is currently vacant. The previous tenant moved out a couple of days ago and Colleen was planning to move in as soon as we had a chance to clean it. We'll stay there." She made a face. "I guess I'll work off my grief scrubbing the place down."

"I'm not sure where I'll go. I noticed the Up A Lazy River

motor court is closed." Tavish pursed his lips. "Where *is* the next nearest hotel?"

Wally took a peek at Skye and she was scowling at him. He shrugged at her as if to say it wasn't his fault her god-father's motel was out of business while Charlie was under investigation by the state police.

Realizing the Wraiges were staring at him, Wally answered, "Laurel." He felt uneasy at the thought of one of his prime suspects being so far away and hastily added, "However, I just remembered, one of my officers is looking for someone to rent a bedroom at her house. Maybe she'd put you up. But she has a dog. Will the cat be okay with that?"

"Sure." Tavish patted the top of the carrier affectionately. "Snowflake is a mellow lady."

For a nanosecond, Wally worried about suggesting that a possible murderer stay with Martinez, but he shrugged it off. Not only was she armed, the dog he'd just mentioned was actually the newest member of their squad. If Wraige tried anything, Arnold would tear him apart.

"Okay. Let me check with her."

Wally texted Martinez, warning her that Tavish was a suspect in the superintendent's murder and had a cat. A few seconds later she replied that she was okay with both facts and would be happy to rent the guy a room.

After passing Martinez's address onto Tavish, Wally walked Skye to her SUV. He asked her to send the summary of her talk with Nanette to his police email and kissed her goodbye.

He'd been thinking about what aspect of the crime he should pursue next and had decided that although both Nanette and Tavish were reasonable suspects, at this point finding out what coins were missing and tracking them down would be the best use of his time.

With that in mind, Wally drove the short distance to the victim's office. The district's administrative building was located adjacent to the elementary school. The board had gotten a deal on a house when the owner had died with no heirs and gutted it to fit their needs.

Wally parked, exited his Hummer, and walked up the cement ramp that had been added to the front of the structure to meet accessibility requirements. He pushed through the double glass doors and entered a small foyer that led to what had to have originally been the house's living room. Now it contained a large U-shaped desk and a wall lined with file cabinets. Two tweed wing chairs were arranged with a small table between them.

A forty-something redhead looked up from her computer screen, smiled, and purred, "Chief Boyd, what brings you here today?"

"Ms. Kline, I'm sorry to inform you that Dr. Wraige died this morning."

Wally watched the administrative assistant's reaction carefully. Rumor had it that she and the superintendent had once been involved.

She paled. "What happened? He wasn't sick. Did he have a heart attack?"

"I'm sorry, Ms. Kline, we aren't releasing that information yet."

Swallowing hard, she visibly pulled herself together, smoothed her hair, and said, "I've asked you several times to please call me Karolyn."

"I'll need to access Dr. Wraige's laptop." Wally's tone was businesslike. He was used to women flirting with him but had no interest in anyone but his beautiful wife. "Is it in his office?"

A tiny frown marred her unnaturally smooth forehead. "I

believe so. He usually leaves it here rather than hauling it back and forth."

"May I?" Wally nodded toward a closed door. It had a gleaming brass nameplate engraved with a small crest and Dr. Shamus Wraige, Superintendent.

"Certainly." Karolyn rose, walked over, and turned the knob, then ran her tongue over her lips and offered, "Anything I can do to help?"

"Not at the moment."

Wally stepped forward, and she arranged herself so that he had to come in contact with her to enter the room. As he eased past her, she thrust out her chest so that her breasts brushed his arm.

Once he made it inside, she trilled, "Just give me a holler if you think of anything. I'll be right out here ready, willing, and able."

Rolling his eyes, Wally stepped back and closed the door, then looked around. It was a typical office for someone of Wraige's stature. A massive cherrywood desk and shelving took up one side of the large office and a leather furniture arrangement occupied the other.

Except for empty in- and outboxes, the desktop was clear. Wally realized he probably should have asked the vic's assistant where he stored the laptop.

Although he didn't have a warrant to conduct a search, both the widow and son had given him permission to look at the computer's files, so he felt comfortable doing that. But if the laptop wasn't in plain sight, he'd have to have the city attorney contact a judge.

Just as Wally was turning to step out of the room to ask if Karolyn knew where Wraige kept the computer, he noticed the slim device sitting on the shelves behind the desk. He tucked it under his arm and strode to the door.

Karolyn was on the phone, but when she caught sight of Wally, she shot him a guilty look. She quickly muttered something into the receiver and hung up.

Smiling brightly, she chirped, "Did you find Dr. Wraige's laptop?"

"I did." Wally headed for the exit, then stopped, turned toward her, and asked, "What time do you start work?"

"Eight." She fluttered her lashes. "And I get off at four thirty. Maybe we could grab a drink sometime."

"I'm married." Wally dismissed her invitation. "Were you on time today?" He waited for her to nod, then continued. "Have you left this office since you arrived?" When she shook her head, he asked, "Can anyone corroborate that?"

"Well, I've been on and off the phone all day with various board members." Karolyn's confused expression morphed into alarm, her eyes widened, and she dropped her flirtatious behavior. "Why are you asking? Wasn't Dr. Wraige's death due to natural causes?"

"I'll need a list of the people you spoke to this morning between eight thirty and ten." Wally returned to her desk. "Now, please."

Karolyn swallowed audibly. "Coming right up." She clicked a few times on her keyboard, then turned as the printer behind her whirred to life. Once it spit out a sheet of paper, she silently handed it to Wally, then evidently her confidence returned. She coyly licked her lips and asked, "Anything else, Chief?"

"I don't suppose you happen to know Dr. Wraige's laptop password."

"Uh." She tucked a strand of hair behind her ear and, not meeting his eyes, said, "It's possible that it's Meat Loaf."

Wally tilted his head. "Was that his favorite food?" The man hadn't struck him as someone with such down-home tastes in cuisine.

"Meat Loaf with a capital *M*," Karolyn explained. "You know, the singer."

"Hmm. I would never have pegged Dr. Wraige as one of that guy's fans."

"It was the song 'I'd Do Anything for Love' that Shamus liked, not the guy," Karolyn muttered.

It took a second, but then once Wally thought about what he knew regarding Wraige's BDSM proclivities, he remembered the rest of the song's title, "(But I Won't Do That)," and he had to hide his grin.

Thanking the admin assistant, Wally returned to his Hummer and booted up the laptop. The password Karolyn suggested worked and with a bit of research, he soon found the inventory of the vic's coin collection.

As he drove to the police station, Wally considered his next move. Was it worth spending a couple of hours figuring out what the collection was worth, or could he assign one of his officers to that task and spend his time on something else?

Groaning, he decided that he'd better do it himself.

It took Wally as long as he feared and when he finished, it looked as if one of the coins that was missing was an uncirculated 1916-D Mercury Dime. According to Google, it could be worth up to forty thousand dollars.

Wally stood up. He was stiff from being hunched over the computer for so long. As he stretched out the kinks in his back, the intercom buzzed.

He pushed the button, and Thea said, "Chief, the owner of the Treasure Chest just called to report that someone left the jewelry box taken in the Wraige burglary on his doorstep."

"I'll head there now," Wally responded, then jogged downstairs and into the garage.

He slid behind the wheel of his Hummer, threw the vehicle in reverse and raced toward Scumble River's only pawnshop.

The Treasure Chest was located on the edge of town, not far from the highway's entrance and exit ramps. As Wally pulled into the empty lot, he was glad to see that there were no other customers. Pawnshop owners were usually more cooperative without witnesses.

The large front window bore the words TREASURE CHEST in gilded letters and the tall neon sign near the road scrolled BUY, SELL, LOAN in red. A blue OPEN sign blinked on and off as Wally pushed through the glass door and strolled over the threshold.

He immediately noticed a poster on the back wall behind the register that read:

WE CASH CHECKS.
WE BUY SCRAP GOLD.
WE REPAIR JEWELRY.
IF IT'S STOLEN, DON'T BOTHER US.

Although a bell had sounded when he'd entered, the owner was nowhere in sight. Figuring the guy had momentarily stepped into the back room, Wally wandered around looking over the items that were for sale.

A wide-ranging array of instruments from guitars to trombones hung from one wall and power tools and electronics lined the shelves of the two. The third had glass cases holding jewelry and guns.

Growing impatient for the owner to return, Wally called out, "Khan, it's Chief Boyd. You here?"

Several minutes went by, and there was no answer. Had whoever dropped off the jewelry box come back to get his money and ended up hurting or killing the pawnshop owner?

Wally rested his hand on his sidearm and yelled, "Khan, are you here?"

Silence.

He moved toward the rear of the shop and raised his voice. "Khan, are you okay?"

This time Wally heard a toilet flush and he moved his hand to his Taser. He edged a little closer to the back room door and toed it open with his foot.

Immediately an alarm blared and a deep voice roared, "What the f—"

An instant later Khan rushed out clutching a shotgun.

"Stop." Wally's heart skipped a beat. "Police."

"Chief?" Khan slowly lowered his weapon. "What're you doing here?"

Earbuds hung around his neck, a newspaper was under one arm, and toilet paper was stuck to his shoe. Clearly, he'd been interrupted during his daily meditation on the porcelain throne.

"Sorry." Wally held up his hands placatingly. "I came about the jewelry box you reported."

"That was quick. I thought I'd locked the outer door." Khan noticed the toilet paper and removed it from his shoe, then stuffed it in his pocket.

Wally grimaced and resolved not to shake the man's hand. "Did you open it?"

"Nah." Khan's posture relaxed. "As soon as I saw that the brass plaque matched the description of the stolen goods you sent out, I put it in a bag and called the station. Figured you want to preserve any prints."

"Terrific." Wally beamed at the man, who was running his fingers nervously through his gray bangs.

Khan had gotten his nickname because he resembled Ricardo Montalbán in his *Star Trek* role.

"How have you and the missus been?" Khan moved over to the register, reached underneath, and pulled out a paper sack. "I bet those babies are keeping you busy."

"You're right about that." Wally took the bag. "Thanks for calling."

"I'm always happy to help the police."

"And we appreciate it."

After thanking the man again, Wally returned to the Hummer. He pulled up the list of stolen items on his phone, then donned rubber gloves and carefully removed the wooden chest from the paper sack. As Khan had stated, the brass plaque read: SHAMUS WRAIGE.

Opening it, Wally noted that a heavy gold signet ring, two watches, diamond cuff links, and a platinum tie tack were still in the box. Only one of the items that had been reported stolen was missing.

He scratched his head. This was easily a couple of thousand dollars' worth of jewelry.

What kind of thief steals things, then dumps them at a pawnshop rather than try to sell them?

CHAPTER 11

At Last

As Skye left the Wraige residence, she realized that she actually had over an hour when she didn't have to be anywhere. She'd taken the afternoon off of work to help Wally with his investigation, and she wasn't due to relieve Dorothy from her nanny duties until four thirty.

She drove aimlessly for a few minutes, thinking about what to do with herself. The twins were probably down for their afternoon nap, so even if she went home, she wouldn't get to spend time with them.

Of course, she could always go back to school and write reports. But she and Wally had both made a pact to stop working so much overtime. Especially since neither of their jobs paid them for those extra hours—either in money or appreciation.

It was a shame that there wasn't enough time to drive to Joliet. She needed to get a wedding present for her friend Judy Martin, the town librarian. Next month, Judy was marrying Anthony Anserello, one of Wally's officers. They were registered at Macy's, and Skye had hoped to get to the chain's Louis Joliet Mall location.

However, with the days flying by, Skye made a mental note to order something for them online the minute that she got to her laptop. Otherwise, she would end up without a gift to give the bride and groom on their wedding day.

Still, Skye wasn't ready to go home yet. Pulling up to the next four-way stop, she realized that she was heading in the direction of her parents' house.

Evidently, even her subconscious had known that what she really needed to do was go and see if there was any way she could help her Uncle Charlie who, with the motor court under lockdown, was currently occupying Skye's old bedroom.

Sighing, she made the turn onto the icy, unevenly paved street. The Midwest had been having a wretched winter and the country roads leading to her folks' place were a slushy mess. The snow had started before Thanksgiving and had continued through December, January, and into February.

There had never really been a warm spell to melt the awful white stuff before the next storm came through. And now there was layer upon layer of rutted ice covering the pothole strewn asphalt.

Thankfully, the big SUV had good traction, and as an Illinois native, she'd grown up driving in winter's treacherous conditions. She took it slow, leaving lots of braking room, but was relieved when she turned into her parents' and could park the Mercedes.

Jed, Skye's father, kept the driveway clear of snow, but since it was pea gravel, there was no way to remove all the slippery patches, and she skidded a little as she got out of the SUV. Teetering, she regained her balance, then carefully made her way to the sidewalk.

Her parents' home sat on a plot of land carved out of the acreage that her father farmed. During the summer, the house would be crowded on three sides by either soybeans or feed corn, depending on the crop rotation schedule, but right now looked as if the redbrick, ranch-style house was adrift on a sea of white.

As Skye climbed the single step to the patio, she noted that her mother's concrete goose wore a yellow smock with large colorful wings attached and a matching cap with a yellow beak.

Skye thought it must be a canary costume, but her mom usually dressed the statue for the season, so it should have had on something representing Valentine's Day. Was May just hoping for an early spring, or did the fowl's clothing choice have a deeper connotation?

Mulling over what a bird could mean, Skye opened the back door and entered the utility room, calling out, "Yoo-hoo. It's me."

When she was home, May didn't believe in locking her doors, and Skye worried that anyone could just walk in and surprise her mom. However, Skye had long since realized that there was no changing May's mind, and she no longer tried to reason with her.

As Skye bent down to unzip her boots, her nose twitched and she hastily pinched it together. If May heard her sneeze, she'd be sure Skye was sick. She'd never believe that it was the Febreze Fresh-Cut Pine air freshener that May liberally sprayed throughout her house rather than her daughter about to succumb to the bubonic plague.

By the time Skye had removed her shoes and coat, May appeared in the utility room doorway and said, "Charlie's on the phone with Loretta about his case, so keep your voice down."

"Okay." Skye stepped past her mom into the kitchen and asked, "Is that good or bad?"

May followed, but instead of answering Skye's question,

she demanded, "What's wrong? Why aren't you at work? Is it the twins?"

"Everything's fine." Skye knew that her mother's go-to response to anything unexpected was to fear that the worst had happened. "Wally found Dr. Wraige dead, and he asked me to take the afternoon off to help him interview the super-intendent's wife and son."

If her mother hadn't been a police dispatcher, Skye would have never mentioned the murder without checking with Wally. But May would know all about it as soon as she reported to work at four o'clock, and as long as Skye warned her not to tell anyone, she wouldn't share the information.

"It wasn't a natural death, I presume?" Suspicion glimmered in May's emerald-green eyes—the same exact color Skye saw every day when she gazed into the mirror. "Why wasn't it on the scanner?"

"Wally kept it off the radio. He didn't want Mrs. Wraige and her stepson to hear about it until they could be notified." Skye leaned against the counter and tried to change the subject. "Where's Dad?"

"Jed's out in the garage working on a new doghouse for Chocolate." May screwed up her face and tsked. "When he comes inside for supper, he'll get those wood shavings all over everything."

Skye walked over to her mom and nudged her shoulder. "Just think of the sawdust as man glitter."

May snickered, but quickly resumed her frown. "I told him that he better strip in the utility room and shower in the half bath."

"Doesn't he always?" Skye teased. Her mother would give you the shirt off her back. But it would come with instructions on how to wear it, wash it, and hang it up.

"No, he does not," May snapped. "Last year, when he was

working on that dang antique tractor of his, he came in covered in grease and tracked it through the whole house."

Skye clamped her lips shut to contain the giggle trying to escape. Her mother had the memory of an elephant with a mule's stubbornness, which meant getting on May's bad side was never a smart move. It was time to change the subject again.

Moving to the fridge, Skye opened it and said, "I missed lunch. Do you have anything I can snack on?"

May nodded, then narrowed her eyes. "Why didn't you eat? I know Dorothy packs something for you and Wally both. I hope you're not starving yourself to get rid of the weight from the babies?"

"Whoa!" Skye blinked. "Who are you and where did you put my mother?"

May's words were a complete turnaround. She had never been a fan of Skye's curvy figure and had had her daughter watching what she ate since she was eight years old. To this day, because of her mother's efforts to keep Skye from gaining a single pound, Skye hated both celery and cottage cheese.

"Don't be silly." May waved away Skye's astonishment. "According to Dr. Boz, new mothers shouldn't attempt to lose weight for six to twelve months. Your body is still adjusting to having given birth."

Skye wrinkled her brow. "Who's Dr. Boz?" That wasn't the name of Skye's ob-gyn.

"He's on TV." May disappeared for a few seconds and came back holding a checkout stand magazine. "See? Isn't he handsome?"

Skye squinted at the picture and accompanying headline, then said, "Yes, he is."

While Skye looked through the article, May busied herself with pulling food out of the fridge. By the time Skye was done reading, her mom had a thick sandwich, chips, and a bowl of fruit chunks on the counter.

She hugged May, then sat on a stool and dug in. At the first bite of baked ham, tangy mustard, and homemade bread, she moaned.

"So why are you here?" May marched to the sink and washed off the knife she'd used. Dirty dishes were not allowed to lie around in her kitchen.

"I came to see how Uncle Charlie was making out and to ask if I could do anything to help him." Skye ate a potato chip, then remembering that May had never answered her, rephrased her original question and asked, "Has there been any news on his case? Is that why Loretta called?"

"We'll soon find out." May dried the knife and returned it to its proper slot in the utensil drawer. "All Loretta said when I picked up the phone was that she needed to talk to Charlie right away."

"Hmm." Skye continued to eat her late lunch, then asked, "Did you know Dr. Wraige?"

May brought over a plate of frosted brownies, took the stool next to Skye, and said, "Not really. I've spoken to him a few times at church events. He seemed a little domineering for my taste."

Skye almost choked on the bite of melon she'd just put in her mouth. If only her mother knew just how true her statement was.

Skye quickly swallowed and said, "That's my impression too. Have you heard anything about him around town? Has anyone mentioned not liking him?"

"Just the usual disgruntled parents." May selected a brownie. "Charlie probably knows more about that, since he's president of the school board and works closely with the superintendent."

"We can't tell him about Dr. Wraige's murder until Wally gives us the go-ahead." Skye took a sip from the glass of Diet Coke her mother had poured for her. "Besides, I don't want to bother Uncle Charlie about it. He has his own troubles."

"Okay." May fingered the crease in her perfectly ironed jeans, then looked up and said, "But that husband of yours better not think Charlie had anything to do with the superintendent's death."

Shoot! Skye hadn't even considered that possibility. But Charlie and Dr. Wraige did have a bit of an adversarial relationship on the board.

"Has Charlie been here all day?" Skye asked, crossing her fingers.

"Yes." May glared at her daughter. "He hasn't left the house since Loretta dropped him off here yesterday. He doesn't even have his car since it was included in the state police's search warrant."

"Well, that's one good thing, then." Skye blew out a relieved breath, then bit her lip. "Did anyone stop by between eight thirty and ten?"

"Maggie was here from eight until eleven." May's put-upon sigh could have powered the windmill they used to pump water for their lawn and garden. "We were picking out which of the bank bus trips we wanted to take next month."

Skye beamed. "Excellent." Maggie was her mother's best friend and a nonfamily member, so an acceptable alibi for Charlie.

"Now that that's settled." May wiped her fingers on a napkin. "What are you wearing to the Valentine's Dinner Dance?"

The newish Stanley County Country Club that had been built between Scumble River and Laurel had opened up their event to nonmembers and sold tickets to benefit the local humane society. When Skye and Wally decided to attend, most of their immediate family and friends had followed suit.

"I ordered a couple of dresses online." Skye worried her bottom lip. "Hopefully they came today. Wally's going to wear his dress uniform since he hasn't had time to replace his tux yet."

"I'm wearing that dress I bought for Maggie's daughter's wedding." May hopped off her stool; returning a few seconds later, she held a wine-colored dress with a tiered skirt and lacy jacket. The color was perfect with her salt-and-pepper hair. "Your father's wearing his dark suit and I bought him a shirt to match my outfit. Should I wear my silver sandals or black pumps?"

"The sandals for sure." Skye bit into the chewy brownie and closed her eyes at the delicious hit of chocolate. "I wonder what Loretta's wearing?" Skye shrugged. "Not that it matters. She and Vince will be the handsomest couple there even if they come in his and hers gunny sacks."

"They are very attractive people." May's voice was firm. "But you and Wally have a special glow when you're together that is hard to compete with."

"Aw. Thanks, Mom." Skye liked this new, sweeter May and hoped the change wasn't something temporary. "Did you hear that Carson is back from his business trip to Texas and is coming to the dance too?"

May's lips formed a hard line and she scowled. "Is he taking Bunny Reid? I can just imagine her trampy outfit. Not to mention her makeup."

Bunny was an ex–Las Vegas showgirl and a thorn in May's side. The two women had gotten along briefly when Skye was dating Bunny's son, Simon, but as soon as that relationship was over, so was the uneasy truce the two mothers had been maintaining.

"Nope. They haven't been seeing each other since just

after Christmas," Skye teased. "I can't believe the queen of gossip didn't hear about their breakup. Bunny didn't take it at all well."

"What happened?" May's eyes gleamed. "What did that floozie do?"

"Carson had wanted to end things for a while, but he's such a gentleman, he waited until after the holidays. But when he finally told her that they just weren't right for each other, she threw a bowling trophy at him and he ended up needing stitches on his chin."

Bunny managed the bowling alley that her son owned. She lived in an apartment above the business and spent a lot of time at work.

"Oh my good gracious." May covered her mouth with her hand.

"Wally thought she should be arrested for battery, but Carson refused to press charges."

"A small price to pay to be rid of her." May didn't seem too upset that there had been bloodshed. "So who is Carson taking, then?"

"Dr. Norris." Skye finished eating and got up to put her dishes in the sink. "I really like her and I think she's perfect for Wally's dad. Did I mention she was at the crime scene this afternoon? I thought it was odd she was there instead of Simon."

"Simon's on vacation." May picked up the used paper napkins and walked into the utility room to put them in the trash can that she kept hidden in the coat closet. "He took that Emmy Jones to the Bahamas."

Before Skye could respond, Charlie stomped into the room and said, "What are you two talking about?"

At the sound of her godfather's voice, Skye whirled around. Although she fought to keep her expression neutral,

Charlie's gray color and rapid breathing scared her. As he took a seat at the dinette table, his color began to improve, but she was still worried.

Skye hastily explained, "Mom was just telling me that Simon and Emmy are out of town." Then she narrowed her eyes and pointed to the cigar in Charlie's mouth. Tapping her fingernails on the counter, she nagged, "Your doctor said you are not supposed to be smoking."

He pounded on the glass tabletop and yelled, "It's not lit!"

"Keep it that way." Skye dealt with adolescents for a living, and his show of temper didn't affect her. "What did Loretta have to say?"

Charlie ran sausage-like fingers through his thick white hair and blew out a breath. "She thinks that I'm in the clear. The state police haven't found a speck of evidence that I was aware of anything illegal going on in the motor court. And of course, there were no drugs or weapons in my personal quarters or in my Caddy."

"That's great." Skye walked over to Charlie, leaned down, and gave him a big hug. "When can you get your car back and reopen the motel?"

"It might be a couple more days." Charlie frowned. "And that old mattress of yours gives me a backache."

"You can come stay with us," Skye offered. "The bed in our guest room is brand new."

"Nah." Charlie shook his head. "I was just teasing. At my age if you don't wake up with pain in every joint, you're probably dead."

"Quit it, Uncle Charlie." Skye stomped her feet. "You always claim to be knocking at death's door."

"I do not. I ring the bell and run like hell. The grim reaper hates that." Charlie chuckled. "Anyway, Loretta is on top of things, and the state police can't stall much longer."

"Awesome." Skye was relieved to hear that he wouldn't have to spend time in jail.

Intense blue eyes under bushy white brows scrutinized her face. "How are you doing? I heard about that stunt Opal pulled at school. I can't believe we have to give the Dooziers money the district can ill afford."

"Everything's fine." Skye really wished she could tell him about Dr. Wraige. "I did the best I could negotiating with Earl, but a lawsuit would cost a lot more than a trip to Beverly Hills."

"Yeah." Sighing, he leaned back and crossed his arms. "I blame Knapik, not Opal, for what happened. I told Wraige we need to force that man into retirement, but for some reason the superintendent keeps protecting him. It's like Knapik has something on him."

"True." Skye frowned. She should mention that to Wally. "I wonder what it is?"

"Whatever it is, Knapik has to go." Charlie shook his finger. "I'm sick of Wraige's excuses. And while we're cleaning house, Wraige's cousin Pru Cormorant needs to retire too. She used to be a decent teacher, but the past ten years she's gotten downright nasty, and I'm tired of all the parent complaints about her playing favorites and sending home snide little notes. Just the other day, Mrs. Brenner called and screamed at me that Corny sent her a letter that said her son is depriving some village of its idiot and that the boy has been working with glue too much."

Shoot! Skye had forgotten that Pru was related to the superintendent. She needed to remind Wally of that as soon as possible.

"It would be great if Homer and Pru both retired." Skye's smile was weak. "Well, I'd better get going." She leaned down and kissed her godfather's cheek, then walked over to her mother, and as she kissed her mom goodbye, she whispered, "Remember. Do not tell Charlie about Dr. Wraige's murder."

As Skye hurriedly shoved her feet into her boots and put on her coat, she looked at May and asked, "By the way, what's with the goose's costume?"

"He's the Birdman of Alcatraz." May shot a pointed glance over her shoulder to where Charlie still sat. "The Birdman was innocent too."

She nodded her understanding, and May thrust a foil-wrapped plate into her hand. As Skye rushed out of the house, she waved her thanks, then ran to her SUV and slid behind the wheel.

While she hastily dialed Wally's number, she thought about Pru and the superintendent. A while back the English teacher had said that she and Dr. Wraige were more like sister and brother than cousins.

Which meant there was a good chance that Pru knew things about her cousin that his wife or son might not. They needed to talk to her before she heard about his death.

CHAPTER 12

Counting Valentines

AFTER SKYE REMINDED WALLY ABOUT THE ENGLISH teacher's relationship with the superintendent, he cursed. "Good gravy! How did we forget about that?"

"It's hard to keep up with who's related to whom in a town where everyone is about three degrees of separation from each other."

"Right." Wally sighed. "I'm on my way back from Laurel, so I'll meet you at home in about twenty minutes."

"Why were you in Laurel?" Skye put him on speaker and started the SUV.

"This afternoon, Dr. Wraige's jewelry box turned up at the pawnshop and I brought it straight to the techs so they could start processing it for clues."

"Interesting. You can tell me all about it tonight." Skye backed out of her parents' driveway and onto the road. "See you soon."

Checking her watch, Skye hastily increased her speed. It was nearly four thirty and she didn't like to make Dorothy work longer than her agreed-upon hours. They were extremely fortunate in securing May's old friend as their live-in housekeeper and nanny, and the last thing Skye wanted to do was take advantage of the woman's good nature.

Unlike her parents' country road, the one leading to Skye and Wally's new house was clear of snow. Even though there were still some icy patches and drifted-over spots, she made good time and pulled into their long paved driveway with a few minutes to spare.

As she passed the site where her old home had stood, she stopped and looked to the right. It was truly amazing that there was no indication that before the tornado, there had ever been a structure in that spot. She had inherited the three-story residence from Mrs. Griggs, an elderly woman who left it to her because she was convinced that Skye was her reincarnated daughter.

At first, Skye had been skeptical about Mrs. Griggs's claim, but after the woman's ghost began to make appearances and leave little gifts, Skye had decided to keep an open mind. Mrs. Griggs's spirit had stuck around for as long as Skye lived in her house, but after it was destroyed, she evidently went into the light.

At least, that was the message she sent to Skye through Millicent Rose, a woman claiming to be the twins' fairy godmother.

Smiling at the memory, Skye drove a bit farther and again paused. This time, she gazed to the left. The RV that she and Wally had lived in after their house was demolished by the twister was finally gone.

Carson had provided them with the motor home while they were having their new place built, and he'd had arranged for it to be taken away once they moved into their forever home. Skye had to admit, it was nice having a billionaire father-in-law and a husband with a hefty trust fund.

It still felt a little surreal to be able to buy anything she wanted without worrying about how to pay for it. But her sister-in-law, Loretta, had come from an affluent family, and she had helped Skye come to grips with Wally's wealth.

With a final look at both locations, Skye drove on. She and Wally had decided to build their new house closer to the river. She'd been worried about the upkeep for the enormous yard and lengthy driveway, but after Wally hired a landscape company to keep the yard mowed and the snow plowed, she was happy they had chosen that site.

She loved the view from their rear deck, and having the house set farther back from the road gave them a lot more privacy.

Once she'd pulled the SUV into the attached garage, Skye grabbed her purse and the brownies, then went inside. She stopped in the laundry room to hang her coat on one of the hooks lining the walls and to take off her boots. Just because she wasn't the one cleaning up, didn't mean she was willing to track mud into the house.

Having divested herself of her outerwear, Skye walked down the short hall that led to the kitchen. From there, she could see both the dining and great rooms.

Although the TV was on, Dorothy wasn't paying it much attention. She had the twins on a pad in front of the fireplace and was blowing bubbles with a wand that she dipped into a bright red bottle.

Eva was gurgling, her brown eyes sparkling as she watched the bubbles dance over her head. Her cute little nose twitched with excitement and her soft pink lips crinkled in a smile.

CJ was moving his hands around excitedly every time a bubble came close to him. His thickly lashed green eyes were wide with wonder as he attempted to close his fingers around the floating spheres.

Bingo, the black cat that Skye had inherited from her

grandmother, was sleeping on the sofa. As per the Feline Law of Comfort Seeking, Bingo had claimed the coziest spot in the room.

"Hi!" Skye raised her voice, not wanting to sneak up and scare the older woman. "I'm home."

Dorothy used the edge of the heavy coffee table to get to her feet and said, "We were having such a good time, I didn't hear your car."

Skye pointed. "I think it was more that guy on TV shouting."

"Televangelists are sort of the pro wrestlers of religion." Dorothy chuckled.

"Does Father Burns know you watch his competition?" Skye teased.

"Hey." Dorothy snickered. "I just like hedging my bets."

"Humph." Skye giggled. "When God decides to communicate with humanity, I doubt his messenger will be a guy on cable with a bad hairstyle and a wife wearing enough makeup to graduate at the top of her clown school class."

"Maybe so." Dorothy shrugged, not at all offended by Skye's gentle ribbing. "But better safe than sorry."

"You could be right." Skye knelt beside her babies and picked up the bottle of bubbles to play with them. "Everything okay with the twins?"

"As right as rain." Dorothy beamed. "Both little darlings have been fed and changed. They wouldn't fall asleep earlier, so I was just about to put them down again and see if they'd nod off now."

"I'll do that." Skye blew a few more bubbles. "You are officially off duty."

"Let me help you," Dorothy insisted, scooping up Eva and heading toward the nursery. "I'll put the princess in her bed and you bring the prince."

"Okay," Skye agreed. "But then you're through for the day." Dorothy would work twenty-four/seven if Skye didn't stop her.

CJ and Eva were asleep before their little heads hit the mattress and Dorothy reluctantly went up to her apartment above the garage.

Skye and Wally had added it to their house plans once they'd realized they'd need live-in help to manage with the twins. It had a kitchen, living room, bedroom with an attached bathroom, and its own outside staircase entrance, giving Dorothy the privacy to come and go as she pleased.

Once Skye was alone, she quickly went into her bedroom to change into a pair of jeans and sweatshirt. She was in the kitchen investigating what Dorothy had planned for her to cook for supper when she heard Wally's Hummer park out front.

She frowned. It was odd that he hadn't put his car in the garage.

A few minutes later, he joined her in the kitchen and said, "Any chance I can get you to come with me to Pru Cormorant's house?"

"Sure." Skye put the casserole dish back in the fridge. "But what about the twins? I'm not asking Dorothy to watch them."

"I called Dad and he said he'd be happy to come over and keep an eye on them for a few hours." Wally stepped closer to Skye and drew her into his arms. "He even said we could go out to eat afterward."

"Oh! That would be such a treat." Skye snuggled against his muscular chest. They rarely had any alone time. "Are you sure he doesn't mind?"

Chuckling, Wally rested his chin on the top of her head. "You know Dad loves being with his grandchildren. Plus, Doris Ann canceled their date because she's busy doing the Wraige autopsy."

"Sold." Skye tilted her chin up so she could look at her gorgeous husband. "I'll just go change back into my work clothes."

"Okay." Wally headed toward the nursery. "While you do that, I'm going to take a peek at the babies. Dad will be here any minute."

After putting on her black wool pants and red sweater set again, Skye took a few extra minutes to comb her hair and freshen her makeup. She firmly believed that it was always a good idea to look your best before tackling a difficult situation.

And any situation involving the prickly English teacher was by definition difficult.

By the time Skye returned to the kitchen, Carson and Wally were sitting at the table. Both had large glasses of milk in front of them and they were demolishing the brownies her mother had sent home with Skye.

Every time she saw her father-in-law, Skye was struck by how much he and his son looked alike. Both were tall, with broad shoulders, trim waists, and chiseled features.

While Wally's dark hair was only threaded with gray at the temples, Carson's thick mane was now completely white. But they both had the kindest, warmest brown eyes that Skye had ever seen.

Carson hastily swallowed, wiped his lips on a paper napkin, rose to his feet, and gave Skye a big hug. When she'd become engaged to his son, he'd asked her to call him Dad. And from that moment on, he had treated her like a beloved daughter.

Hugging him back, Skye said, "Thanks for watching the twins on such short notice. I don't like to take advantage of Dorothy."

"Anytime." Carson sat back down and reached for the remaining brownie. "Especially if you have treats like this for me."

"Glad you enjoyed them." Skye couldn't believe the men had gone through the whole plateful. "But I can't take the credit. Mom made them."

"I'm sure yours are just as good as your mom's," Carson said gallantly.

"Don't let May hear you say that." Skye winked. "She guards her saucepan brownie recipe with her life. She says I can have it when she dies or stops baking, but I have to promise never to share it."

"And I thought southern women were fierce about their cooking secrets." Carson chuckled, then asked, "When will my grandbabies be up? They better not sleep the whole time like my last visit."

"They went down about a quarter to five, so I'd say around seven, but now that they're getting older they're sleeping less, so it could be even sooner."

"I reckon that will have to do." Carson leveled a finger at his son and squinted. "That is, if you and your pretty wife go have a nice long dinner after you take care of business. I made a reservation at the Prime Tomahawk Steakhouse in Laurel."

"Thanks, Dad. You didn't have to go to all that trouble." Wally hugged his father, grabbed Skye's hand, and asked, "Ready, darlin'?"

"Yep." Skye waved goodbye to Carson. "Call us if you need us."

Once Skye and Wally put on their coats and boots and got into the Hummer, she said, "You know, this might be a wasted trip. It just dawned on me that Nanette might have already notified Pru."

"I doubt it." Wally made a three-point turn, headed down the driveway, and turned onto the road. "Tavish said that Nanette didn't get along with any of the vic's extended family. Something about how she'd been the other woman when Wraige had divorced his first wife."

"Then maybe Tavish called Pru." Skye watched the scenery rush by as Wally headed toward town. "She'd be his cousin too."

"I supposed he might." Wally frowned. "But he didn't strike me as a guy who would think to do that. I guess we'll find out."

"True." Skye bit her lip, then shrugged. "It would be great to see Pru's reaction to the news of her cousin's death, but either way, I bet she'll have some insight as to Dr. Wraige's enemies."

It felt like déjà vu when Wally turned into Pru's street. They'd been there a couple of months ago to talk to the English teacher about another case. One where she'd been the suspect.

Thankfully, that interview had gone better than expected and Pru hadn't been so upset with Skye that it had caused any awkwardness between them at school. Or at least, any more than usual.

The English teacher and Skye had polar opposite viewpoints on education and barely tolerated each other as colleagues. Friendship had always been out of the question.

Wally parked the Hummer by the curb in front of Pru's house, and he and Skye walked up the sidewalk. The English teacher lived in a well-maintained beige brick ranch with an attached two-car garage. The driveway looked as if it had been recently plowed, the sidewalks were cleared of ice, and the yard was a pristine white, unmarred by a single footstep.

All of which Skye could have predicted from her knowledge of Pru's personality. Before her previous visit, she would have been surprised at the extensive Valentine's decorations, but during that encounter, she'd learned that Pru was an avid crafter and made ornaments for her home to commemorate every holiday.

Tonight, there was an elaborate red-and-pink wreath on the front door, a colorful cupid in the picture window, and foil hearts hung from the trees.

As Skye and Wally approached the front door, it swung open. Pru stood framed in the entryway with her hands on her hips and a frown on her face.

"Good evening, Pru," Skye said. "I hope we're not interrupting your supper."

"We eat *dinner*." Pru folded sticklike arms across her narrow chest. "Only the uneducated refer to the evening meal as *supper*."

"Actually…" Skye started.

She was about to inform the infuriating English teacher that dinner was whichever meal was heaviest—midday or evening—but she caught herself and remained silent. There was no use alienating the woman they wanted to interrogate.

"Actually?" Pru's expression was smug. "Would you care to complete your thought?"

"No." Skye waved it away. "It wasn't important."

"That seems true of a lot of what you have to say." Pru smirked.

"I highly doubt that." Wally put his hand on Skye's back and shot Pru a look that said *I dare you to insult my wife*.

"You would." Pru's thin lips tightened and she suddenly demanded, "To what do I owe your presence?"

"I'm afraid we have some bad news," Skye said gently. "May we come in?"

"What's wrong?" Pru's normally pale complexion went dead white.

"It would really be better if we came inside where you could sit down." Skye took Pru's arm and lightly steered her into the living room. Once she was seated on the sofa, Skye sat next to her and said, "I'm sorry to have to tell you that Dr. Wraige has passed away."

"Shamus is gone." Pru's voice cracked. "What happened to him?"

Wally ignored her question, took the chair directly across from the couch, and explained, "I was called to Dr. Wraige's house late this morning because he reported that someone had been trying to get inside but that they had left when they couldn't open the door."

"Another break-in?" Pru's watery blue eyes were malicious. "It just goes to show you how inept the police department is in this town."

Skye stole a glance at Wally and notice a muscle in his jaw was twitching. Giving him a chance to cool down, she said, "Wally went to Dr. Wraige's house to take his report, only to have no one respond when he rang the bell or tried the superintendent's cell."

"At that point, I entered the premises through the unlocked sliding glass door off the deck." Wally's expression was impassive. "And I found your cousin dead in the master suite's sitting room."

"Was it his heart?" Pru clutched her own chest as if in sympathy.

"We won't know for sure what caused his death until the autopsy is complete." Wally paused, then added, "But we don't believe it was natural causes."

"Are you saying he was murdered?" Pru's overplucked eyebrow rose.

"Sadly, we are." Skye patted the woman's skeleton-like hand. Skye shivered. Pru's fingers were as cold as ice. "And we're hoping that you might be able to give us a list of people who might want him dead."

"You don't need a list," Pru chuckled nastily. "If someone killed Shamus, it was that witch of a wife of his. She only married him for his money."

"His money?" Wally echoed.

Pru's pointy nose twitched, making her look like a rabbit on the trail of a tasty carrot. "You aren't the only one with a trust fund, Chief."

CHAPTER 13

Doctor, Doctor

IT WAS A LITTLE BEFORE SEVEN WHEN WALLY AND SKYE finally left Pru and returned to their car. They'd stayed with the distraught woman until her housemate got home—both so she wouldn't have to be alone and to continue questioning her about Dr. Wraige's enemies.

Pru had maintained that her cousin's wife was the only one who wished he was dead. Scoffing at the idea that Nanette and Shamus had really been trying to get pregnant, Pru had declared that at his age, her cousin wasn't interested in having another child. She'd also sworn that he had reformed and no longer engaged in sexual activity outside of his marriage.

As Wally pulled the Hummer away from the curb and headed toward Laurel, Skye massaged her temples. An awful hunger headache throbbed behind her eyes. She should have nabbed one of her mother's brownies before she went to get dressed and her husband and father-in-law scarfed them all down.

Evidently, Wally noticed her discomfort because he asked, "Are you okay?"

"My head hurts a little, but it'll be fine once I eat."

Realizing she had another problem, she squirmed in her seat. "And I need a bathroom sooner rather than later."

"Why didn't you ask Pru to use hers?" Wally shot a confused glance at her.

"I was afraid that she'd think I wanted to snoop," Skye explained. "You know, on all those crime shows the cops always request either a glass of water or to use the bathroom to sneak around a suspect's home."

"You need to stop watching those programs," Wally teased. "Stick to your romance novels. I like it a lot more when you get ideas from Nora Roberts's latest book rather than when you use information from *Law & Order*."

Skye ignored his exaggerated leer and said, "It just occurred to me that your dad said he made reservations for us at the Prime Tomahawk. How did he know what time we'd get there to eat?"

"He invested in the place." Wally arched a brow. "I'm sure if he told them to hold a table all night, they'd be happy to do it for him."

Skye frowned. "I feel bad if they're turning people away to accommodate us."

"It should be fine. I doubt if Tuesday is one of their busier nights." Wally patted her hand. "Don't worry. Dad makes sure people are well compensated for any favors he requests."

"I just hate for people to think that we expect special treatment because we have money." She chewed her bottom lip. "I'm doing better, but it's hard to get used to this lifestyle."

"That's because you're the most caring, kindhearted person that I've ever met."

"Aw." Skye squirmed again. She really should have asked to use Pru's bathroom.

"Can you hold it until we get to Laurel?"

Crossing her legs, Skye said, "I think I can make it, but it will be close."

"I can always use the sirens," Wally said with a lopsided grin. "Good thing when Dad gave me this vehicle, I had it modified."

"I'll let you know if you need to do that." Skye settled back into the comfy seat, determined to forget about her full bladder. "While I'm thrilled that we're getting some alone time, I hope your father's okay with the twins. CJ's been cranky. I think he's teething, and you know if he's out of sorts, Eva is too."

"I mentioned that when I called him, and he's fully prepared. He bought this new baby teething mitten while he was in Texas and is anxious to try it out." At Skye's inquisitive glance, Wally added, "It's a tiny glove that CJ can wear and chew on."

"Your dad is so cute," Skye giggled. "Mom just uses a frozen bag of veggies."

"Of course she does," Wally chuckled, then changed the subject. "Have you heard much about the Prime Tomahawk? All I know is that Dad arranged a deal for them to get fresh farm-raised Wagyu and Black Angus beef from one of the ranches he owns in East Texas."

Skye's mouth watered. "Everyone who has been there says it's awesome."

They discussed food for a while, then Wally said, "I asked the city attorney to get a warrant to search the superintendent's office. Any idea how bent out of shape the board will be about that?"

"I doubt they'll be upset." Skye relayed Charlie's comments about Dr. Wraige, assuring Wally that she had not told her godfather the superintendent was dead. Then she added, "And Uncle Charlie has an alibi, so don't go there."

Wally sped up to pass a slow-moving tractor, then said, "Nope. Never. Did Charlie say how things stood with the state police? I never did get a chance to call the lead detective today."

"He was on the phone with Loretta when I got to Mom's, and it looks as if he's in the clear." Skye's stomach growled and she put her hand on her midriff. "He's still not officially released, but they admitted to Loretta that there was no evidence to link him to the drugs or weapons, or the people selling them, who were staying at his motel."

"That's terrific." Wally beamed. "I'll try to contact the investigator tomorrow and see what I can find out about the case."

"How long do you think it will it take them to return Uncle Charlie's car and allow him to reopen up the motor court?" Skye asked.

"If they've really cleared him, they'll release his personal vehicle soon." Wally glanced at her out of the corner of his eye and tensed, as if aware what he was about to say would upset her. "But the motel will depend on whether the perps they arrested make a deal."

"You mean they could keep it closed until the trial!" Skye screeched, then regretted it when her head throbbed even more than before.

"Yep." Wally lifted a brow. "Although they probably won't keep it that long, they might if they're concerned that they may need additional evidence for a conviction."

"That could drive him out of business." She hadn't been prepared for that answer and her chest tightened, but then she smiled. "No way will Loretta allow that. She'd sue the state police if they try to pull that stunt."

Wally turned the car onto the road leading into Laurel. "I'm sure she's informed them of that intention, so Charlie is probably good."

"Loretta would definitely do that." Skye nodded vig-orously. "I remember when she was president of our Alpha Sigma Alpha chapter. It was the year after I joined, and the university administration found some nitpicking issue with our house and tried to move us off campus. Loretta pulled up every single little legal loophole she could find, and we were able to stay in it. The sorority was really grateful to her and she even got an award."

Skye crossed her legs. They were still a few minutes from the restaurant and she hoped she could last that long. She really had to go.

"Why am I not surprised?" Wally traced a finger gently down Skye's cheek. "I bet you were right there helping her do the research."

"Maybe." Skye grabbed his hand and kissed his palm. She was silent until she remembered what she'd wanted to do at home before Wally sidetracked her. "Shoot! I forgot to look to see if the dresses I ordered for the Valentine's Dinner Dance arrived."

"Dresses? Plural?" Wally turned into the Prime Tomahawk's lot, parked the car, and got out to open Skye's door. "How many of these shindigs are we attending? Or are you changing halfway through?"

"Don't be silly. I ordered two of the same dress, just in different sizes. I'll return the one that doesn't fit right." Skye kissed his cheeks, then swiftly walked toward the restaurant's front door and entered before Wally could hold open the door. Once he joined her, she said, "You go ahead and sit down. I'll meet you at our table."

She looked around for the restroom and when she spotted it, she took off at a jog. She could only pray that there wasn't a line of women waiting for a free stall.

After she took care of business, Skye exited the bathroom

with a sigh of relief. She located Wally in a corner booth and quickly headed toward him. With that pressing issue gone, her hunger headache felt that much worse.

Since Wally was in uniform, he was sipping a glass of iced tea and there was a Diet Coke with a lime wedge waiting for her. She slid onto the bench and took a long drink, then, her stomach growling, she grabbed the menu sitting on the table-top and scanned the selections.

A few minutes later, a server came to take their orders, and once he was gone, Skye finally had a chance to really look around the restaurant. It had a sleek feel with granite top tables, stylish black leather seating, and muted lighting provided by low-hanging pendant lamps suspended from a wooden-slat ceiling.

White stacked stone panels alternated with reclaimed wood on an accent wall and the other three were painted a soft gray. Several strategically placed large steel-framed mirrors made the space look bigger.

The bar area was also decorated in wood and metal elements with LED light boxes used to display the restaurant's wine inventory. A bright red sofa in the lounge provided a pop of color.

Skye sighed in satisfaction. The air was redolent with grilled meat and caramelized onions, and she was about to enjoy a yummy supper with her handsome husband. This was true contentment.

Gazing at Wally, she could tell that he was itching to talk over the case. He probably didn't want to bring it up, afraid he'd ruin their evening. But even if she wasn't a fan of the superintendent, he did deserve justice.

Hoping they could get that discussion over with before their entrée arrived, or at least before dessert, she said, "I wonder how much of what Pru claimed about Nanette and

Dr. Wraige we can believe. From my experience dealing with parents and students, I've become very aware that folks often kept secrets from their closest family, and those same people often chose to ignore their loved ones' flaws."

"It'll be difficult to check out what Pru said about the trust fund"—Wally took out his memo pad and made a note—"but the city attorney should be able to get me a look at the vic's will."

"If Wraige was still playing around, someone must know something about it," Skye mused. "Although, after all the gossip when he and his secretary were involved, he was probably smart enough to do his cheating out of town this time."

Wally nodded. "Keep your ears open. News of his death might stir up the rumor mill."

"I'll try to hang around the faculty lounge a bit more than usual." Skye looked around, hoping their food was coming soon, then asked, "Have you heard if the crime scene techs or Doris Ann found anything interesting?"

"Wraige had a locked armoire full of some pretty intense fetish gear." Wally tilted his head and quirked his lips. "But as Nanette indicated to you, it seemed as if it hadn't been used in a long time. They said it was covered with dust and smelled moldy."

"That's interesting." Skye's cheeks warmed. She might be a psychologist, but it was still a little embarrassing discussing someone else's sex life. She chose her words carefully, then said, "According to that class on human sexuality that I took in graduate school, a person who needs that type of stimulation would have a difficult time finding satisfaction in more conventional ways."

"Interesting." Wally winked. "How about the other way around? Folks who are mostly conventional but do a little exploring? Do they get hooked and aren't able to go back to their usual ways?"

"Absolutely not!" Skye choked on the sip of water she'd just taken. Was Wally suggesting what she thought he might be? "Why?"

"Just wondering, since the police academy didn't have such an enlightening class in this curriculum." Still chuckling, Wally asked, "What do you think Nanette meant when she told you that she and her husband had come to some sort of compromise that they both could live with and that he no longer had other sex partners?"

"I thought"—Skye paused as the server put a basket of warm bread on the table, then when the man walked away, she continued—"although Nanette wasn't into that kind of lifestyle, she allowed Dr. Wraige tie her up and spank her. But nothing kinkier."

"You figure she was really okay with that?" Wally asked, tearing off a piece of the loaf. "And that it was enough for him?"

"I have no idea." Skye broke off her own slice. "It could have caused resentment on both their parts or it could have been the perfect solution. I don't know either of them well enough to even guess."

"Wraige was certainly an interesting man. I'm guessing he had a lot of secrets." Wally buttered his bread, then popped it into his mouth.

"That reminds me—" Noticing that their server was approaching, Skye waited for the man to place their salads in front of them, ask if they needed anything else, acknowledge their refusal, and leave before she continued. "You mentioned getting a warrant to search Dr. Wraige's office, and I know you processed the crime scene, but how about the rest of his house?"

Wally moved his plate next to Skye's. She began to pick off the items on her salad she didn't like and put them on his, smiling at the cozy routine they'd formed as a couple.

As she de-cucumbered her salad, Wally said, "I'm hoping to get a warrant for the residence as well, but the city attorney said we only had a fifty-fifty chance. It depends on the judge."

"Can't the lawyer choose which judge he approaches?" Skye asked.

Waiting for his answer, she forked a big bite of blue-cheese-drenched lettuce into her mouth. It tasted heavenly. Either the Roquefort dressing was exceptional or she was really hungry. Probably both.

Wally watched her in amusement, then after sampling his own salad, said, "Stanley County only has three judges. Whoever is sitting Wednesday morning is the one we get."

"Shoot!" Skye shook her head. "It's so much easier on *CSI*."

Once they were finished with their first course, the server cleared the table, refilled their drinks, then brought out their entrees. Skye nearly drooled as the man placed her New York strip in front of her. Next to the sizzling steak, a double baked potato oozed buttery goodness, and several stalks of asparagus glistened with olive oil.

Wally had opted for the T-bone, but his side dishes were the same.

"What do you know about Wraige's secretary?" Wally asked, cutting a piece from his perfectly seared steak and popping it into his mouth.

"Not much." Skye wrinkled her brow, thinking. "Karolyn was the talk of the district when I first started working in the schools because she was sleeping with the superintendent. Then they broke up and she wasn't a hot topic anymore. I haven't heard much about her for the past couple of years or so."

"You're sure they broke it off? Could they have just kept it on the down low?" Wally ate half of his baked potato while Skye thought about her answer.

Finally, she shook her head and said, "I doubt it." She chewed a bite of steak, savoring the hints of rosemary, thyme, basil, and garlic, then explained, "First of all, Karolyn isn't the subtle type. And second, she's been on the prowl for another lover. I remember that she sort of blackmailed Uncle Charlie into taking her out."

"Blackmailed?" Wally polished off the last of his asparagus.

"I can't recall what it was exactly. He wanted something and she got it for him." She shrugged. "It wasn't a big deal."

Both Skye and Wally focused on their food until Wally pushed away his empty plate and Skye followed suit. She was stuffed.

"Is there anything you can think of about the vic or his son or his wife?" Wally signaled the server and asked for the dessert menus. Once they were delivered and the waiter walked to another table, he said, "Has there been any talk about Wraige having a substantial trust fund?"

"None. But that explains his expensive house, car, and coin collection." Skye scanned the list of tempting treats. "That reminds me, did you figure out the value of the coins that are missing?"

"I did." Wally read from his memo pad. "Most were in the hundred-to-two-hundred-dollar range. However, there was an uncirculated 1916-D Mercury Dime. And according to Google, it could be worth up to forty thousand dollars."

Before Skye could respond, the server returned. She had intended to skip dessert, but although her mind said, *Do crunches*, her taste buds said, *Eat cupcakes*. So she caved in and asked for the mocha caramel ones.

She'd do a few extra laps at the pool the next time she had a chance to take a morning swim at the high school. After all, sugar was plainly God's way of saying he didn't want her to be thin.

Wally and Skye chatted about the pricey coins and the stolen items left at the pawnshop until the waiter returned.

After he placed their desserts in front of them, the server poured decaf for each of them and left.

Once Skye was sure he was out of earshot, she said, "This probably doesn't mean anything, but did I mention that Dr. Wraige seemed under the weather Monday morning?"

"In what way?" Wally mumbled around a mouthful of walnut turtle pie.

"He was pale and sweaty." Skye put down her fork. "And his face was a little gaunt, as if he'd lost some weight."

"Well since he wasn't poisoned, he might have just been getting over the flu, or…" Wally stiffened. "We were thinking whoever shoved him into the cupid statue had to be pretty strong, but if he was weak from being sick, that's a whole other ball game. I need to contact Doris Ann right now and make sure she checks that out."

"That reminds me," Skye said, "are you releasing the cause of death or the details about the arrow?"

"Definitely not." Wally grimaced. "Hopefully, there won't be any leaks from the lab or ME's office." His frown deepened. "In fact, I'll remind Doris Ann of that and ask her to warn the crime techs."

As Wally made the call, Skye thoughtfully finished her cupcake. Something wasn't right. She just couldn't figure out what it was they were missing.

CHAPTER 14

Won't You Be My Valentine?

WALLY OPENED ONE EYE, PEERED AT THE BRIGHT RED numbers displayed on his clock radio, and flung back the comforter. It was already seven fifteen and he had to be at the station by eight. Why hadn't Skye gotten him up? Although a better question was how he'd managed to sleep through her a.m. routine?

His wife might be the sweetest woman alive, but she was anything but quiet in the morning as she showered and dried her hair. Then there were the sounds of distress that seeped from her walk-in closet as she moaned about having nothing to wear.

When they'd first gotten married, Wally had made the mistake of suggesting to Skye that if she showered the night before, her hair would be dry in the morning, thus saving her at least ten minutes. He'd also mentioned that it would be a good idea to choose her outfit before going to bed.

Neither of his helpful hints had met with her approval. She'd scowled at him and muttered something about her hair not laying right if she slept on it. She'd also pointed out that unlike him, her job did not come with a uniform, thus the weather and her activities had to be taken into consideration when she was deciding what to wear.

Luckily, he'd bit his tongue and hadn't mentioned that the next day's temperature and her schedule were available to her before she went to bed. If he'd learned anything from his disastrous first marriage, it was when to shut up.

With the minutes ticking by, Wally pushed those thoughts aside and leaped out of bed, then hurried into the adjoining bathroom. He quickly washed his face, brushed his teeth, ran an electric razor over his stubble, and combed his hair.

Skye had been right about the convenience of wearing a uniform. He didn't have to waste a second choosing his wardrobe. Donning the navy pants, navy long-sleeved shirt, necktie, and black leather oxford shoes, Wally was set.

He vaguely remembered Skye mentioning that she had an early meeting at the elementary school, so he wasn't at all surprised to find only Dorothy occupying the kitchen. Wally's resolve to skip breakfast flew out the window when he sniffed the air and realized that she was frying bacon.

They'd just received their monthly shipment from Pederson's Natural Farms, and that company's uncured cherrywood smoked bacon was the best. Wally grabbed his favorite Bubba insulated stainless steel mug from the cupboard, put it in place on the coffee maker's drip tray base, popped in a dark roast K-Cup, and pushed start. No way was he letting a single strip of that bacon go to waste.

"Morning, Chief." Dorothy looked up from the stove. "How do you want your eggs?"

"Good morning. Whatever way's easiest," Wally answered as he waited for his cup to fill.

Dorthey nodded and turned back to her cooking. "Scrambled coming right up."

A few minutes later, Dorothy slid a plate in front of him. Thanking her, he buttered his toast and dug into his meal.

"Skye told me that the school district superintendent bought the farm yesterday." Dorothy was a no-nonsense woman with a wicked sense of humor. "I'm betting you have a truckload of suspects for that murder."

Last night, around ten o'clock, Wally had gotten a phone call from Kathryn Steele, owner of the *Scumble River Star*, the town's weekly newspaper. She'd somehow found out about the Wraige homicide and advised him the story would be in Wednesday's paper.

With the story appearing in the paper, there was no longer any reason to try to keep the superintendent's death by unnatural causes quiet, so Wally had given Skye the go-ahead to text her mom and tell her that she could give Charlie a heads-up before the whole town was talking about it.

Kathryn Steele had also requested a quote from Wally regarding the case. Although he knew that wouldn't satisfy the journalist for long, he'd given her the standard line—the police are unable to comment on an ongoing investigation.

Kathryn had keep pressuring him for information that she could include in next week's edition until he finally had hung up on her. He could only hope she didn't get anything about the cause of death or any other details from someone else. He was sure that Doris Ann would keep quiet but not as confident in the rest of the forensic staff's discretion.

Swallowing a mouthful of fluffy eggs, Wally refocused on Dorothy and asked, "What makes you think there'll be a lot of suspects?"

"Well…" Dorothy shrugged, suddenly finding the pan she was washing fascinating. "You know, for one, his kinky personal life."

"Right. I forgot you knew about that." Wally picked up

a slice of crispy bacon. "You said for one. What are the other reasons?"

"He ran the school district like it was his own personal kingdom." Dorothy dried her hands and put them on her hips. "He figured out people's weaknesses and used them against them."

"Oh?" Wally was surprised Skye hadn't mentioned anything about that, but she had said that she had very little to do with the man.

"He pretty much leaves the teachers alone because they have a union, but support personnel are hung out to dry." Dorothy made herself a cup of coffee, then joined Wally at the table. "Not too long ago, Wraige really screwed the district's bus drivers."

"How so?" Wally stopped eating, took out his memo pad, and waited.

"He makes sure they are kept part-time so they get no benefits." Dorothy sipped her coffee. "But worst of all, they're not allowed to discipline the kids and he doesn't back them up when parents complain that their little darlings were bullied by other kids and the driver didn't do anything about it."

"Was any particular driver unhappy with him?" Wally asked.

He wrinkled his brow. How many drivers did the school employ? The district included quite a few miles of far-flung rural territory and all those farm kids would have to be bussed into town to attend classes.

Dorothy shrugged. "I've heard grumbling from a lot of them." She pursed her lips. "But if I were investigating, I'd look at the last one fired. I can't recall his name or what exactly happened, but there was definitely a ruckus around the guy's dismissal."

"Thanks for the tip." Wally resumed eating, then realized

Dorothy was still looking at him. He swallowed and asked. "Someone else?"

"Rumor has it that he'd been seeing a lot of Neva Llewellyn lately."

"Seeing her as in dating?" Wally had met the junior high principal on several occasions and from what Skye said about her and his own impressions, she didn't strike him as someone willing to be the other woman.

"I doubt Neva would have an affair with him." Dorothy made a face. "But they had been having heaps of closed-door meetings in his office."

"How do you know that?" Wally finished his breakfast, got up and put the plate in the dishwasher.

Dorothy followed Wally, took the plate out of the dishwater and rinsed it off. "Karolyn's in my bowling league and I overheard her telling one of her cronies that Neva had been meeting with Wraige a couple times a week since winter break."

"Interesting." Wally refilled his travel mug and snapped on the lid. "Thanks for breakfast and the tips."

Once he was in his Hummer, he hit the remote for the opener, then dug out his cell phone. While he waited for the door to rise, he sent a quick text to Skye asking her to call him when she had a chance. Maybe she knew, or could find out, why the junior high principal had been meeting so often with the superintendent.

Among the advantages of living in a small town was the short, traffic-free commute to work, and Wally arrived at the station within minutes of leaving home. He parked the Hummer in the attached garage, noting that the K-9 modified police vehicle was missing from its usual spot. Evidently, Martinez was already on duty.

After checking with the dispatcher to see if he had any

messages and picking up the midnight shifts' logs, Wally headed upstairs to his office. He was a few minutes late, but Dorothy had given him some great leads, so he wasn't too worried about it. At least not until Dante barged through his door, huffing like a penguin-shaped dragon.

"Where the hell have you been?" Hizzoner demanded, tapping his watch.

"Gathering information regarding yesterday's homicide." Wally sat behind his desk, put down the papers he'd been carrying, and took a leisurely sip from his travel mug. "Can I help you with something?"

"Yes. You can wrap up this case toot sweet." Dante scowled. "Kathryn Steele had the nerve to call me last night to demand a statement. And since you hadn't bothered to inform me that our beloved school superintendent had been murdered, I sounded like a fool."

"Hmm." Wally refrained from mentioning that Hizzoner was perfectly capable of sounding like a fool even when he was fully up-to-date and instead explained, "You told me never to bother you at home unless Scumble River was about to be invaded by terrorists or aliens." Wally calmly continued to savor his coffee. "By the time we finished with the next-of-kin notifications, I would have had to interrupt your dinner to advise you on the case. I figured this morning was soon enough."

"You figured wrong." Dante glared, then seeming to realize he was standing while Wally was comfortably ensconced behind his desk, he plopped down in one of the visitor chairs and ordered, "Fill me in."

Wally summarized finding the body and the missing coins. He gave the mayor the minimum amount of information that he could get away with revealing and wasn't surprised when Dante demanded more.

At Wally's silence, Hizzoner narrowed his beady eyes and said, "If there are burglars in my town who aren't afraid to kill people, I need to know about it."

"I'm not completely convinced that the homicide was committed by some random thief." Wally leaned forward. "And by keeping the details quiet, you won't have to face concerned citizens afraid they're about to be murdered in their beds."

Dante sagged back in his chair. "Why can't things ever be simple with you or your nosy wife?"

Wally narrowed his eyes. Insulting Skye was a hot button for him. But he'd learned that the first step in staying calm was recognizing that the person you were upset with was *born* an idiot and couldn't help himself.

Dante fidgeted under Wally's lethal stare and flinched when the telephone rang. On the second ring, when Wally made no move to answer it, Dante jumped to his feet and scurried to the door.

Just before exiting, he leveled his finger at Wally and commanded, "From now on keep me informed. Even if it is after hours."

Wally gave Hizzoner a curt nod, then deliberately turned his head away and scooped up the receiver. "Chief Boyd speaking."

"Chief, we got the warrant for the school administration office. I'm sending a copy to your phone." Neal Boulder, the city attorney, had initially sounded jubilant, but now his tone changed. "The judge wouldn't okay the residence though."

Neal's high-pitched voice grated on Wally's ear and he quickly asked, "Anything we can do to change that decision?"

"The judge indicated that you need evidence that suggests one of the occupants was involved in the crime you're investigating," the lawyer answered. "Right now, everything points toward a random burglary, which gives us no due cause to search the residence."

"Okay." Wally ran his fingers through his hair. "I'll contact you if I come up with anything you can use to get the warrant. Oh, and see if you can get the contents of the vic's will released to us."

Once he disconnected, Wally looked at his cell to see if Skye had responded to his message, but there was nothing. He checked the time.

It wasn't even nine o'clock. She was probably still in her meeting.

A quick glance at the afternoon and midnight shifts' reports revealed that nothing out of the ordinary had happened during those sixteen hours. After filing the papers away, Wally rose to his feet and went downstairs.

Informing Thea that he was going to the school district administration building, he proceeded to the garage and headed over to the superintendent's office. He'd kill two birds with one stone. Conduct the search and find out what Karolyn knew about Neva Llewelyn's frequent meetings with Wraige.

As he drove, Wally thought about Karolyn Kline's seductive behavior. During most of his adulthood, depending on his marital status, Wally's attitude toward flirtatious females ranged from amiable tolerance to mild interest.

But once Skye came back into his life and then into his arms, other women's attentions just became an annoyance. Wally knew that his wife was still insecure about her curvier than socially acceptable figure, and he was always afraid that she would be upset when those ladies came on to him.

It wasn't that Skye didn't trust him. It was more that she had to endure the gossip about her husband caused by those predatory females. The last thing he ever wanted to do was hurt her, but sometimes the matter was out of his control.

Even if he expressed no interest whatsoever, the rumor mills in Scumble River would ensure that Skye was made aware of the encounter. And occasionally, the women who were unsuccessful in their attempts to flirt with him would be so incensed that he ignored them, they would out-and-out lie about the incident. Skye wouldn't believe their stories, but others would.

Sad to say, he suspected that Karolyn would fall into the group of women who didn't take being snubbed by men very well. Which meant getting information from her would be tricky.

Thankfully, her alibi had checked out and he didn't have to deal with her as a suspect. He had assigned Anthony to verify Karolyn's call list and she'd been on the phone almost continuously during time of death window.

Wally was still planning his strategy when he arrived at the admin building. After parking the car, he entered and found Karolyn reading a novel.

She hastily stashed the book out of sight and purred, "Chief, what brings you back here so soon? Do you need my help again?"

"I do." Wally had decided to attempt the delicate feat of being friendly without stepping over the line. "I have a warrant to search this office, but before I do, I'm hoping you can give me some information."

"If I can," she cooed and waved at the two visitor chairs. "Have a seat."

Wally sat down and took out his memo pad. "I heard that Neva Llewellyn had been having several meetings a week with Dr. Wraige. And I believe that the frequency of those meetings was unusual."

Karolyn rose, walked around her desk and perched on the edge so that her knees were nearly touching Wally's. "That's correct."

Wally forced himself to remain where he was instead of following his instinct to move his chair back and maintain his personal space. "Do you have any idea what Neva and Wraige were discussing?"

"Well…" Karolyn leaned forward so the deep V of her tight purple sweater gapped, putting her considerable cleavage on display.

"Yes?" Wally prompted, keeping his gaze firmly on Karolyn's eyes.

Frustration flickered across her face, and she flipped her long red hair off her shoulders, then shrugged. "I can't remember what I was going to say."

Smothering his irritation, Wally forced some warmth into his voice and said, "You were about to tell me what Neva and Wraige discussed."

"Right." Karolyn shifted, crossing her legs. Her hemline slid up her thigh, revealing the lacy tops of thigh-high stockings. After a solid minute, she pulled her skirt down and continued. "As you can see, my desk is only steps away from Dr. Wraige's office, so even though his door was closed, when they raised their voices, I couldn't help but hear some of what they said."

"Of course you couldn't." Wally nodded encouragingly. "And what was it they were discussing?"

"Neva wanted Dr. Wraige to appoint her assistant superintendent. She'd just about finished with her PhD and needed experience for her résumé in order to apply for superintendent's positions in other districts."

"And Dr. Wraige refused?" Wally frowned and jotted down a note to himself to talk to the junior high principal.

"Not at first. She was all set to start in the fall." Karolyn's hazel eyes sparkled. "But evidently, Neva reneged on her part of the bargain."

"Which was?" Wally had a good idea but wanted it confirmed.

"She was supposed to sleep with him." Karolyn's mouth twisted in disgust. "And people talked about me. I didn't screw for a paycheck. I did it because he was different. I liked that he took charge and made me do what he wanted. The guys around here are too nice."

"I see." Wally tucked that bit info into his mental file and resolved to be extra nice to Karolyn since that wasn't what she liked. "Then Neva was out of luck?"

"Nope." Karolyn leaned even closer and Wally almost choked on her heavy perfume. "It was Shamus who was out of luck. Neva recorded his job-for-sex offer and threated to make it public if he didn't make her assistant superintendent. She had something else on him, too, but I never managed to catch exactly what it was. They were still hashing out the details of her new position when he died."

CHAPTER 15

The Cupid Shuffle

THE PARENT CONFERENCE AT THE ELEMENTARY SCHOOL scheduled for seven fifteen to eight fifteen that morning had gone on and on. Instead of the hour Skye had allotted for the meeting, it hadn't ended until eight forty. And only then because the kids arrived to start their day, which meant the teachers had to get to their classes.

Now, dodging both students and staff, Skye flew down the hall leading to the exit, praying that none of the teachers would stop her to chat or ask for her assistance with anything. It was difficult to explain to anyone who was assigned to a single building that she had to split her time equally among all of the district's schools and she absolutely couldn't be late for her next appointment.

Having only one supervisor, most of the faculty couldn't conceive of the delicate balancing act it took for Skye to appease her trio of bosses, especially, with two of the three being über competitive with each other.

Thank goodness for Carolyn! The elementary principal was the only one Skye's principals who didn't see a cancelation or a skipped day at her school as a hideous insult to her personally and to her building.

Thoughts of Neva's displeasure at having already waited twenty-four hours for the boy with the suspicious pocket watch to be interviewed had Skye increasing her speed to an all-out sprint. Patience wasn't the junior high principal's strong suit. Neither was accepting excuses.

On the bright side, the parents that she and the grade school team had been working with for the past three years had finally agreed to having their son, Larson, evaluated. The boy had been struggling academically since the second semester of kindergarten, but his dad had always insisted that his son would catch up with his peers and had resisted all recommendations for testing.

Ultimately, Larson's father had had to acknowledge that his child was falling further and further behind the other students. It probably helped that his son's behavior had become defiant and unruly at home rather than just at school.

Happy that Larson would now have a chance to get the help he urgently needed, Skye slid behind the wheel of her Mercedes and immediately unzipped the insulated bag waiting for her on the passenger seat. She pulled on her seat belt with one hand and unwrapped her sandwich with the other.

Although it was super early for lunch, she'd skipped breakfast and this was probably her only chance to eat until late afternoon. Biting into the BLT, she decided to call it brunch.

Thankful that Dorothy insisted on packing a lunch for both her and Wally, Skye took a second to enjoy the homemade bread and crispy bacon. When her husband had first insisted on special ordering the breakfast meat from a company in Texas, she had thought he was being extravagant, but she had to admit there was a definite difference between it and the package she usually picked up at the supermarket.

Chewing slowly to savor the flavor, she drove the short distance to the junior high. It was a shame that the tomato and lettuce were what you would expect for February in Illinois, but the rest of the sandwich was delicious.

As she pulled into the school's parking lot, Skye's thoughts turned to the reason that her morning conference had ended later than planned. Usually, it would have been a tardy parent throwing off her schedule, but this time it was Carolyn Greer, the elementary principal, who caused the delay.

Afterward, she'd explained to Skye that she and the other two principals had been summoned by the school board to a meeting at the administration building. They had been informed that district superintendent had been murdered and instructed to send out notices via email, text, and/or letters to the parents informing them of Dr. Wraige's death and asking them to break the news to their children.

Skye had asked if Carolyn wanted her to do crisis intervention with the students. Carolyn had declined her offer, telling Skye that there would be no formal announcement at any of the schools, and all three principals doubted the students would need intercessions since so few had any contact, let alone any relationship, with the superintendent.

Still, Skye was glad that last night, once Wally had given her the green light to reveal Dr. Wraige's death, she'd contacted Piper, alerting her to the situation. There was always the off chance that the kids might already be aware of Dr. Wraige's death when they got to school the next morning and even if they didn't know him very well, some students could experience difficulties with the idea of any adult authority figure passing away.

Skye had instructed Piper to review the crisis plan and be prepared to act with or without Skye's presence. Although, of course, she could call Skye to help if she felt overwhelmed.

So far, she hadn't heard anything from Piper, who was at the high school, and as Skye arrived at the junior high and checked in, she crossed her fingers. But there were no messages in her box, and the school secretary didn't even look up when she greeted her.

So far, so good. Blowing out a thankful breath, Skye headed to her office. It was such a relief not to have to deal with any crises that would force her to change her plans to talk to the pocket watch boy.

Entering the room, Skye smiled at the upgraded space. The new arrangement allowed her to do her job so much better than the smelly closet she'd been stuck in for the past seven years.

Using part of her furnishings budget and some of her own money, she'd created an inviting counseling nook. The room had been painted a soothing aqua blue, the broken blinds had been removed from the windows and replaced with white woven shades, and a comfy gray tweed love seat now resided on an area rug with two coordinating chairs facing it. A sturdy coffee table between them completed the inviting area.

After locking her purse in the bottom desk drawer, Skye took out a few fidget toys. Occupying his hands with something fun should help Tyson relax while they talked. Satisfied that she was ready, she went to fetch the young man from his classroom.

Violet Lawrence, Tyson's special education teacher, was expecting her, and as soon as she spotted Skye at the door, Violet sent Tyson out into the hallway. He slipped out of the classroom and slouched against the wall.

He was small for his age, appearing closer to twelve then fourteen and wore jeans along with a gray hoodie. As Skye greeted him, he kept his hands in the sweatshirt's front pockets and his gaze on the floor.

Skye introduced herself, then, inviting him to walk with

her, she said, "Ms. Lawrence asked that I chat with you, but I promise you'll be back in time for lunch."

"Okay." His voice was monotone and his face expressionless.

When they got her office, Skye opened the door and waited for him to step inside, then said, "Do you have any idea what she might want me to talk to you about?"

Tyson shrugged, then like most students she brought here, he headed straight for the large aquarium against the rear wall. It took some work to maintain, but it was worth the trouble because it helped the kids feel comfortable.

Skye studied him as he watched the colorful fish. He seemed mesmerized by their languid movements.

As she joined him at the tank, she said, "See that big blue fish?" When he nodded, Skye continued, "It's a neon blue discus. It's my favorite."

Tyson looked at her, suspicion glinting in his eyes. "Why is he your favorite?"

"Because, although he's a little harder to take care of due to his special needs, he's worth it." She waited, allowing Tyson to digest what she'd said, then asked, "Would you like a flavored water?"

"That would be awesome." Tyson turned away from the aquarium.

Skye smiled to herself at his sudden change in attitude. It was truly amazing with the offer food or drink could do to build rapport.

Tyson followed Skye to the mini fridge that she'd installed behind her desk. It was another purchase that she'd squeezed into the refurbishing budget, although she bought the refreshments she kept inside.

"Black raspberry, cherry limeade, orange mango, or kiwi strawberry?"

"Orange mango." He pointed to the one he wanted. "Is it fizzy?"

"It is." Skye grabbed two bottles—she was thirsty, too—then led Tyson to the counseling nook. After he sat down on the couch, she handed him his drink and took the chair facing him. "Have you thought about why Ms. Lawrence might want me to talk to you?"

"Uh…" Tyson twisted open the cap on his bottle and took a long swig. "It might be about that watch. But it was Ray's, not mine."

"Ms. Lawrence was pretty sure you said it was yours." Skye sipped her cherry limeade, then said, "Unless you stole it, you're not in trouble. And even if you did take it, I'm sure we can fix this."

"I didn't steal it!" Tyson shouted, then shrank back against the sofa cushions as if afraid that she'd punish him for yelling.

Skye ignored his outburst; instead, she smiled at him and said, "That's great. We didn't think you would do that." She waited for him to relax, then added, "All we want to know is where you got it."

"It's not mine." Tyson thrust out his bottom lip and reverted back to his original defense. "I told you that it's Ray's."

"Hmm." Skye put down her drink. It was time to stop this line of questioning for a while and circle back around later. She picked up a blue-and-green tangle toy and offered it to Tyson. "Have you ever tried one of these?"

He gingerly took the smooth plastic knot. "What do you do with it?"

"I just like to twist and bend it." Skye chose the orange-and-yellow one and demonstrated. "It's sort of like looking at the fish. It helps me calm down and think through things more easily."

As Tyson manipulated the twisty plastic, Skye saw his

shoulders loosen and his breathing become less agitated. He'd come into their school diagnosed with a learning disability, but she suspected he also suffered from anxiety, something she wanted to look into during his upcoming reevaluation. Most likely, his severe processing deficits made the school environment feel overwhelming and she wanted to see if he would be eligible for counseling or maybe her eighth-grade boys group.

"Can I ask you something?" Tyson stole a glance at her before returning his gaze to the toy.

"Sure."

"Since bread is square, how come bologna is round?" He frowned. "They know we're going to put it in a sandwich, right?"

"I don't really know the answer to that, but my best guess is that it's cheaper to make in that shape."

"Hmm." He nodded. "It's always about the money, isn't it?"

"Not always." Skye wondered where that response had come from. "But you're right, it is a lot of the time."

She waited several minutes until he was absorbed in the tangle again, then said, "We really need to know where you got the watch."

Without looking up from the brightly colored toy, Tyson blew out an annoyed breath, then seemed to realize he wasn't getting away with the lie about his friend, and muttered, "I found it."

"Where?" Skye had learned that the less she said—single-word responses were best—the more likely the kids would keep talking.

"The graveyard south of town. The one out by all those rich people's houses." Tyson glanced at her, then put down the fidget toy.

"How did you get all the way out there?" Skye asked, handing him an Infinity Cube.

According to his file he lived on the opposite end of

Scumble River. That put him a good five miles from the cemetery.

"I rode my bike." Tyson examined the silver gadget. "I like looking at all the old tombstones." He flipped the cube and it opened. "Did you know they have people buried there that were born in the 1700s? And the names are really cool too. Like Lettice and Ibot."

"Are you interested in the past?" Skye asked.

If he was, she'd let his teacher know that he was keen on history. Finding a subject that he enjoyed might be good way to draw him into reading more. There were several companies that produced high-interest, age-appropriate biographies for struggling readers.

"Yeah." Tyson reassembled the cube. "I like to find out about people in the olden days. You know, how they lived and dressed."

"That would be fun to investigate." Skye nodded, then asked, "Do you remember where in the cemetery you found the pocket watch?"

"Let me think." He played with the cube for a few seconds as he screwed up his face and chewed on his lips, then he snapped his fingers. "It was near the edge. Right by the trees that separate the houses from the graves. I saw something shiny and when I went over to see what it was, I saw the watch half-buried in the snow."

"Where do you have it now?" Skye leaned forward. "You must have hidden it really good since your parents couldn't find it when they looked. Did you stash it somewhere here at school or outside?"

"Nah." Tyson shook his head. "I had a better spot. I put it in a plastic bag and buried it in the kitty litter." He grinned. "It's my job to clean Simba's box so I knew they wouldn't find it."

Skye made sure that her voice conveyed admiration. "Smart."

Kids like Tyson often took compliments as sarcasm. If they thought they were being patronized, they reacted poorly.

"I guess." He shrugged, his cheeks reddening. "But I have it with me now."

"I know you found it and all, but I'm going to need you to give it to me." Skye held out her hand, hoping he wouldn't make a big fuss about giving it up. "Someone must have lost it, and from the description, it sounds as if it's been in their family for a long time."

Tyson stared at her without moving. His expression was defiant or maybe just unhappy.

"I bet whoever misplaced it is really upset." Skye kept her hand out.

Tyson reached into the pocket of his hoodie, but before he pulled it out, he hesitated and grumbled, "I always heard that it was finders keepers, losers weepers. That's what my dad always says when he brings something home from the landfill that he works at."

"Only if you can't locate the true owner." Skye's mind raced for a solution. She didn't want the situation to escalate to the point Neva had to get involved. "How about you choose one of these gadgets as a reward for finding the watch and turning it in?"

"Can I have one for my friends Ray and Jeremy too?" Tyson bargained.

"Absolutely." Skye bought the fidget toys in bulk for less than six dollars apiece. "Hand me the watch and choose the ones you want."

Once the transaction was completed, Skye glanced at the time and said, "Yikes!" She jumped to her feet and motioned for him to follow her. "We have to get you back to your classroom ASAP. Lunch starts in two minutes and I know you don't want to be late for that."

"I have one more question for you." Tyson's eyes sparkled with mischief and Skye braced herself. "I've been streaming *Gilligan's Island*, and I can't figure out why, if the professor can make a radio out of a coconut, he can't fix a hole in the boat."

"Probably because that would have ended the show." Skye grinned, then hurried Tyson down the hall.

She gave his teacher a thumbs-up to indicate the watch issue had been resolved and returned to her office. She had twenty minutes before Neva would be available to be briefed on Tyson's interview.

The junior high principal always took the first lunch duty. It was a chore none of the other district principals chose to undertake in their schools, but something that Neva's staff greatly admired.

While Skye waited, she took out the baggie that she'd stashed in her purse. Dorothy had baked chocolate chip cookies and sent a couple in Skye's lunch.

While she finished her cherry limeade and munched on the cookies, she checked her phone. She frowned when she saw a text from Wally.

He wanted her to call as soon as possible, so she tapped the icon. As the phone rang, she worried that something else bad had happened.

Wally picked up on the third ring, and she asked, "Is everything all right?"

After assuring her that nothing was wrong, Wally commented, "You're starting to sound like your mother. Every unexpected call does not mean there's been a disaster or that I have horrible news."

"Last time you called me during work was about Dr.

Wraige's murder," Skye pointed out. "So I believe my concern is justified."

Wally chuckled and recapped his conversation with Dorothy and his interview with Karolyn, then said, "Any possibility you could sound out Neva regarding the assistant superintendent thing? Maybe find out if she still gets the job with Wraige dead."

"Hmm." Skye swigged the last sip of her drink. "I'm meeting with her this afternoon and I'll try to steer the conversation in that direction."

"Great. This must be what she meant when she told you Wraige would do what she wanted." Wally paused, then added, "But what did the superintendent have on the school board? Maybe try to find out that too."

"I'll give it my best shot." Skye rolled her eyes wondering how she'd get that out of Neva. "Any other miracles you'd like me to perform?"

"Nothing comes to mind, but I'll let you know," Wally teased.

They chatted for a few more minutes, then when Skye noticed it was time to go talk to Neva, she muttered a hasty goodbye and hung up.

Rushing toward the door, Skye noticed that her chest was covered in cookie crumbs. That wouldn't do.

She returned to her desk, brushed off her sweater and put on some lipstick. Looking much more professional, she headed to the main office.

With any luck, the principal would be so pleased that Skye had secured the pocket watch and gotten the story behind it, she'd be in a talkative mood. Otherwise, prying information out of Neva was about as tough as convincing Skye's mother her grandbabies weren't the smartest, most beautiful children on earth.

CHAPTER 16

Your Cheatin' Heart

URSULA NELSON, THE JUNIOR HIGH SECRETARY, GLANCED up as Skye entered, then quickly became engrossed in her work, refusing to acknowledge Skye's presence. Skye had been instrumental in revealing that Ursula's nephew had been involved in criminal activity, and even though the woman knew the boy had been in the wrong, she wasn't Skye's number-one admirer. Or even number five hundred, for that matter.

Skye tried to wait out Ursula's silent treatment, but when the secretary continued to ignore, she finally cleared her throat and said, "Hi! Is Neva ready for me?"

"Actually"—Ursula's beetle-brown eyes flashed from under her prominent forehead and bored into Skye—"Ms. Llewellyn has been waiting for you."

"Didn't she have lunch duty?" Checking the time, Skye moved toward the principal's door. "The bell for the next period only rang a minute ago."

"Which is when she expected you," Ursula snapped.

Her clawlike fingers returned to scrabbling through the stack of index cards in front of her. She had flatly refused to convert to the district's computer system and once a week someone else had to type in the information from the cards.

"Right."

Ursula hunched over the white paper rectangles on the desktop. She leaned over and moved a pile closer; her long torso and beady eyes made her look like a crow protecting its eggs.

Glancing up, Ursula waved her talon. "What are you standing there watching me do my job for? Go on in and do your own job."

Gritting her teeth to avoid a nasty comeback, Skye entered the principal's office. Neva had redecorated when she took over from the last occupant, and the room had gone from resembling a sports bar to having the ambiance of a Victorian parlor.

The athletic memorabilia that had decorated the space was gone, replaced with reproductions of paintings by Marie Spartali Stillman and Eleanor Fortescue-Brickdale. The drab brown walls had been painted an attractive ballet pink and floral curtains now hung from the windows instead of utilitarian white metal blinds.

Skye seated herself in a Queen Anne chair and faced Neva across a gleaming wooden desk. While she waited for the principal to look up from the file she was reading, Skye breathed in the pleasant odor of vanilla and lemon that wafted through the air from a silver bowl of potpourri residing on a small butterfly table positioned next to an antique rose velvet love seat.

Neva straightened the sleeve of her wine-colored suit jacket and leaned forward. "How did your talk go with Tyson Howe?"

"Very well." Skye beamed, happy to have good news. "It took a bit to gain his trust, but once he relaxed, he was very cooperative."

"I'm a little surprised." Neva frowned. "His teachers tell me he's been extremely difficult to motivate ever since he's moved here."

"Although I'm not shocked to hear that, it's unfortunate." Skye pursed her lips. "I suspect when we complete his upcoming re-eval, I'll be adding him to my counseling caseload, either seeing him individually or in a group. A kid like Tyson, who's bright but has a such a severe learning disability, needs help with his emotions, and most parents aren't able to provide that assistance."

"When is his annual review?" Neva tapped a few keys and gazed at her computer monitor. "I don't see him on this month's schedule."

Skye took her appointment book out of her tote bag, flipped through it until she saw Tyson's name, then ran her finger down the page. "I'm hoping to have everything finished for him before spring break."

"So, six more weeks?" Neva tapped a perfectly manicured nail on the desktop. "Is there a chance we can speed that up any?"

"I'd have to move him to the top of the list." Skye leafed through her planner. There were no openings. "Is that fair to the others that would be pushed back?"

Neva considered Skye's question for a few seconds, then asked, "Do you think any of the students who are presently scheduled ahead of him will require an alteration in placement or services?"

"The teachers haven't made me aware of any they feel might need changes," Skye answered cautiously. "And I did just establish rapport with Tyson, so now would be a good time to test him."

"That's an excellent point." Neva tented her fingers. "Please make him your priority and inform the rest of the team of his new standing on the list."

"Will do." Skye jotted down a note and put away her appointment book.

"Now"—Neva folded her hands on the desktop—"tell me about the pocket watch."

Skye explained where and how the boy had found the watch, and once Neva had nodded her understanding, Skye continued, "Although Tyson didn't steal it, I didn't feel he should keep it."

"Why is that?" Neva drew her eyebrows together. "Didn't you believe his story about finding the watch abandoned in the cemetery?"

"I did." Skye tilted her head. "But the watch appears to be an expensive family heirloom. It was most likely lost, not purposely discarded. Which is why I thought it best that we try to locate the owner." Neva opened her mouth to respond, but Skye held up her palm to stop her. "I know it isn't technically the school's place to do that, but I felt it was a good lesson for Tyson to learn."

"Fine. I won't stop you from pursuing this matter." Neva gazed firmly at Skye. "But I expect you to handle that on your own time."

"Absolutely." Skye nodded. "Should I talk to Tyson's special ed teacher, or do you want to let her know the results of our talk?"

"I'll speak to Ms. Lawrence," Neva answered. Then, when Skye didn't get up, she raised a brow and asked, "Was there something else?"

"I…" Skye stuttered to a stop. How in the world was she supposed to bring up the issue of the assistant superintendent position?

"Yes?" Neva's fair brows met above her nose, and she tilted her head.

"I wanted to tell you I was sorry about Dr. Wraige's

unexpected passing," Skye said carefully, hoping Neva would open up. "I know you and he worked closely together, so if you need to talk…"

Neva stiffened, then seemed to force herself to relax and leaned back in her chair. "That's very kind of you, but Shamus and I didn't have a personal relationship, and our professional one was"—she paused—"let's just say, cool at best."

"Oh." Skye's mind raced. How could she find out the information Wally requested? "I guess I assumed you were closer to the superintendent than that, because you told me you could get him to approve additional psych services in the next budget."

"One doesn't have to be on friendly terms to influence the boss." Neva's smile was predatory. "In fact, often it's better if there's not that type of association."

"Really?" Skye encouraged. "I can't see how that would work."

With Skye's response, Neva's forehead furrowed, then she seemed to realize she was probably revealing more than she had intended to divulge and hastily added, "Please keep this confidential, but Shamus and I had recently agreed that I would become the district's assistant superintendent in the upcoming year."

"Congratulations!" Skye said. "Do you think Dr. Wraige's death will influence your promotion at all? I mean, will his intention to create a new position be honored by the school board?"

"It had better be." Neva's voice hardened. "I have a signed contract."

"That's great." Skye smiled, then mused, "I wonder how Dr. Wraige convinced the board to add an assistant superintendent to the staff?"

Neva leaned forward. "I'm only guessing, but Shamus was

good at exchanging favors with people. Favors that those individuals wouldn't necessarily want made public." She stood, walked around her desk, and waited for Skye to get to her feet, then continued. "And all it would take was the idea that Shamus might expose the fact that he'd pulled some strings for a board member and that board member would make sure Shamus got his way."

"Wouldn't that hurt Dr. Wraige too?" Skye asked. "After all, he was the one who had used his influence to get special treatment."

Neva shook her head. "Shamus had a five-year contract. If he had to, he'd be able to retire with full benefits before he had to negotiate the next agreement."

"But board members have to run for election every four years." Skye finished Neva's explanation. "Wouldn't it take more than one member to get a budget item like that passed by the board?"

"Not really." Neva shrugged as she and Skye walked out the door together.

"How so?" Skye questioned. "They'd need a majority to vote yes."

"True." Neva tapped Skye's arm. "But you'd be surprised what one motivated man can do to influence the rest of the board members."

Once they were in the hallway, Neva headed toward the resource room and Skye went in the direction of her office. If Tyson's reevaluation was being moved to the head of the line, she had to alert the rest of the team ASAP so they could adjust their schedules.

After unlocking her door and settling behind her desk, Skye turned on her computer. While she waited for it to boot up, she took the pocket watch out from where she'd stashed it in her locked drawer.

She hadn't really looked at the piece of jewelry before, but since she was now tasked with finding the rightful owner, she spent time examining it. It was a beautiful pocket watch, and as Violet had indicated, definitely heavy enough to be real gold.

Running her fingers over the intricately engraved monogram on the watch's back, she squinted until the image came into focus. She could just barely make out the word FORTITUDINE curved over the image of an arm holding a sword aloft. It looked like it might be a family crest. If so, there was a good chance that it might help her identify the owner.

Three hours later, a shrill ringing of the bell yanked Skye out of the report she was writing. Blowing a curl out of her eyes, she looked at the time. It was three fifty and classes were over for the day.

Or at least classes at the junior high were done. The district schools all got out at staggered times to allow maximum usage of the buses. Because so many of its students drove themselves, the high school ended earliest, at three twenty-five. The junior high was next, and the elementary was last at four fifteen.

The same was true in the morning with the high school staring at seven fifty, the junior high at eight fifteen, and the grade school at eight forty. Which was fine, except for the itinerant staff like the nurse, speech pathologist, and Skye.

The pupil personnel services staff served all three buildings and frequently began their day at one and ended at the other. This often resulted in them working longer than any of the other employees.

During their last contract negotiations, Skye, Belle, and Abby had banded together and managed to get their expected hours in writing. This new clause replaced the sentence that obligated them to follow the school's schedule.

None of them were able to completely adhere to their contracted hours. However, they had all agreed to make an effort to do so.

Given that Skye had had a seven-fifteen meeting at the elementary school, she was entitled to leave at three forty-five. She'd already stayed a few minutes over and hurriedly backed up her document, grabbed her purse, and headed for the door.

Just as she slid into her SUV, her phone vibrated in her pocket. She quickly checked and saw that it was a text from Dorothy that the twins didn't go down for their afternoon nap until late. The housekeeper warned Skye to be prepared for the babies schedule to be off that evening.

As Skye replied to Dorothy, another message came in. This time it was from Wally.

If you have time after you're finished at work, stop over at the PD before you go home.

She smiled happily when she saw that he'd signed it with a cute emoji of two happy faces kissing. He really was the sweetest guy.

Deciding that it would take more time to text a reply than to just drive the two miles from the school to the station, Skye started the SUV and steered the Mercedes out of the school's lot. A few minutes later, she parked and walked toward the red brick building.

In order to avoid being waylaid by the dispatcher, Skye used her key to let herself into the station through the garage entrance. It wasn't that she objected to exchanging pleasantries with Thea; it was more the length of the discussion. There seemed to be a twenty-minute minimum, during which the weather was thoroughly debated and their families' well-being confirmed.

Walking down the short corridor that led to the staircase, Skye heard Thea talking, but no one answering. She realized that her evasion hadn't been necessary as the dispatcher seemed to be tied up on the emergency line.

Abruptly, Thea's voice change from her usual soothing tone into an annoyed bark. From what Skye could tell, it sounded as if the dispatcher was explaining to whomever was on the other end of the phone that being served onions on a sandwich when the order had been for a plain cheeseburger was not cause for either the caller to dial 911 or for the restaurant chef to be arrested.

Evidently someone was a very picky eater. And they didn't know how to scrape off a disliked item from their burger. Handling the police, fire, and ambulance lines sounded almost as tricky as Skye's job as a school psychologist. And she got paid a heck of a lot more than the fifteen dollars an hour the dispatchers earned.

Shaking her head at what people considered an emergency, Skye climbed to the second floor. When she got to the top but before she moved into the hallway, she carefully peered to her left.

The mayor's office had a clear line of sight to the stairs' landing, and her uncle had pounced on her one too many times to be comfortable stepping into the corridor without making sure he wasn't around.

When she was certain that the coast was clear, it only took a second to walk to Wally's office. Not bothering to knock, Skye pushed open the door and froze.

Why was Wally holding a strange woman in his arms?

CHAPTER 17

Can't Help Falling in Love

SKYE WAS STILL STANDING SPEECHLESS IN THE DOORWAY when Wally noticed her and said, "Thank goodness you're here, darlin'." He kept talking as he eased his burden into one of the visitors' chairs. "This is Colleen Vreesen, Nanette's friend. She came to the station to turn in her key for the Wraige's house, but she started to feel dizzy while I was questioning her. I just barely caught her in time or she would have faceplanted on the floor."

It was now evident to Skye that the woman was unconscious, or at least pretending to be. Skye was pretty sure that while Wally was explaining things to her, she'd seen the Vreesen woman's eyes open for a nanosecond. There also might have been a tiny frown crawl across her lips.

"Can you take over while I call for an ambulance?" Wally asked, attempting to keep Colleen from slipping out of her seat.

"Sure." Skye approached the supposedly comatose woman and got a grip on her shoulders. She noted that Colleen's head was lolling against the back of the chair. "But wait a second on that telephone call."

Wally stopped moving toward the phone. "Okay." Clearly puzzled, he waited for her to clarify her request.

Skye took the woman's arm and lifted it over her face. According to the continuing education seminar that she'd taken on factitious disorders, if Colleen allowed it to hit her nose, she really was out cold. But as Skye had suspected, when she let the woman's hand drop, Colleen jerked it away.

The class instructor had explained that not many conscious people will allow themselves to be smacked in the snout. Prior experience has taught them that it really hurts and a defensive instinct takes over.

Although Colleen tried to continue the pretense, Skye said, "We know you're faking, Ms. Vreesen, so you might as well sit up and talk to us."

"Where am I?" Colleen's eyelids fluttered like hummingbird wings and she looked around as if in a daze. "What happened to me?"

"You seem to have fainted." Wally exchanged a glance with Skye.

"Oh my." Colleen clutched her chest. "It's just all been too much for me. First, the accident, then the news about Shamus."

"I'm sure it has." Skye pushed aside the fact she was ninety-nine percent sure the woman had faked her blackout and put on her therapist persona. "Would you like something to drink, or I can help you to the restroom so you can splash your face with cold water?"

She'd instinctually disliked the woman, but that was probably due to jealousy. Seeing her in Wally's arms had stirred up a slew of negative emotions about herself. Skye had almost rid herself of the insecurity she felt being married to such a rich, handsome man, but evidently there was still a little hanging on.

"Who are you?" Colleen's baby-blue eyes narrowed. "You weren't here before."

"This is my wife, Skye." Wally stepped over and put his arm around Skye's waist. "She's also the psychological consultant for the police department."

"Scumble River needs a psychologist? How interesting." Colleen twisted a strand of ash-blond hair as she gazed at Wally. "I didn't realize you were married, Chief."

"Really?" Skye raised a brow. "Hard to miss the honking big wedding ring on his left hand."

Wally tried to hide a chuckle as he flashed the wide platinum band on his ring finger, but Skye noticed his amusement and pinched his side.

He cleared his throat and his tone became professional as he said, "Just before you fainted, I had asked you to tell me your whereabouts between eight thirty and ten yesterday morning."

"Right." Colleen nodded. "I was actually on I-55 driving into the city, but I never got there. I ended up turning around and coming back here."

"But didn't you say that you arrived in Scumble River after midnight last night?" Wally asked. "That's what you told me before you fainted."

"That's where the accident I mentioned comes in." Colleen wet her lips. "A pickup swiped my car. I was able to take the Bolingbrook exit. I pulled into the nearest parking lot to see how much damage there was to my Prius."

"How awful for you," Skye said. "Did your car end up being undriveable?"

"No. As it turned out, the only damage was a bit of paint scraped off and my driver side mirror was smashed. Actually, the mirror was totally gone. Only a few wires were left sticking out of the hole." Colleen shook her head. "I would have guessed there would have been more damage, but it seems as if I was lucky."

"Then why did it take you so long to get back to Scumble River?" Skye asked.

"A Good Samaritan followed me. He wanted me to call the police, but what was the use?" Colleen sighed noisily. "I didn't get the truck's license plate and it was doubtlessly long gone."

"You should always make a report," Wally advised. "For your insurance if nothing else. Now you probably won't be able to collect."

"I wouldn't make a claim anyway. My premium would go up more than it would cost me to just pay to replace the mirror myself."

"Probably," Wally agreed. "What you've told us still doesn't explain why you were so late getting back to Scumble River."

"When my Good Samaritan saw how shaken I was from the incident, he said he lived in a nearby housing development and insisted on taking me to his place so that I could rest," Colleen explained.

"You got into a car with a strange man and went to his home?" Wally scowled. "That was an extremely reckless thing to do."

"You're right." Colleen's pupils dilated. "I don't know what I was thinking. I must have been in shock." She shrugged. "But all's well that ends well. The guy was a sweetheart. I ended up sleeping for several hours, then when I woke up and saw the text from Nanette that Shamus was dead, I was so stunned."

"I imagine you wanted to get back to Scumble River right away to be with your friend in her hour of need," Skye said dryly. So far, she didn't believe a word the woman had uttered. "To comfort her."

"I did, but I felt woozy when I stood up and my Good Samaritan told me that I needed to eat because my blood sugar was probably low." Colleen touched her hair. "He made me dinner, then we started watching this movie while I ate, and well, I didn't end up getting back on the road until after ten."

"Let me get this straight," Skye said slowly. "After being hit by a truck on I-55 and finding out your best friend's husband had been killed, you basically went on a date with a guy you just met?"

"I guess you could say that I did." Colleen giggled and tugged on her ear. "You probably think that I'm terrible, but life's too short to worry."

"Hmm." Skye made a noncommittal sound, then having nothing else to say, gave Wally a look indicating she was done.

"I'll need the Good Samaritan's full name and address." Wally took out his memo pad, clicked on his pen, and stared at Colleen.

"Uh…" She bit her lip. "Let me see. It was Merle, or maybe Burl?"

"How about his surname?" Wally prompted. "Merle or Burl what?"

"It might have been Brown, no maybe Green." Colleen closed her eyes. "I know it was definitely some color. Possibly Black or White or Gray?"

"How about where he lives?" Wally encouraged. "Did you notice the street?"

"Sorry." Colleen tapped her chin. "As I mentioned, I think I was in shock, and the area was really twisty. And then when he drove me back to my car it was dark."

"Did the development have a name?" Wally asked, and when she shook her head, he said, "Could you find the house if we took you there?"

"Probably not. At the best of times, I have a terrible sense of direction." Colleen widened her eyes. "Why is this important?"

"We need to confirm your alibi." Wally leaned a hip against his desk. "Did you get his phone number?"

"My what!" Colleen squealed. "You think that I killed Shamus?"

"At this point, we're still ruling people out," Wally explained.

"I didn't get his number, but I gave him mine. If he calls, I'll have him get in touch with you. And you can come down to the parking lot with me and see the damage on my car." Colleen crossed her arms and frowned. "I can't believe you're being so mean about this. Nanette can tell you I didn't get to the apartment until nearly midnight."

Wally asked a few more questions, then accompanied Colleen downstairs to look at her vehicle. While he was gone, Skye checked in with Dorothy, who reported that Eva was playing with her Crinkle and Roar Lion and CJ was on the twins' Kick 'n Play Piano Gym.

She sent Skye a picture of them both and Skye thanked her, then admired her beautiful babies. With all the photos and videos Dorothy sent throughout the day, Skye didn't feel as if she was missing her children's progress as much as she had feared.

After telling Dorothy that she and Wally would be home within the hour, Skye hung up. She looked around, trying to decide what to do until Wally returned, then walked behind his desk.

Taking a seat, Skye searched for a clean legal pad and found one in his top drawer. She grabbed a pen and started writing.

There was something off about Colleen, but she couldn't

put her finger on what exactly was bothering her about the woman. She jotted down her questions:

1. Why had she pretended to faint? Was it to seduce Wally or was it to distract him from his line of questioning?
2. Would a thirtysomething woman really go off with a stranger? And if so, why had she stayed so long at his house?
3. If she and Nanette were such close friends, wouldn't Colleen hurry back after finding out Nanette's husband had been killed?

Skye chewed on the end of the pen. What was wrong with this picture?

She was still trying to come up with an answer when Wally strode into the office.

He did an exaggerated double take, smiled broadly, and teased, "Chief Boyd, my how you've changed. Why are you out of uniform?"

"That's Mrs. Chief Denison-Boyd," Skye joked back at him. "The department has never issued me a uniform. Should I complain?"

"Well…" Wally drawled. "You would look adorable in a Scumble River Police Department pants and shirt, but I think plain clothes"—he winked—"or no clothes, is better for your position."

"That could be considered harassment." Skye wagged her finger at him. "But because you're cute, I'll let it go this time." She rose, picked up the legal pad she'd been using, and moved to a visitor's chair, then after Wally was seated behind his desk, she said, "I suspect a good deal of what Colleen told us was a lie."

"Not that I disagree, but why do you think that?" Wally leaned back in his chair.

"One, she spontaneously provided way too much minutiae." Skye glanced at her notes. "Two, she became testy when you questioned her about the Good Samaritan's details. Three, it's odd she couldn't recall anything that would help us identify the guy. And lastly, her pupils were dilated, which happens when the nervous system is stressed."

"Good to know." Wally leaned forward. "Before I forget, I spoke to the state police investigator today, and Charlie's in the clear. They've released his car and will let him reopen the motel on Monday."

"That's awesome!" Skye beamed, then asked, "Was that why you want me to stop by?"

"No. I have couple other things to discuss." Wally selected a folder and flipped it open. "And once we're home, I know we'll get distracted with bath time for the twins and supper for us, and all the other stuff that takes up our evenings now that we have kids."

"True." Skye sat back and crossed her legs. "Then let's get to it. I told Dorothy we wouldn't be too long. You know it's her bowling night."

"Okay, what did Neva have to say?" Wally stared expectantly at Skye.

"How do you know I got anything from her?" Skye studied her nails.

"Because you're amazing." Wally's lips twitched upward. "Spill."

"She has a signed contract for the position of assistant superintendent, so Dr. Wraige's death doesn't affect her one way or another."

"And?" Wally encouraged. "What else?"

"She said that Dr. Wraige tended to hold board members'

secrets over them to get his own way." Skye fingered a chip in the pink polish on her thumb. When had that happened? "She also said it would only take one motivated person on the board to sway the vote."

"Hmm." Wally tapped his pen against his cheek, then said, "Great. Now I have to interview the entire school board as well as the whole transportation department." Once he'd recounted what Dorothy had told him about the bus drivers, he asked, "Have you heard about anyone else at school that has a beef with Wraige?"

"Not that I can think of offhand." Skye closed her eyes and thought about the rumors floating around the schools. "The teachers and support staff are pretty well insulated from the superintendent due to their contract." She chewed her bottom lip. "The secretaries and custodians answer directly to the principals."

"Neva seemed to have him where she wanted him. How about the others?"

"Caroline doesn't make waves, but..." Skye stuttered to a stop. "You know, he has been threatening to force Homer to retire."

"Could he really do that?" Wally asked, his expression disbelieving.

"I doubt it." Skye rolled her eyes and smirked. "Homer would be hard to blackmail because he's too dumb to hide things very well."

"I'll check on his alibi, but I think we can eliminate him."

Skye glanced at her watch. "What have you found out today?" They needed to hurry it up. Dorothy liked to go out for dinner with her friends before their bowling league, which meant she needed to leave the house no later than five thirty. "Any forensics?"

"Nothing from the lab yet." Wally flipped through some

papers in the file. "But Doris Ann did send over her preliminary findings."

"Anything interesting?" Skye asked leaning forward to see the report.

"There was something odd in his stomach contents." Wally tapped the page. "Doris Ann said that normally, with an obvious cause of death like bleeding out from a wound, she wouldn't have been too concerned with an unidentifiable item in a body's stomach, but because you mentioned Wraige had seemed ill, she's having it analyzed and will get back to us with the results. She wants to know his exact symptoms as that will help her figure out what tests to run."

"He was pale and sweaty and his hands were trembling." Skye wrinkled her brow. "He swayed as if he were dizzy, and then while we were hiding, he complained about diarrhea and nausea. If you'd made us a wait a few minutes more, I think he would have had to use a bucket in the corner."

Wally made a note. "I'll pass that on to Doris Ann."

"Why would it matter what's in his stomach?" Skye asked, frowning. "As you said, the arrow in the neck caused exsanguination, which led to his death."

"True." Wally tented his fingers. "But what if there had been a previous attempt on his life?"

CHAPTER 18

I've Got You Under My Skin

EARLY THE NEXT MORNING, WALLY HEADED TO THE BUS barn. He yawned and gulped down a mouthful of coffee. Returning his travel mug to the Hummer's cup holder, he yawned again. It was still dark, and after dragging himself out of bed before dawn, he needed all the caffeine he could hold in order to wake up enough to conduct coherent interviews with the drivers.

Or at least, not fall asleep at the wheel and end up in one of the deep ditches along his route. It would be beyond embarrassing for the chief of police to have to call a tow truck for a one-car accident, and Dante would never let him live it down.

Last night's storm had coated the street with a slippery layer of snow, requiring him to concentrate on keeping the vehicle from sliding every time he had to stop at a crossroads or slow down for a deer with a suicide wish.

According to the car's thermometer, it was currently below freezing, but it was supposed to get up to near forty by the afternoon and Wally hoped the rise in temperature might help melt some of the accumulation.

The meteorologists were calling for warmer weather and

no precipitation for the near future. If the radio's predictions could be trusted, Central Illinois might finally get a respite from winter.

With that positive thought cheering him up, Wally went over his plan for handling the upcoming questioning of the bus drivers. He intended to keep things casual, not wanting any of them to decide they wanted a lawyer present or refuse to talk to him at all.

Yesterday, when Wally had contacted Sally Anserello, the Scumble River School District director of transportation, who just happened to be one of his officers' mother, she had told him her people clocked in at six and were usually on the road thirty minutes later.

Figuring on that half hour being his best bet to find all the drivers in one convenient location, he'd set his alarm for the ungodly hour of five o'clock. With less than his usual eight hours of sleep, he tended to be short-tempered, and he would have to be careful not to alienate the drivers.

Thank goodness he had an inside source. Sally was a nice lady and she'd given him the scoop about the lesser-known workings of the school district's transportation department.

There were twelve drivers and twelve bus monitors, as well as six substitutes. Wally figured the subs wouldn't be the ones with the biggest beef against Wraige. With no set hours or guarantee of work, they probably drove in order to make a bit of extra cash rather than to provide a living for their families.

Making the turn into the long asphalt lane that led to the bus barn, Wally studied the facility's layout. A six-foot-high chain-link fence with a rolling gate surrounded the large property that included two asphalt areas and a large green metal pole building.

Currently, the gate was wide open and buses were lined up diagonally on the lot in front of the structure. Off to the side, a smaller paved rectangle held employees' cars. Wally left the Hummer next to a battered Toyota Corolla and walked to the barn.

As he entered, Sally greeted him with a big smile and asked, "How are those adorable twins of yours?"

"Cute as two bugs in a rug." Wally's Texas expressions tended to come out when he bragged on his children. "They're growing faster than the bluebonnets in the Hill Country during April."

Sally led him toward her desk and sat down with a grunt, rubbing her hip. "Is Skye happy to be back at work? I was wondering if she'd be able to leave the babies and end up quitting."

"It was hard for her," Wally admitted. "But she wouldn't be happy staying home. Her mind's too restless and her need to help people is too strong."

"Yeah." Sally nodded. "She's a real smart woman and has one of the biggest hearts I've ever seen. Good thing you were able to hire Dorothy Snyder. That had to take a load off both your minds."

"She's definitely a treasure." Wally beamed, then winked. "Especially after Skye's brother and sister-in-law stole our last nanny."

Sally snickered. "The way I heard it, your father and Skye's mother drove away that babysitter. Besides, you're better off with Dorothy."

"That's true." Wally scratched his head. "But what I can't figure out is how Loretta controls May so much better than the rest of us."

"It must be some kind of lawyerly secret." Sally narrowed her eyes. "Those people are trained to exploit people's weaknesses."

"Could be." Although Wally liked Loretta as a person, he

wasn't a fan of the legal profession, but being fond of his hide, he kept that opinion to himself.

"I hope I can control myself and be a bit less obsessed with Anthony's life than May is with her kids'." Sally patted her gray ponytail and smiled. "Then again, he and Judy are going to make some beautiful babies, so maybe not."

"Are they all set for the wedding?" Wally asked.

"As far as I know." Sally frowned. "What does he say to you?"

"Not much." Wally shrugged. "I guess most guys aren't that involved in the preparations. All they have to do is show up in their tux."

"On time and with the ring." Sally pointed a finger at Wally. "No police emergencies."

"I promise, no matter what, Anthony won't be on duty that day," Wally vowed, then asked, "Are all the drivers here?"

Sally glanced down at her open laptop, then said, "Everyone's clocked in." She waved to the group of men and women seated at picnic-style tables, flipping through bright red binders. "The ones you want to talk to are closest to the coffee urn."

Wally had told Sally that he was investigating the superintendent's murder and wanted to chat with any of her drivers that had a grudge against Wraige. She'd given him the name of the recently fired driver that Dorothy had mentioned but advised him that that guy was probably not who Wally should interview first.

According to Sally, Libby was the ringleader of the malcontents and if anyone wanted the superintendent dead, it was her. She encouraged the others to do her dirty work for her. She stirred everyone up, then hung back and watched the fireworks from a safe distance, all the while staying under the radar herself.

While this Libby woman didn't sound like the kind of person who would commit murder herself, she did sound like the kind of person who might have pushed someone else into it. And Wally wanted to know whom among her colleagues Libby had been provoking lately.

Thanking Sally and promising to show her some recent pictures of the twins once he'd talked to the drivers, Wally left her by her desk and walked toward the table she'd indicated. He took his time, sizing up the group before he got to them.

There were three women and two men varying in age from early twenties to late fifties. Four of the five wore jeans and sweatshirts, but one woman, an older brunette with shoulder length hair and glasses, had on neatly pressed khakis, a white button-down shirt, and a navy blazer. She was also the only one wearing makeup.

Wally would bet his bottom dollar that was Libby Jenson. And although she was the one that he wanted to talk with the most, he changed course to approach the man sitting to her right. From Sally's description, Wally reckoned that someone like Libby would never be able to stand that he'd chosen another driver to question rather than her.

Wally held out his hand to the man he'd selected and said, "May I have a few minutes of your time, sir?"

The guy blinked, then tilted his head and asked, "What can I do for you, Chief?" He shook Wally's hand and added, "I'm Gene Ringkamp."

"Nice to meet you." Wally wasn't surprised Gene had known who he was. His picture had been in the paper often enough that most Scumble River citizens recognized him without an introduction. Especially in uniform. "Have you heard that Dr. Wraige was killed yesterday?"

"Of course we did," Libby piped up. "It was in the *Star* yesterday."

Wally hid his smile. It hadn't taken her long to nibble at his bait. Now he had to reel her in and make her want to tell him everything.

Ignoring Libby, Wally turned to the three others at the table and asked, "I was hoping one of you could explain to me the superintendent's role in the transportation department?"

Even though the question hadn't been directed at her, once again, Libby answered, "His role was to treat us like dirt and make sure we couldn't make a living wage by keeping our hours just below full-time."

Evidently, Dorothy had been right about the situation. Wally made a metal note to slip a few extra bucks into the housekeeper's pay envelope. He wouldn't have thought of the bus drivers as possible suspects, and he doubted that Skye would have considered them, either.

"Doesn't your union protect you from that?" Wally egged Libby on.

"Wraige pretty much destroyed every attempt the drivers made to unionize." Libby's attractive face reddened and her voice rose.

"How could he do that?" Wally asked. "It's against the law to interfere with a union being organized."

"There are ways around everything," Libby muttered, then shot a look of loathing at some of the drivers at the other tables.

Gene finally spoke up. "The thing is, like everybody else, Dr. Wraige had the right of free speech. He made his disapproval clear and insinuated that if we organized a union, he would then outsource the bussing to one of the big companies that handle transportation in the Laurel and Clay Center school districts."

"I see." Wally shoved his hands in his pockets, the better to subliminally convey that this was a casual conversation, not an interrogation. "I suppose quite a few employees were pretty upset by those tactics."

"Some more than others." Gene glanced at Libby, then added, "But most were afraid of losing their jobs and backed off. A lot of the drivers like the work because the hours are good for their families."

"I think I heard that a man was fired recently?" Wally glanced around the table. "Did he do something wrong on the job? Or was it because he objected to the way Dr. Wraige operated?"

"Keith Makowski was a great driver." Libby crossed her arms. "The kids and parents loved him and I...uh, I mean he thought that would protect him against any of Wraige's reprisals."

"But I take it his popularity didn't save him?" Wally asked, and when Libby shook her head, he continued, "What got Mr. Makowski fired?"

Gene gave Libby the side-eye and said, "Some people thought that since Keith seemed to be bulletproof, he was the ideal person to publicly confront Dr. Wraige at a school board meeting."

"And that didn't go over very well?" Wally hazarded a guess.

Gene sighed. "At the meeting, the superintendent placated Keith by saying that he and the board would look into the drivers' grievances. Particularly the lack of full-time hours and the absence of support when disciplinary issues were raised on the buses."

"Of course, that never happened," Libby snapped. Adjusting her glasses to stare at Wally, she gritted her teeth and continued, "As soon as the parents' interest died down, and they forgot about Keith's presentation, Dr. Wraige made his move."

"Which was?" Wally asked, shifting to look at the angry women.

"Our contract forbids us from posting anything on social media about our students," Libby began, and Wally nodded his understanding.

"Most of us follow that rule, but occasionally we'll post something about a kid. We won't use his or her name, but we'll mention what they told us," Gene explained.

"Okay." Wally made a mental note to ask Skye if that kind of contractual clause was common for employees of school districts.

"I've been driving here for ten years and no one has ever gotten in trouble for one of those posts about an anonymous student," Libby added.

"I see." Wally had a good idea where this was going. "What happened?"

"Keith loved social media." Gene shook his head. "I don't see the attraction myself, but he's a lot more friendly and out-going than me."

"He also couldn't stand to see a kid upset." Libby picked up the story. "So one day after school, this student gets on the bus and tells Keith that he's hungry. Keith asks him if he ate his lunch."

Wally raised a brow.

At his inquiring look, Libby explained, "He asked because sometimes students throw away the cafeteria meal if they don't like it. The kid says he couldn't buy a hot lunch because he was twenty-five cents short and the cafeteria lady said that he already owed too much and according to board policy, she couldn't give him any more credit."

"And Keith was angry and posted it online?" Wally guessed.

"Yep." Gene pulled out his phone, found what he was

looking for, and handed it to Wally. "Here's Keith's post. I got a screen shot before the superintendent ordered him to take it down."

Wally squinted and read the tiny print:

How in the world is it okay to deny a child who is already on reduced lunch something to eat? Wouldn't we all rather feed a child than throw leftover food away?

Giving Gene back his phone, Wally said, "Dr. Wraige fired him over that?"

"Normally, only Keith's social media friends would have seen his post and the superintendent would have never even known that it was out there." Libby tapped her neatly trimmed nails on the Formica tabletop and the subtle pink polish gleamed in the overhead lights. "But he didn't have his settings as private, and the post got shared and reshared, and then it was everywhere."

"And as more and more people saw the post, they called the superintendent to complain." Gene shrugged. "Keith was summoned to the administration building and told that he had violated the terms of his contract, and he was terminated without severance pay."

Wally glanced at the big clock on the wall behind the drivers and saw that he had less than five minutes before they'd need to leave on their routes, so he quickly asked, "How did he take that?"

"About like you'd expect." Gene stood up and walked toward the exit.

Libby got to her feet too, but paused to add, "If Keith hadn't spoken out at the board meeting about our poor working conditions, Dr. Wraige would have probably just ordered him to delete the post and made him take a week off work without pay." She frowned. "But because Keith had publicly outed the superintendent's poor treatment of us bus drivers,

Dr. Wraige used his infraction of the rules to get rid of what he considered a troublemaker."

Wally followed the woman as she headed to the lot. "Do you know of anyone else that Wraige fired under those circumstances?"

"No." Libby opened the bus's door and climbed aboard, then leaned down and said, "But that's because everyone else was too afraid to go against him." She got behind the wheel. "The cowards."

Wally watched the woman drive off, then returned and got Keith Makowski's address from Sally. The man sounded like a wonderful person and not someone who would commit murder. But even a nice guy can be pushed beyond his limits and get in a shoving match with someone who ends up accidently dead.

CHAPTER 19

Cat's in the Cradle

AT PRECISELY SIX FIFTY-NINE A.M., SKYE WALKED OUT OF the house and into the garage. She had a seven-thirty PPS meeting at the elementary, then planned to spend the rest of the day at the high school.

Although normally she was at the grade school on Thursday mornings and the junior high in the afternoons, between the lockdown on Monday and the superintendent's murder on Tuesday, she'd had to rearrange her schedule. It wasn't uncommon for her to have to make changes, but it was still a pain in the butt to have to notify the principals and demonstrate that their schools weren't being shortchanged of her time.

Sliding behind the wheel of the Mercedes, Skye placed her thermal lunch bag, tote, and purse on the passenger seat, then hit the button underneath the review mirror and waited for the garage door to open. While it rose, she fastened her safety belt and started the SUV.

As she reversed onto the driveway and drove around the half circle in front of the house until the Mercedes was heading toward the road, she glanced from side to side until she spotted the black Escalade backed into a position between some trees. It had a clear view of the entire property, as well as the street running in front of the acreage.

When the babies were born, Carson had talked Wally and Skye into allowing him to put a security team on his grandchildren. This was in addition to the top-of-the-line home security system that he'd already installed in the RV that he'd provided for them to live in while they built their new home.

Skye's father-in-law had claimed that his men were among the best in the country and that most of the time she wouldn't even be aware of their presence. But he was wrong. Even when she couldn't see them, she could feel them watching her. And she could almost always spot them.

Even now, although she couldn't see the man, she knew there was a guard stationed at the rear of their property. Considering that the house's backyard abutted the river, she wondered if Carson thought they might be attacked via submarine or destroyer.

During their negotiations with her father-in-law about the babies' security, Skye had asked Wally why he didn't have guards keeping an eye on him. She'd pointed out that Carson's son was just as likely to be abducted as his grandchildren.

Wally had said that he had had security until he graduated from college, but chose not to once he was out of his father's limelight. He had added that the twins were much easier targets than he would be because they wouldn't put up a fight, which was why he agreed with his dad that they needed protection.

It was one of the few drawbacks of having a billionaire father-in-law. And since the pluses were so many more than the minuses, Skye had been willing to live with the guards to keep her babies safe.

She'd been afraid that Dorothy would resent both the

electronic and live surveillance, but the housekeeper had taken it in stride. She even regularly provided the men on duty with home-baked treats.

Although Skye couldn't see into the darkly tinted windows of the Escalade, she still waved as she drove by the vehicle. She had no idea if the guard waved back, but it seemed rude to just ignore the man.

Putting aside all thoughts of security teams and billionaire fathers-in-law, Skye spent the rest of the ride to school mentally preparing for the conference. PPS at the elementary was both her easiest and most difficult meeting. Easiest because the principal was the nicest, and hardest because often this was the first time the younger students were being referred, which meant they had very little educational history to consider while making their decisions.

One good thing about an early appointment was that Skye scored a parking spot right next to the entrance. Grabbing her purse and tote bag, she quickly walked into the building and headed to the special education classroom where the PPS team held their meetings.

Ninety minutes later, she was back in her SUV and on her way to the high school. There had only been two kids on the agenda and both had landed on the speech and language pathologist's to-do list instead of Skye's.

With the meeting being shorter than expected, she was running a little ahead of schedule. Pleased to have some extra time, Skye stopped by Tales and Treats and picked up a couple of boxes of the café owners' assorted pastries. She'd put one in the faculty lounge with a note that if anyone wanted to talk about the superintendent's death, she was available for the rest of the day.

So far, it had been a heck of a week and everyone deserved a little indulgence. Plus, if any of the staff were upset about Dr.

Wraige's murder, it was good way to invite them to explore their feelings with her.

Skye planned to share the smaller box of treats with Piper and Trixie. They could all get together during the school librarian's planning period to chat and decompress. Skye hadn't seen either her BFF or her intern since Monday and she had no idea how they were doing.

But first, she had to get the treats through the lobby and past the principal's office. If Homer spotted the distinctive aqua-blue-and-gold-foil bakery boxes, he'd swoop down and cherry-pick the most desirable pastries for himself before anyone else had a chance.

Fortunately, early on, Skye had cajoled Homer into giving her a key to the rear door. She'd demonstrated the heaviness of her evaluation equipment to him by handing him the cases and swiftly walking away. He'd followed her from the front entrance to the faculty parking lot around the building in an effort to give them back to her.

Once she'd relieved him of the test kits, sweat dripping from his beet-red face, he'd reached into his pocket and took his own key from the ring. Skye assumed he had a spare in his desk but didn't ask. She was just happy to finally be able to come and go with ease.

Now, as Skye entered the back hallway juggling her tote bag, thermal lunch container, purse, and the two bakery cartons, she really appreciated the convenience. Not to mention the ability to stay under Homer's radar.

As it was between periods, Skye made it to her office without anyone seeing her, and when she entered, she was pleased to find Piper inside. The intern looked up from her desk, then hurried over to help Skye with her load. They exchanged greetings while Skye walked to the closet and hung up her coat.

"How's it going around here?" Skye asked as she put her purse and lunch bag in her desk drawer. "Anyone seem upset about Dr. Wraige?"

"Not that I've seen." Piper returned to her seat. "Like you suggested, I've been hanging out in the faculty lounge and walking through the hallways during passing period, but everyone appears to be fine."

"That's a relief." Skye explained her plan for the baked goods, grabbed the large box, and headed for the door. "I want to drop these off before second period ends and the hallways fill with teachers and students. I'll be back in a few minutes."

Hurrying down the corridor, Skye kept a watchful eye out for Homer. The annoying principal tended to pop up at the most inopportune times.

However, today was her lucky day, and Skye made it to the faculty lounge without seeing him. She quickly arranged the treats on one of the platters stored in the cupboards by the sink and covered them with the plastic wrap kept in a nearby drawer.

Then, taking a piece of construction paper and a marker from another cabinet, Skye made a sign inviting the staff to talk to her if they wished. She folded it into a tent and started toward the door, but before she made it, the bell rang and she decided to wait until the halls cleared.

Fighting the crowd in the corridors always made her feel like a salmon going upstream. She usually ended up caught on someone's hook and had to wiggle off by suggesting the teacher come see her when they had more time.

A few minutes later, Skye thought it was probably safe to leave. She had her hand on the knob when the door abruptly swung inward.

Once again, it was Tavish Wraige who had narrowly missed giving her a black eye. He barreled into the room and stopped abruptly when he saw Skye. He jumped back as if she'd Tasered him, ran his fingers through his hair, and stared at her.

He seemed unsure what to say, so Skye smiled and murmured, "Fancy meeting you here." When he appeared even more confused, she tried again. "How are you and your stepmother doing? I know you both had a horrible shock."

"Fine." Tavish ducked his head. "I…uh…haven't seen Nanette since, uh…"

"Well, at least she has her friend Colleen staying with her, right?"

"Yeah." He shrugged. "I guess so. The last I heard, that was the plan anyway."

Skye nodded. Making conversation with Dr. Wraige's son was about as easy as ending one with May.

"So, uh…" Tavish paused, then said, "Sorry. I wasn't expecting to see anyone and I was thinking about something else."

"I understand." Skye gestured to the platter. "As the sign says, if you ever what to talk…"

"Thanks for the offer. I'm good." Tavish strode over to the table. "But I will have a bear claw. My father always raved about this bakery."

"The café owner makes all his own pastries." Skye waited to see if Tavish would say anything more, but when he was silent, she opened the door.

He spoke just as she took a step into the hallway. "Thank your husband for helping me find a place to stay. Zelda's a real sweetheart."

"I'll do that," Skye called over her shoulder.

As she proceeded to her office, Skye wondered if Tavish had a little crush on the young officer. After all, Zelda *was* gorgeous. Not to mention smart. And both she and Tavish loved animals.

When Skye arrived, Piper was still typing away on her tablet, but a few seconds later, she looked up and said, "Report number thirty-two is officially done. I just sent it to you to look over."

"You don't have to do that anymore." Skye walked to her desk and retrieved the bakery box she'd left there. "Your reports are excellent. You only need to show them to me if the results could be controversial and you might need some backup."

"Thanks!" Piper beamed. "That means a lot. I know you gave up some of your maternity leave to supervise me when the co-op psych went AWOL and I appreciate it. As difficult as it was at first, this district has been a great learning experience."

"That's one way of looking at it." Skye chuckled, wondering if she should mention to Piper the possibility of a permanent job for next year, then decided to wait until she was sure there was a position available. Instead, she asked, "Do you have an eval or counseling session scheduled this period? Trixie's free so I'm going to go share some pastries with her. You're welcome to join us."

"I've got a student coming to test." Piper stood, smoothed her navy slacks, and pulled down her baby-blue sweater.

"Oh, darn." Skye was glad to see that the young woman had taken her suggestion and finally stopped wearing suits every day. She had told Piper that if she dressed in the type of clothing most of the teachers wore, it might help her establish a better rapport with the faculty.

"Will you need the office, or should I find somewhere else to set up the assessment?"

"You can have the office. I'll camp out somewhere and do paperwork." Skye stuffed her laptop and a few files into her tote bag, then flipped open the bakery box and held it out. "Want one?"

"Thanks! I'd love one to have for lunch." Piper helped herself to a bismarck, carefully wrapping it in one of napkins inside the carton before stashing it in her desk drawer. "Say, did I tell you what I heard when I was observing a student in history class?"

"No," Skye answered cautiously. Observations could be pretty tricky. "What?"

"The teacher asked what a resident of Moscow was called," Piper giggled. "He told her that they were Mosquitos."

"Not a horrible answer," Skye chuckled. "My latest funny experience was in the junior high social studies class. The teacher asked if anyone knew what a census taker did. One of the girls said that it was a man who went from house-to-house increasing the population."

Piper and Skye were both laughing as Skye waved, and headed to the school's multimedia center aka the library. She wasn't entirely sure Trixie would be there, but it was the best place to start her search.

In addition to being the high school librarian, Trixie also cosponsored the school newspaper with Skye, coached the cheerleading squad, and had recently started a community service club to promote volunteerism among the teenagers.

Skye knew Trixie thrived on the constant vortex of activities, but she sometimes wondered if her friend kept too busy. Was there something her cheerful BFF didn't want time to think about?

As Skye entered the multimedia center, Tavish Wraige walked out. He was absorbed in the tablet he carried, and only distractedly returned Skye's greeting before rushing off. What had the attendance and residency investigator been doing in the library?

Turning to watch Tavish march down the hall, his black oxfords clicking on the worn linoleum, Skye wondered if he was on the trail of a student who was playing hooky. They had been known to hide out in the library because if the kid had a good sob story, Trixie would look the other way.

Once Tavish was out of sight, Skye gazed around the room. The walls were lined with bookshelves and the middle of the space contained an assortment of tables, chairs, and study carrels.

Because this was Trixie's free period, the multimedia center was empty, but Skye could hear country music coming from the rear. Smiling, she walked around the counter and into the workroom.

The comforting smell of coffee greeted Skye, and when Trixie spotted her, she sprang from her stool and said, "Tell me all about the murder."

With her first mystery finished and having recently been accepted by one of the top New York literary agents, Trixie was on the lookout for her next plot. She was particularly fascinated by Skye's involvement in real-life cases. Although, with all the kids the librarian saw every day, she often knew more about what was happening around Scumble River than anyone else.

"Can I have some coffee first and share these pastries with you?" Skye showed the box to Trixie, who snatched it from her hand.

"Sure. Help yourself." Trixie waved to the Keurig and proceeded to pull out small paper plates and napkins from a nearby cupboard.

Skye selected her favorite French vanilla and popped the K-Cup into the machine. Once it completed the brew cycle, she added Sweet'N Low and creamer, then took a seat next to where her friend was perched.

Trixie punched a button on the MP3 player parked in the dock on the counter, and as the speakers went silent, Luke Bryan's crooning was cut off mid-word.

Skye selected a cinnamon streusel scone, then asked, "How's Owen? Is he keeping busy?"

Like Skye's father, Trixie's husband was a farmer, and February was a slow month for him. Still, being a farmer's daughter, Skye knew that men like her dad and Owen always had had some project to keep them occupied.

"He's at the big farm show over at the Kankakee Fairgrounds. There were quite a few agriculture dealers, suppliers, and companies that were going to be there that he was interested in seeing."

"I wonder if he'll come home with a new tractor." Skye winked. "That's what happened last year when Dad went to the show."

Once they'd exchanged news on their families and talked a bit about the babies, Trixie demanded, "Now tell me about Wraige's murder."

Wally had given Skye the green light to share everything except for the cause of death and what ME had found in the superintendent's stomach, so she answered. "Wally was called out to Dr. Wraige's house because he'd reported that someone had tried to break in through the patio door."

"Go on," Trixie ordered, taking a huge bite of the blueberry lemon muffin that she'd chosen from the assortment in the box.

Skye told her about Wally finding Dr. Wraige dead, the missing coins, and their interviews with the superintendent's wife, son, and houseguest, then she snapped her fingers and said, "Which reminds me, I saw Tavish Wraige leaving the library when I got here. What did he want?"

Trixie beamed. "He's offered to help me with the community service club."

"Really? He just volunteered out of the blue?" Skye was shocked.

Tavish hadn't struck her as the type to get involved, but

maybe she'd misjudged him. After all, he had served his country in the military.

"Well, not exactly." Trixie suddenly found something in the depths of her coffee mug fascinating and stared at the dark liquid as she explained, "While you were on maternity leave, I may have mentioned to Homer that the teachers were contractually obligated to work on an extracurricular activity, so the other staff should have to as well."

"You mean like those of us who are assigned to the entire district?" Skye tapped her fingers on the countertop. "That is a totally unreasonable requirement. What if all the buildings insisted on that? The nurse, the speech path, and I would have three times the after-school obligations as everyone else covered by the contract."

"I didn't think of that." Trixie played with the layers of her red chiffon skirt and refuse to look at Skye. "But you already volunteer."

"*Volunteer* is the important word in that statement." Skye narrowed her eyes. "If I'm forced to do something at each school, I may have to think about quitting. There's only so much time I'm willing to spend away from my children."

"Shoot!" Trixie's round cheeks turned pink. "I'll fix this. I promise. I'm pretty sure if push came to shove, Homer couldn't enforce it since it isn't a part of your contract."

"Good." Skye crossed her arms. "Belle and Abby would be even more upset than I am. Abby helps her boyfriend at his veterinarian clinic in the afternoons and Belle has private clients she sees for speech therapy."

"Well, none of you have to worry." Trixie grinned. "There aren't a ton of candidates eager for any of your jobs."

"True."

"What are you thinking?" Trixie demanded. "You have a funny look on your face."

"I was just wondering how things in the district would change now that Dr. Wraige is gone." Skye but her lip. "You know the saying, better the devil you know than the devil you don't. What if the next one is worse?"

"Hmmm," Trixie murmured, then said, "Circling back to Dr. Wraige's murder. Who's your top suspect?"

"Wally hasn't really said, but I'm guessing it's between the widow and the son."

"How about the houseguest you mentioned?"

"She's definitely on my list." Skye crossed her arms. "Her alibi has such big holes in it you could drive a semi through it."

"Maybe you just don't like her because she made a play for Wally," Trixie teased.

"Unfortunately, ever since he did that interview with the newspaper and revealed his family's wealth, women have been throwing themselves at him like mad."

"I was afraid of that." Trixie nodded sagely. "He was already too much of a hunk for his own good."

"Yep." Skye glanced at her watch. "This period's about over and I need to find a place to work while Piper uses our office to test."

"You can set up right here." Trixie hopped off her stool. "I'll be out front with Corny's honors English class." She paused. "Wait, wasn't Pru related to Dr. Wraige?"

"Yes. She was his cousin." Skye pulled her laptop from her tote bag. "Why?"

"Any chance she killed him?" Trixie's eyes twinkled with mischief. "That would be a good way to get rid of her since she's never going to retire."

"No chance. She has an alibi and no motive." Skye whacked her friend's arm. "Now get out of here. I have a report to write."

"Fine." Trixie walked out the door, but then stepped back

into the room. "I just remembered something Tavish said. I didn't really make anything of it at the time, but we were talking about the community service club, and he said something about donating his father's gold-and-diamond signet ring to raffle off for our next fundraiser."

"Interesting." Skye muttered. "You'd think that would be something he'd want to have as a memento for himself or his future children."

"Only if he wanted to remember his father, but I had the feeling he wasn't too fond of him." Trixie shot Skye a significant look, then hurried away.

CHAPTER 20

Everybody Loves Somebody Sometime

IT HAD TAKEN LONGER THAN WALLY HAD EXPECTED TO track down Keith Makowski. The ex–bus driver no longer lived at the address Sally had provided, and Wally had had to do some investigating to find him.

If Wally had worked for a larger police department, he would have had his IT department scour their databases for the information. But in a small town, it was quicker to make a few telephone calls and ask the local gossips for the guy's current location.

He'd been a little surprised to hear that the man Wraige had ousted in a fit of pique was now living along the river, deep in Red Ragger territory. He'd moved from a relatively nice neighborhood to literally the wrong side of the tracks.

As Wally slowly drove by the Doozier property searching for Makowski's new residence, he noticed that even covered in a blanket of pristine snow, Earl's place looked awful. Car parts, dead appliances, and broken-down furniture led to a peeling front door. The ramshackle fence surrounding the backyard still leaned inward, one strong breeze from falling over.

204

However, there was something new sitting up next to the road. A rudimentary plywood booth with a satellite dish perched on top of the decrepit roof. A crudely painted sign proclaimed:

**FREE WHY-FRY
SMOOCHES $1 EACH
WET ONES $5**

As Wally drove by, he saw that inside the slapdash structure, there was an old worn-out recliner. Surrounding the chair was a carpet of beer cans.

He scowled at the sight of Earl's latest get-rich-quick scheme. Which Doozier family members worked the booth? It had better not be any of their underage children.

Wally's lips tightened and he narrowed his eyes. He allowed the Dooziers quite a bit of leeway, but if Earl was forcing his kids to kiss strangers, he'd throw the man's scrawny butt in jail so fast it would make his head spin faster than Linda Blair's had in *The Exorcist*.

Afraid that he'd forget if he waited until he got back to the station, Wally radioed Thea and instructed her to have all patrols swing by the Doozier property. They were to log in who, if anyone, was manning the kissing booth and to notify Wally immediately if the worker appeared to be under the age of eighteen.

Before signing off, Wally gave the dispatcher his intended location. A few seconds later, he stopped the Hummer in front of a tall wooden gate blocking the entrance to an evergreen-lined lane. He turned off the SUV, then studied the chained and padlocked entrance.

It looked as if Makowski didn't want any unexpected visitors.

Wally's cop instincts kicked into high hear. What was the man hiding?

Exiting the Hummer, Wally opened the back and put on his body armor and his tactical jacket with *POLICE* stenciled across the back. He checked that the side waist zippers were open for access to his duty belt, then he maneuvered around the gate. He'd have to walk the rest of the way.

There hadn't been a No Trespassing sign, so Wally was fairly certain he didn't need a warrant to approach the house. To be absolutely certain, he should have contacted the city attorney. But he was only here to chat with a person of interest, not make any arrests, and sometimes it was better to apologize than ask permission.

Trudging down the long icy path, Wally tried to be as quiet as possible. The uneven dirt surface made it a challenge, but in a situation like this, with a possible murder suspect, it was best to approach the man's residence and reconnoiter before making his presence known.

As he rounded a slight bend in the lane, Wally suddenly stopped. What was that odor? It almost smelled as if someone was baking bread. He sniffed again. It was definitely yeasty. He couldn't put his finger on it, but it was vaguely familiar.

He moved noiselessly toward the scent. Abruptly, he stepped behind a huge Douglas fir. Peering between the branches, he saw a guy kneeling by a large copper container that had to be over five feet tall. It had tubing coming out of the top that bent toward the ground.

Having grown up in Texas Hill Country, Wally recognized the apparatus, and now that he'd seen the equipment, he realized the smell was alcohol distilling. Both the equipment and the unlicensed production of liquor were illegal in Illinois.

Earlier, Wally had pulled up Makowski's driver's license photo, and although the man looked worse for wear, the moonshiner was definitely the ex-bus driver. His new occupation explained why the guy had moved from his pleasant house in town out to the sticks. Here, there were no snooping neighbors to turn him in for his unlawful activities.

Well, that is except for the Dooziers. And they were probably Makowski's best customers.

Retrieving his phone from the case attached to his duty belt, Wally swiped the video button and aimed it at Makowski. The recording wouldn't be admissible in court, but the ex-bus driver probably didn't know that, so it was good leverage when Wally questioned him about the superintendent's murder.

When Makowski finished up and left the little clearing, Wally returned to the driveway. He wanted to approach the residence from the front so as not tip off the guy that he knew about his illegal moonshining activities.

Wally walked up the neatly kept sidewalk to the front entrance and rang the bell. A few seconds later Makowski opened the door.

"Mr. Makowski?" Wally said, wanting the guy to formally confirm his identity.

"Yes." Although Wally could tell the man was nervous, the ex-bus driver's tone was genial. "Chief Boyd. What brings you out here?"

Wally's smile was affable. "I'd like to speak to you about Dr. Wraige."

"What about him?" Makowski leaned casually against the doorframe, giving no indication that hearing his previous employer's name alarmed him.

"I understand you and he parted ways under unpleasant circumstances." Wally took a step forward.

The man didn't budge. *Interesting!* Usually, people instinctively moved aside.

"That's not exactly a secret." Makowski shrugged. "He

brought the incident in front of the board and made sure that it became a matter of public record. It was his way of guaranteeing that I wouldn't be hired by any other district or school bus company."

"Why was he so vindictive?" Wally moved closer to the threshold. "It's mighty cold out here. Could we go inside and talk?"

"Sorry, the place is a mess." Makowski's grin didn't match the expression in his eyes. "My wife would be mortified if I let you see it this way."

Wally pasted a concerned expression on his face and chuckled. "I wouldn't want you to get in trouble with the missus."

"Speaking of that." Makowski inched backward and started closing the door. "I'm going to have to ask you to leave. I can hear the wife putting lunch on the table so I need to go eat."

"That's a shame because the food might end up going to waste." Wally stuck his foot in the doorway, whipped out his phone, and said, "Take a look at this, Mr. Makowski. Now do you have some time to chat?"

As the man focused in on the little screen, his face reddened and he gasped. He glanced behind him, then hurriedly stepped out onto the front porch. When he attempted to run, Wally blocked his path.

"Get out of my way." Makowski thrust out his chin. "You're on private property and you didn't show me no warrant."

"You're right." Wally nodded. "But I'll argue that I heard suspicious noises and smelled the distilling process." He shrugged. "There's a fifty-fifty chance the judge will accept my version."

Wally was banking on the guy not realizing that at most

he'd have to pay a hefty fine and have his equipment confiscated. He wanted him to think that he'd end up in jail, which might loosen his tongue.

"No. Please," Makowski begged. "I only started doing this because that son of a motherless goat fired me and stopped me from getting another job. I begged him to let me work a few more months, just until I turned sixty-five and my Social Security and Medicare came through, but he laughed and said I should have thought of that before embarrassing him in front of the whole town with my whining."

"Wraige certainly wasn't a very compassionate man." Wally nodded sympathetically. "How about you answer some questions for me and then we'll talk about the issue of the still? Sound like a plan?"

"Thank you for the chance, Chief." Makowski jerked his chin at the house. "Why don't you come in and have lunch with me and Faye? She made her famous pulled pork and potato salad."

"Are you sure you want to answer my questions in front of your wife?"

"We been married forty years. I ain't got any secrets from Faye."

"Lead the way." Wally gestured for Makowski to proceed and they walked inside.

In a big city, sitting down to a meal with a suspect might raise some eyebrows, but in a small town like Scumble River, no one would say a word. Of course, Wally would have to keep alert for trouble.

When they entered the kitchen, a tiny woman was taking a pie out of the oven and the smell of cinnamon perfumed the air. She turned, and when she saw Wally, she tilted her head as if asking what was up.

Makowski studied his feet, then said, "Chief Boyd here

caught me with the still and now I have to answer some questions or he'll show the city attorney the pictures and I'll be arrested."

She rolled her eyes, then smiled at Wally and said, "Have a seat, Chief. Thank you for giving my idiot husband a chance to get himself out of this mess. I told him becoming a moonshiner was not the way to make ends meet and that I could get my old job back at the factory."

"No problem." Just in case Makowski decided to make a run for it again, Wally sat down nearest the back door. But the man took what Wally guessed was his regular seat at the table, tucked a napkin inside the collar of his flannel shirt, and appeared more anxious for lunch than to try to escape the long arm of the law.

Without asking, Faye got a plate and silverware for Wally, then poured him and her husband a glass of milk. Wally thanked her and looked around.

Although the appliances and furniture had to be a good forty or fifty years old, everything was spotless. Faye's cleaning habits would give May a run for her money, and that was saying a lot.

As she sat down, Faye gave Wally a shrewd look and said, "If your questions are about Dr. Wraige, Keith didn't kill the man."

"What!" Makowski shouted, then glared at Wally. "You didn't say nothing about that son of a biscuit eater being deceased. When did that happen?"

Apparently, Mrs. Makowski was more informed than her husband. Either she read the hometown paper and he didn't, or her sources for the local gossip were better than his. Of course, he could be faking his surprise.

"Yesterday's *Star* said he was found dead," Faye explained to her husband as she dished out potato salad and passed homemade rolls around the table.

"Why didn't you tell me that?" Makowski demanded spooning a huge portion of pulled pork onto his bun. "That's not exactly minor news."

"You always get mad at me when I tell you stuff before you get a chance to look at the paper." Faye shrugged. "I didn't want to spoil it for you."

Wally broke into the couple's squabbling. "So you weren't aware of Dr. Wraige's death?"

"No," Makowski mumbled around a huge mouthful of potato salad. "I would have been celebrating if I'd have known that turd was dead." His wife gave him a hard stare and he hastily added, "But I didn't kill him."

"Where were you Monday between eight thirty and ten a.m.?" Wally asked.

"Me and Faye were over to Laurel that morning." Makowski took a swig of milk.

"Where exactly in Laurel?" Wally's stomach growled and he picked up his sandwich.

He'd watched Makowski consume both the pulled pork sandwich and the potato salad. Assured they were safe to eat, Wally took a bite as he waited for the man to answer.

"I'd rather not say." Makowski inspected the contents of his plate. "It's private."

Wally raised a brow. "I promise not to take out an ad in the *Star*."

"It's none of your business." Makowski returned to his meal. "Faye can tell you I was there and that's all you need to know."

"Can anyone else verify your location?" Wally asked. A wife's alibi wasn't worth a hill of beans. Most would lie for their husbands, whether it was out of love, loyalty, or fear. Sometimes a combination of all three. "Preferably someone not related to you."

"I'm not saying." Makowski polished off his sandwich and made another one.

"Oh, for the love of heaven." Faye blew out a sigh. "We were at the proctologist getting his piles removed." She snickered. "All those years sitting in that hard bus seat caused hemorrhoids."

Wally hid his smile and said, "I'll need the doctor's name and Keith will have to give him the go-ahead to tell me you were there."

"Consider it done." Faye got to her feet, picked up the receiver from the phone attached to the wall, and dialed. After she explained the situation, she gave the handset to her husband and ordered, "Tell them it's okay to talk to Chief Boyd about your procedure."

Makowski glared at her, then mumbled into the phone. When he had given his permission, he passed the receiver to Wally who spoke to the nurse. She verified the ex–bus driver's alibi and Faye hung up the phone.

"Are we square?" Makowski asked, then shoveled potato salad into his mouth.

"There is the matter of the illegal distillation of alcohol." Wally finished eating and pushed his plate to the side.

"Couldn't you forget about that?" Makowski's brown eyes had a sly glint. "If I was able to tell you something that might give you a lead on who killed the superintendent, maybe you'd be inclined to sort of pretend you never saw the still and it could just disappear."

"That depends." As long as he stopped making moonshine, Wally intended to give the guy a pass anyway, but if Makowski was willing to cough up a clue, all the better. "Let's hear it."

"About a week ago, I went to the superintendent's office to see if I could get him to reconsider giving me my job back.

When I got there that secretary of his wasn't around and Wraige's door was closed so I just sat in the lobby and waited for someone to show up."

"And?" Wally prodded.

Wally liked hearing a good story as much as the next guy, but the man needed to keep it moving. There was a lot that needed doing back at the police station.

"I heard Wraige and a woman yelling at each other and…" Makowski paused as Faye put a slice of apple pie in front of him.

When Makowski didn't continue, Wally asked, "Who was the woman?"

"I didn't know at first, but I saw her when she left and it was his wife." Makowski scooped a forkful of pie into this mouth.

"Could you tell what they were fighting about?" Wally asked, taking a bite of his own dessert.

"Yeah." Makowski nodded vigorously. "It was pretty clear."

"What was pretty clear?"

Makowski squinted as if trying to remember exactly. "Mrs. Wraige was screaming at the superintendent about his trying to screw her friend. I think this woman was living with them and it sounded like Mrs. Wraige wanted to kill her husband right then and there."

"Well, that's certainly a motive for murder." Wally rose to his feet. "You may have just given me what I needed to get a warrant to search Nanette Wraige's residence." As he headed to the door he said, "I'll be back to make sure that moonshining equipment is gone."

"It will be, Chief," Faye answered and glared at her husband. "One close call is enough, even for this old idiot."

CHAPTER 21

All You Need Is Love

SKYE SMILED AT THE GIRL SITTING ACROSS FROM HER AND said, "We made some good progress today, Hailey, and your teachers are very pleased with your efforts to participate more during classes." Skye slid a glance at her watch, then added, "The final bell is going to ring in a few minutes. Is there anything else you'd like to talk about before this week's session is over?"

"I know that I'm doing better in school." Hailey twisted a limp piece of mouse-brown hair. "But it's harder at home. My brothers are so mean and if I try to tell them to stop or complain, my dad just says that I'm being too sensitive. I wish Mom were still around."

"Is being insensitive something you think you should strive to achieve?" Skye asked, wanting the girl to really think about the meaning of the word.

"No. I don't want to be like my father or brothers." Hailey shook her head. "But maybe it would be good if I could feel less hurt by their nasty comments."

She leaned forward, wishing she had as good a counseling space at the high school as she'd created at the junior high. Maybe once Piper's internship was up and she could get rid of the second desk, there would be room for a couple of comfy chairs. Now that she'd accepted that she had disposable income, she'd realized that she could just pay for them herself and not worry about trying to squeeze them into the psych budget.

Meeting the girl's uncertain gaze, Skye asked, "What's a helpful way you could respond to your families' unkind remarks?"

Hailey had originally been referred for counseling because a teacher had been concerned that she might harm herself. The woman had noticed that whenever the girl felt overwhelmed, she'd scratch deep gouges in her arms and when she'd approached Hailey's father, he had claimed his daughter only did that to get attention.

However, he had given permission for Hailey to talk to the school psychologist. Skye had been working with the girl for the past six weeks and seen some good progress. Now she wanted to check if Hailey remembered some of the strategies they'd previously discussed.

"I can walk away from the person that's being mean to me." Hailey furrowed her brow. "If they follow, I can imagine an invisible shield around me that doesn't allow negative energy to get through it."

"That's a good one." Skye nodded encouragingly. "Anything else?"

"I can set boundaries." Hailey bit her chapped lips. "I can tell them that it's not okay for them to talk to me like that and let them know that I don't need their opinions because I have my own."

"That's great too." Skye hadn't exactly put it in those words, but if that was how Hailey could use the tactic, more power to her. "Why don't you try those two things for the coming week and let me know how what happens?" She rose from her chair and Hailey followed suit. As they walked toward the door, Skye added, "We talked about you maybe sharing some of these feelings with your grandmother when she comes to visit next month over spring break. Are you still considering that possibility?"

"Uh-huh." The girl tilted her head. "I might even ask her if I can live with her. Ever since Mom died, Dad has sort of given up."

The bell rang, and as Skye turned the doorknob to show the girl out of the office, she said, "Let's talk more about that in our next session. We have six weeks before you need to decide what you want to do."

"Okay." Hailey waved and walked out into the teeming hallway.

Before Skye could close the door, Piper hurried over the threshold and said, "Mr. Knapik would like to see you before you go home."

"Shoot!"

Skye had been successfully avoiding the high school principal all day. Undoubtedly Homer wanted to discuss Dr. Wraige's murder.

Well, not so much discuss as blame Skye. For some reason he was convinced that all homicides in Scumble River were her fault.

Not so much that he thought that she committed them—at least she hoped he didn't believe that she was the killer. It was more that Homer was convinced that Skye was some sort of jinx who attracted dead bodies.

"If you don't want to talk to him, I'll wait until you leave and then tell him that I couldn't find you," Piper offered.

"Thanks, but it would only be postponing the inevitable." Skye locked her desk, grabbed her purse, coat, and tote bag, then walked to the door. "I might as well get it over with while I'm still on the clock."

After wishing Piper a good night, Skye made her way to the main office. Opal held the phone to her ear, but she put her finger up for Skye to wait.

A few seconds later, the secretary hung up and said, "Could you look at this note and tell me what you think it means?"

Skye took the piece of notebook paper from Opal and read:

> Please excuse Jimmy for being.
> It was his father's fault.

Skye swallowed a giggle and said, "It looks to me as if there's a word or two missing." She smiled at the secretary. "I doubt Jimmy's mom really blames his dad for her son's existence, but you never know."

"Right," Opal said solemnly. "And if she did, why should she want us to excuse it?" The secretary reached for the receiver. "I guess I'd better call and ask what she meant."

"Good idea." Skye nodded, then walked toward Homer's lair.

When she knocked on his door and announced herself, he yelled for her to come in.

As she stepped across the threshold, Homer said, "I've been looking for you all day. So happy you could finally squeeze me in."

Uh-oh. Homer sounded even more belligerent than usual. He'd actually been pretty nice to her since she'd saved his bacon last December. This had to be about the superintendent's death, but why was he angry at her? For once, she hadn't found the body.

Homer Knapik had been the high school principal for as long as anyone under the age of fifty could remember. For the past five years, at the end of the school year, he'd announced that he was stepping down. But like a stink bug, he had always returned in the fall.

Skye was pretty sure Homer never even put in his paperwork, because once the forms were signed and turned into the Teachers' Retirement System, it was difficult, if not impossible, to reverse the process.

She wondered if the superintendent's death would hinder or help Homer's cat-and-mouse retirement game. She looked in the direction of the aggravating principal and her chest tightened when she saw the man sitting across from him. What was Tavish Wraige doing here? This couldn't be good.

Taking a deep breath and hoping the attendance and residency investigator was on his way out, Skye said, "Good afternoon, gentlemen. What is it that you wanted to see me about, Homer?"

"Have a seat." Homer gestured to the empty chair. "This could take a while."

"I can come back when you and Mr. Wraige are through," Skye offered.

"Tavish wants to speak to you before he takes off," Homer informed her from behind his massive desk. He nodded at the man and said, "Go ahead."

After several long minutes of silence, the only sound in the room being Homer slurping from a can of grape soda, Tavis said, "Mrs. Boyd."

"Actually." Skye smiled to take any sting out of her correction. "It's Denison-Boyd, but why don't you just call me Skye? When there are no students present, we're pretty informal around here."

"Thank you." Tavish nodded. "I'd be honored if you'd call me by my nickname. Tavish was my grandfather's name, and I've always used Tav."

"Excellent! Tav it is." Skye beamed, heartened by his request.

Maybe he'd turn out to be as helpful as Scott Ricci had been. She frowned. That is, if he didn't end up having committed patricide.

"The reason I wanted to speak to you"—Tav interrupted her thoughts—"is about the home visit I made this afternoon. My father had directed me to look into the situation before he died, and I felt I should follow through."

"Oh?" Skye's heart skipped a beat. Which of her kids was in trouble? Keeping an affable expression on her face, she asked, "Was there some kind of issue with one of the students I see?"

"I believe so." Tav tapped the file in his lap. "It seems that Karl Krause, a boy who is in special education, is here as a foreign exchange student."

"Right. He has a mild learning disability and receives some accommodations and one resource class," Skye explained. "When he came to live with the Glassman family, he brought the paperwork from his home school."

"But he isn't paying tuition." Tav tilted his head as if assessing Skye's true knowledge of the situation. "According to the policy manual my father issued to me, the district requires that an exchange student enrolling in our schools must pay nonresident tuition."

"I've never heard of that." Skye frowned, then said, "We've had foreign exchange students before. Have they been charged tuition?"

"Not that I'm aware." Tav glanced at Homer, who shrugged. "However, this is a relatively new policy and Krause might be the first foreign exchange student enrolled since it's been in place."

"Or is he the first one who required special education?" Skye suggested. "Thus, costing the district more money to instruct."

Tavish looked uncomfortable. "Anyway. Mr. Knapik was aware of my father's concern and asked me to report back to him once my investigation was complete. I did so about an hour ago and he suggested we bring you into the loop."

Skye stared at Homer. "What is my involvement in the situation?" Doubtlessly it was something that the principal didn't want to handle.

Homer jerked his chin at Tav, who answered, "Mrs. Glassman has stated that neither she and her husband nor Karl's parents are able to pay the young man's tuition to attend our high school. This means that regrettably, tomorrow will be his last day here."

"That's unfortunate. But why are you telling me?" There were only three months of school left and Skye knew this wasn't a battle she could win in that amount of time, if ever.

"The Glassmans have asked that you inform Karl, and Homer agreed that would be best."

"Fine." Skye blew out a sigh. "I'll add him to my list."

Tav stood and strode toward the door, but paused with his hand on the knob and looked at Homer. "I'll look into the other matter you asked me to investigate tomorrow."

Once Tavish disappeared, Homer slapped down the file he'd been leafing through and snarled, "Why didn't you warn me that Dr. Wraige had been found murdered?"

"Why would I?" Skye raised a brow. "It's not my place to make notifications."

Homer shot to his feet and waddled toward her. His stooped stature, protruding belly, and extreme hairiness reminded Skye of an orangutan. That impression was reinforced when he stopped in front of her and she could have sworn his arms hung nearly to the floor. Had they always been like that?

"You should have given me a heads-up." Homer thrust out his bottom lip.

"Why?" Skye was confused. "The board president was informed, and it was up to him to advise whomever he felt needed to know about the death."

"Your godfather"—Homer emphasized the word—"told Neva and Caroline before he told me."

"So?" Skye couldn't fathom why he cared who was first on the phone tree. But then again, Homer had a *Titanic* intellect in a sea of icebergs, so it was difficult to understand his priorities.

"I have the most seniority." Homer pouted. "How does it look that I wasn't first?" He narrowed his eyes, which made them disappear into his face until all Skye could see was a tiny glint of brown. "Is there something going on? Do you know anything? You'd tell me right now if I'm being forced out, right?"

Skye protested, "How would I know what's happening with the board?" No way would she be the one to tell Homer that in all likelihood, Neva was getting a promotion and would soon be his boss.

"Because." Homer crossed his arms. "Your godfather is the board president." He glared. "And you're in bed with the chief of police."

"Hey," Skye complained. "Don't make it sound so crude. I'm married to the guy, not sleeping with him to get information out of him."

"Whatever." Homer shrugged. "The real issue is what are we going to do about Tavish Wraige? You know he probably killed his father."

"What makes you think that?" Skye thought Homer might be right, but she wanted to hear what the principal had to say.

"Don't be a wisenheimer with me," Homer barked.

"I'm not trying to be."

"You know why he'd do it."

"No, I don't." Sometimes she just didn't speak Homer's dialect of crazy. "What would be his motive?"

"Shamus and his son have been on the outs for years." The hair growing out of the principal's ears bristled. "Before a month ago, they hadn't spoken since Shamus dumped the kid's mother."

"Really?" Skye kept her tone mildly disinterested to keep Homer talking.

If he thought she really wanted to know what he was saying, he'd stop. But why hadn't Pru mentioned anything about that? Was she protecting Tavish?

"Yeah." Homer made a sound like Chewbacca snoring, which evidently was his way of tsking. "Tavish got into some trouble in the army, and Shamus heard about it. He stepped in and got him an honorable discharge, then offered the kid a job to keep an eye on him."

Skye cringed at Homer's cruel expression. She had to remember that Homer's skylight was a little leaky and he enjoyed others' suffering.

"Aren't you going to ask me what the kid did?" Homer demanded.

"Do you know?" Skye had dealt with the principal long enough that she was adept at getting information from him. The secret was to imply he wasn't in possession of the facts in question.

"Of course." He held up two entwined fingers. "Shamus and I were like that." Homer's face turned a mottled red and a tear slipped down his cheek. "We were pals. Which is another reason I should have been informed first about his death and not heard about it last."

"I'm sorry for your loss." Skye found herself actually patting the principal's arm. "I had no idea you were personal friends."

"Thank you." Homer wiped his face with the back of his hand and retreated to his chair where he took a gulp of soda. "Since for once you're being respectful and nice to me, I'll tell you about Tavish."

"Okay." Skye crossed her legs. She was dying to know, but attempted to continue to look indifferent. "What caused him to be kicked out of the army?"

"He was caught in bed with his superior officer's wife." Homer snorted. "He claimed that he didn't know she was married and she came on to him, but evidently, adultery is in violation of Article 134 of the UCMJ."

"UCMJ?"

"The Uniform Code of Military Justice." Homer harrumphed. "Evidently, Article 134 is mostly ignored, but not when the woman you're screwing is married to the boss."

"Hmm." Skye processed the information, then mused, "I wonder how Dr. Wraige found out and was able to fix things for his son?"

"Shamus was keeping tabs on his son." Homer shrugged. "And I believe he paid off the officer to withdraw the charges. Shamus guaranteed the man that Tavish would leave the army once his service commitment was over and never speak to the guy's missus again."

"What you told me doesn't sound like a motive for murder." Skye frowned. "Wouldn't Dr. Wraige's actions make Tav grateful to his father?"

"Would it?" Homer raised a hairy brow. "You're the psychologist. You figure it out."

CHAPTER 22

Kiss and Say Goodbye

EVEN WITH THE DETOUR TO HOMER'S OFFICE, SKYE WAS IN her SUV and pulling out of the high school parking lot by three twenty-nine. Dorothy was taking off early on Friday and had insisted on making up the time by working longer today, so she was on the clock until five thirty.

Skye slowed the Mercedes down to a crawl. She was undecided what to do with the nearly two hours of freedom that had fallen into her lap.

It wasn't that she didn't have anything to do. There were always tons of errands. The question was, which one to tackle first?

Dorothy had slowly taken over all of the grocery shopping. When Skye had tried to help, the housekeeper had gotten a stubborn look on her face and stated that as long as she did most of the cooking, she wanted to choose her own ingredients, but Skye suspected it was because she accidently brought home a cucumber when Dorothy had requested zucchini.

She had also been removed from dry cleaner duty. Ever since the little mix-up in December when she'd accepted an order without checking to see if her husband's winter uniforms were present and accounted for—they weren't—and Wally had ended up having to wear a summer shirt and pants, he had claimed that chore.

Running through her mental list, Skye realized that for once there were no checks to deposit in the bank, they didn't need cash from the ATM, and she couldn't mail the birthday gift to her sorority sister in New Orleans because the post office wasn't open—it closed at two on Fridays. All of which meant that she had nothing pressing to accomplish.

Grinning, Skye put her foot on the accelerator and steered the SUV out of town. Twenty minutes each way still gave her an hour and a quarter to shop.

As she carefully maneuvered down the winding road between Scumble River and Kankakee, Skye prioritized the items she needed to buy. The dresses for the Valentine's dance that she'd ordered had finally arrived and thankfully one of the two sizes fit, but now she needed a strapless bra for the off-the-shoulder neckline.

Skye could have sworn that she had the required undergarment, but it must have been lost when the tornado destroyed their house. Over six months had passed since the twister, and she was still discovering that items she thought she owned were gone.

It was too late to order a strapless bra online, which made it her first shopping priority. She also hoped to get some less necessary but more fun lingerie, as all of her current unmentionables were strictly utilitarian and not at all enticing.

Then, if she had time, she wanted a pair of strappy sandals. Although she could wear her trusty nude pumps, they weren't really the cool, flirty image she wanted to portray for Valentine's Day.

This would be the first occasion since the twins were born that she and Wally would have an entire evening together as a couple. They even had reservations for a suite at the Laurel Inn for after the dance. And Skye had big plans for both the dance and the hotel stay. Plans that would definitely be improved with a sexy new nightie.

Thanks to their friends Frannie and Justin, who had been happy to earn some extra cash by babysitting the twins overnight, Skye and Wally didn't have to be home until noon. Frannie and her new fiancé, Justin, had been students that Skye had worked with when she first came to Scumble River. After they had graduated high school, the couple had remained in touch with Skye and the relationship had slowly transformed from professional to personal.

Having finished college, Frannie and Justin were off on their own adventure working for the Normalton newspaper. They had recently become engaged and were coming back home for a few days to start making some decisions about their wedding.

Refocusing on what she needed to buy, Skye thought about the twins. Eva and CJ had everything a baby would ever require. Between May and Carson, their closets and drawers were stuffed with clothing and their shelves were filled with so many toys, they'd never play with them all before they outgrew them.

Sometimes, Skye felt a little put out that she rarely got to buy anything for her own babies. Maybe she'd start donating some of the doting grandparents' gifts to the women and children's center. Then she wouldn't feel so guilty if she purchased an outfit or two and a couple of stuffed animals.

Turning her attention to Wally, Skye realized his wardrobe was almost as complete as the babies'. He'd replaced most of the clothes that he'd lost in the tornado by ordering online and the rest he'd managed to snag at Meijer while grocery shopping.

Men were so lucky. Unlike women's clothing, the vast majority of time their sizes ran true, so he hadn't even had to try them on.

This would be the first time Skye had been able to shop for herself while she was alone. Usually, she had the babies with her and her mom. All three of which required a lot of her attention.

Perhaps May more than the twins. Shopping with her mother was always a trial. Not because May didn't want Skye to get anything, but because she tended to wander away if Skye stopped to browse in a department that didn't hold her interest, which required Skye to lose precious time tracking her down.

Chuckling at the image of the last time she'd had to find her mother in a huge department store—they'd ended up playing hide-and-seek for an hour and she was about to make a lost mother announcement over the PA—Skye pulled into the Kohl's parking lot.

Surprised that it was so crowded, she had to circle several times until she found a spot. Then it was quite a journey to the entrance. Who knew that Thursday afternoon would be such a big shopping day?

Draping her purse strap across her body, Skye jogged toward the door. She paused once she was inside to get her bearings, and it took a few seconds for her to spot the lingerie department.

Finding a strapless bra in her size was as challenging as she'd feared. Evidently most designers felt only smaller women should wear pretty undies.

Thankfully, not all the manufacturers felt that way, and Skye finally found one. She also picked up some sexy black lace underwear to match.

While she was in the area, she scooped up a baby doll

nightie. The cream stretch lace was embellished with a black ruffle along the bottom and tiny black bows around the molded bra cups.

It was just what she needed for a romantic evening at the hotel with her handsome husband. They might have two children, but they'd only been married fourteen months, which in Skye's book meant they were still newlyweds.

After trying on her selections, she headed to the shoe aisle. Finding cute dress sandals in a ten wide was another challenge. But she got lucky again and nabbed a pair in black patent leather. The heel was a little higher than she usually wore, but they made her legs and ankles look amazing, so she'd suffer.

Glancing at her watch, Skye saw that if she wanted to get home on time, she only had fifteen minutes to check out. As she hurried toward the registers, she wished she had time to try on some clothes for work, but she was thankful she'd done as well as she had in her limited window of opportunity.

While Skye waited in line to purchase the items she'd chosen, she dug out her cell phone to call Wally. She'd talked to him just before she left school to make sure he didn't need her at the police department, but at the time, she hadn't known that she'd end up in Kankakee and she wanted to make sure there wasn't anything he'd like her to pick up while she was there.

Although if he wanted her to stop anyplace, he'd have to get home to take over for Dorothy. Wally's cell phone went directly to voicemail and Skye left a message. Before she could try his number at the PD, the line moved forward and Skye put away her cell. She would never be one of those people that made others wait because she was too absorbed in her telephone.

After Skye paid for her items, she walked out to the

parking lot. She was loading her bags in the back of the SUV when she noticed Colleen Vreesen standing next to a car one row over. The annoying woman was giggling and making exaggerated hand motions to whoever was still in the vehicle.

As Skye drove away, she saw Tavish and Nanette Wraige join Colleen, then the trio strolled toward the entrance. Skye had gotten the impression that Tav wasn't close to his stepmother or her friend. If that was the case, and she was pretty sure it was, it seemed mighty odd that the three of them were out together.

***

Shopping had been fun, but once Skye got home, she'd had to hit the ground running. As soon as she dropped her bags in the master bedroom and changed into yoga pants and a sweatshirt, she'd told Dorothy that she'd take over the twins' care.

Thanking her for working the extra hour, Skye shooed the housekeeper upstairs to relax. After coping with the babies and everything else around the house for the past ten-plus hours, Dorothy deserved some time to unwind.

Once Dorothy was gone, Skye spread a large mat on the great room floor and put twins on their tummy in the center. Then she grabbed a few toys and sat opposite them.

Choosing a ball from her pile, she rolled it slightly to CJ's right. According to the experts, this activity helped strengthen muscles and improve coordination. She alternated between her son and daughter, noting that they were both attempting to roll over and succeeding every couple of tries.

She praised Eva and CJ for their efforts and pressed kisses to their precious faces. While Eva had inherited her father's high cheekbones and olive skin, CJ's chestnut curls and emerald eyes were from Skye's side of the family. But both were the cutest babies on earth.

When the twins were both giggling and cooing, Skye selected their favorite stuffed kitty from her stash and a fuzzy yellow blanket and started to play peekaboo. This was supposed to teach them that objects aren't gone just because they can't see them and ease separation anxiety.

A half hour later, Skye heard the roar of Wally's Hummer entering the garage, and he walked inside soon afterward. Together they fed the babies, read them several board books, then put them to bed.

Once Eva and CJ were asleep, Skye reheated the food Dorothy had prepared and they had dinner. They both were starving, and conversation was sparse as they ate the excellent sweet potato and ham casserole accompanied by corn bread muffins.

When they finished eating, they cleaned up the mess they'd created from caring for the babies. Then they washed the dishes from their own meal.

Finally, they took their dessert and coffee into the great room and cuddled together on the huge leather sofa facing the fireplace. Bingo was snoozing in his favorite spot near the couch's arm and let out an annoyed meow when they joined him, then went back to sleep.

After taking a sip from his mug, Wally asked, "How was your shopping trip?"

"Successful." Skye smiled contentedly. "I got everything I wanted."

"What were you after?" Wally put his arm around Skye and squeezed.

"You'll find out Saturday." Skye laid her head on his shoulder.

"Tease." Wally gave a mock growl. "I had a hard day. How about a preview?"

"Not happening." Skye patted his thigh. "But you can tell

me about your trials and tribulations. Sharing with your own personal psychologist might make you feel better."

Wally recapped his interviews at the bus barn, then asked, "Does your contract prohibit you from posting anything about your students on social media?"

"Definitely." Skye shuddered at the thought of how easily kids could be exposed online. "And I'm pretty sure the teachers' does as well. At least, I hope so."

"Right." Wally nodded, then told her about his experience with Mr. and Mrs. Makowski, ending with, "I reported the conversation he overheard to the city attorney, and Boulder thinks with that information he can get a warrant to search Wraige's place."

"That's great. Hopefully you'll find something useful." Skye beamed, then shook her head. "Knowing what I do about the superintendent, I can't say that him hitting on Nanette's friend surprises me."

"Me, either." Wally released Skye and leaned forward to retrieve his dessert from the coffee table. "I wonder how Nanette found out?"

"You don't think Colleen was livid when Dr. Wraige made a pass at her and told her friend?" Skye asked.

"Probably." Wally paused and forked a bite of red velvet cake into his mouth. Once he swallowed, he continued. "But after her story about going to that stranger's house and spending hours there, she doesn't strike me as the type who would be outraged at a man coming on to her."

"True." That thought had crossed Skye's mind, but she didn't want to sound catty. A few seconds later, she snapped her fingers. "That reminds me, I saw Nanette, Colleen, and Tavish in the parking lot at Kohl's."

"The three were together?" Wally polished off his cake and put the plate down. "That seems odd. I thought Tavish and Nanette weren't exactly on friendly terms. Wasn't that your impression?"

"Definitely." Skye nodded her agreement, then picked up her fork.

She took a tiny bite of her dessert, letting the cream cheese frosting melt on her tongue. She liked to savor her food, while Wally devoured his. Which was fine, until he finished his portion too fast and then stared at her plate like Snoopy impersonating a vulture.

"Why would the three of them go shopping together?" Wally mused.

"Funeral clothes?" Skye suggested. "With Tav just out of the service, he might not have a dark suit and need help selecting one."

"I suppose." Wally's expression was skeptical. "But both women?"

"Who knows?" Skye shrugged. "Tav does seem to be a bit of a ladies' man and Colleen comes off as the female equivalent."

Wally narrowed his eyes. "And why do you keep calling him Tav?"

"He asked me to." Skye hid her smile. She liked that Wally was a little jealous. Not too much, but a little possessiveness was nice.

A tiny muscle in Wally's cheek twitched, then he blew out a breath and asked, "So what makes you think Wraige was some kind of player?"

"Because Homer told me the reason *Tavish*," Skye emphasized the man's whole name, "left the army." Wally waved his hand, gesturing for her to go on. "He was caught sleeping with his boss's wife and was given a choice of a dishonorable discharge or not re-upping when his service commitment was over, which was right about the time all this was happening."

"I had no idea that a solider could be dishonorably

discharged for committing adultery." Wally rolled his eyes. "If that were true in civilian life, a lot of folks would be in trouble."

"Yep." Skye cringed. "But wait until you hear the interesting part." She quickly recapped the conversation she'd had with Homer and said, "What do you think about that?"

"From what you're telling me, Tavish should be grateful to his father for getting him out of a jam and not wanting to kill him," Wally muttered. "But that wasn't how he came off when I interviewed him. It didn't seem as if he had much, if any, affection or regard for Dr. Wraige."

"I've been thinking about that." Skye tapped her nails on the arm of the sofa, noticing she needed to fit in a manicure sometime before Saturday night. "Since Tavish and his father didn't have a good relationship to begin with, Dr. Wraige stepping in unasked to rescue Tavish might not have been appreciated. Tavish could have seen it as his father just wanting to save face and not have a son with a dishonorable discharge on his record."

"Good point." Wally frowned. "People often bite the hand that feeds them."

"Sadly, that's true." Skye yawned and began to gather up their dirty cups and plates. Then as she walked into the kitchen she said, "Shoot! I forgot that I needed to go online and see if I can find out anything about the pocket watch one of my students found."

"You never mentioned that to me," Wally yelled from the great room. "Wraige reported a pocket watch stolen the first time his house was burglarized, and it wasn't recovered with the rest of the jewelry."

Skye stiffened and waited to see if her husband's shouting had disturbed the babies. Her shoulders relaxed when she didn't hear any crying, and she was thankful once again that the nursery was in the opposite wing of the house.

She quickly put the plates in the dishwasher and rushed into the great room. Wally was just coming back from the bedroom, flipping through his memo pad.

"Do you have the pocket watch here?" He asked looking up from his notes.

"It's in my tote bag." Skye trotted into laundry room and retrieved the watch. Returning, she sat next to Wally, who had resumed his seat on the couch, and handed it to him. "See, it has what I think is a coat of arms on it. Is it the one stolen from Dr. Wraige?"

"It fits the description." Wally ran his finger over the word FORTITUDINE curved over the image of an arm holding a sword aloft. "Wraige said that it's the MacRaith crest. It seems when his ancestors emigrated to America, the name was changed to Wraige."

"Interesting." Skye wrinkled her forehead. "If someone stole it, how did it end up in the cemetery?" She nibbled a fingernail. "Do you think that was the thief's escape route and he dropped it?"

"Maybe." Wally got up from the couch and helped Skye to her feet. Bingo stretched and jumped off the sofa too. "But that doesn't explain why the rest of the jewelry was left at the pawnshop."

Skye followed Wally into the master bedroom, with the black cat at her heels. "I wonder if the pocket watch was discarded because it would be so easy to identify."

"That doesn't explain why the other stuff was just abandoned instead of pawned. The jewelry box had Wraige's name engraved on it." Wally began to undress. "But the burglar could have gotten a lot of money for the items inside."

"That is odd." Skye went into the adjoining bathroom to get ready for bed.

Wally joined her and just before he stuck his toothbrush

in his mouth, he muttered, "I just wish Doris Ann would get back to me about whatever was in the vic's stomach and the crime scene techs would send me their report. Maybe then we could start finding some answers to all these questions."

CHAPTER 23

Toxic Valentine

WALLY WAS SURPRISED TO SEE NEAL BOULDER IN THE police station when he entered the lobby on Friday morning. The man always reminded him of that cartoon ambulance chaser on *The Simpsons*.

The city attorney had been chatting with the dispatcher, but Boulder turned and beamed at Wally as he presented him with the search warrant for the superintendent's house and said, "Here you go, Chief. Let me know if I can do anything else to help you nab the killer."

"Thanks." Wally shook the lawyer's hand, then examined the document. He was relieved to see it was for the entire premises with no restrictions. "Why the personal delivery service? You usually send warrants to my phone."

"I have an eight o'clock appointment with the mayor and figured I would go old-school." Boulder glanced at the wall clock. "Speaking of which, I'd better get upstairs. I don't want to keep him waiting." He glanced at Thea. "Can you buzz me in?"

"Sure thing." Thea reached down and pressed the button under the counter.

"See you later." Boulder half waved, half saluted, then strolled through the door.

Wally watched until the lawyer was out of sight, then shot a questioning glance at the dispatcher and asked, "Any idea what was all about?"

Thea made a face, then said, "My guess is he's trying to get on your good side because he's running for state's attorney for Stanley County in November."

"Right. I did hear that." Wally walked into the dispatcher's office and headed to the Xerox machine. "I won't support either candidate publicly, but Boulder would be my personal choice."

"Mine too." Thea crossed her arms. "It's about time Scumble River had more say at the county level."

Finished making copies of the warrant, Wally said, "I'm going to the Wraige house. Send Martinez over to assist with the search. We'll see how much progress our new K-9 officer is making in his training."

Although not required by law, Wally first headed to Nanette's CPA firm. He thought it best to inform her that he would be conducting a thorough search of her property.

Nanette's business was located on Basin Street, not too far from the bowling alley, and when he passed by the large, windowless building, Wally sent up a little prayer of gratitude that his father was no longer dating the lane's manager, Bunny Reid. She was about the last person on earth he wanted as a stepmother, let alone anywhere near his children.

As Wally walked into the CPA firm, Colleen Vreesen glanced up from her position behind the reception desk and smiled prettily. "Chief Boyd, what a pleasant surprise." Widening her big blue eyes, she drawled, "I see you're looking as handsome as ever."

Ignoring her tone, Wally asked, "Is Mrs. Wraige available for a quick chat?"

"Party pooper." Colleen giggled and waved toward Nanette's office. "Go ahead in."

Nanette was behind a desk piled with papers. She was tapping rapidly on a keyboard, but when Wally entered, she looked up and frowned.

Before he could speak, she demanded, "Do you have some news about my husband's killer?"

"Sorry, not yet, but I wanted to notify you that I've obtained a warrant and I'll be conducting a search of your house."

He handed her one of the copies that he'd made of the document, and after she read it, she asked. "What exactly are you looking for?" She wrinkled her smooth brow. "I told you the thief didn't touch anything in the rest of the place."

"I'm not convinced your husband was killed by a burglar." Wally watched her reaction carefully. "New evidence has come to light that indicates that it may have been someone with a more personal motive."

"What do you mean by that?" she snapped. "Who are you accusing?"

"We have several suspects." Wally kept his expression bland. "I'm sorry, but because it is an ongoing investigation, that's all I can share at the moment."

Nanette sighed. "Fine, but when can we move back to the house?"

"If there aren't any questions raised by either the search or the report from the crime scene techs, in all likelihood you'll be allowed to move back into the house no later than Monday." Wally turned to leave, then added, "Will all three of you be moving back?"

"I believe Tavish will choose to remain where he is currently." As Nanette returned her attention to the computer, she said, "Now, if you'll excuse me, I really have to get this done."

Wally wasn't surprised that Nanette hadn't been happy with the prospect of him digging through her things. Suspects rarely were thrilled with the actions of the police. It was a shame that the innocent had to be inconvenienced, but at times it was the only way to convict the guilty. And no one wanted a killer running around loose, because once an individual has taken a life, odds are they won't hesitate to do it again.

Martinez was waiting for Wally when he pulled into the Wraiges' driveway. The young woman and her K-9 partner were standing outside her squad car and as soon as Wally parked his Hummer, they met him at the door.

The instant he stepped out of the vehicle, Martinez announced, "Chief, the vic's coin collection turned up in Joliet at the A-1 Coin store."

"Oh?" Wally had sent out the list of missing coins to all the area dealers in a hundred-mile radius, but he hadn't really expected to find it.

"The owner said that the albums were just sitting on the doorstep of her shop. She found it when she opened up this morning," Martinez explained. "She said there was no one around, and as soon as she realized they were the coins from the inventory that you sent out, she called the station."

"Hmm." Wally took a minute to think about the implications of that information. He scratched his jaw and muttered, "So just like the jewelry box at the pawnshop."

"Yep." Martinez agreed, but didn't comment further.

"Okay. After we finish here, I want you to head up to Joliet and get the collection, then transport it to Laurel and have the crime techs check it for fingerprints or any other evidence."

"Will do." Martinez nodded.

Wally popped open the Hummer's rear hatch and grabbed the duffel containing the items he needed to complete a search.

He swung the duffel's strap over his shoulder, then looked at the K-9 officer sitting at Martinez's feet. The animal stared at Wally and yawned.

"What types of items has the dog been trained to detect?" Wally studied the animal.

Martinez patted the giant schnauzer's head. "Arnold and I are working on hidden explosives, firearms, drugs, alcohol, and nicotine. The thinking is that we can use him in school searches and also suspicious vehicles that have been pulled over."

"Excellent. Let's get him started looking for any of those items in the victim's residence."

Wally made a circuit of the house, documenting that the police tape wrapped around the exterior was intact. This provided proof that the interior had remained undisturbed since the murder.

Returning to the front, he cut through the strips sealing that entrance, unlocked the door, and gestured for Martinez and the dog to begin their search. He'd let them do the initial examination of the rooms, then follow in their path looking for items that Arnold couldn't smell.

Once Martinez and her K-9 partner finished with the communal living areas, Wally sent them on to investigate the guest wing while he searched the kitchen. He opened all the appliances, cabinets, and drawers, but found nothing more significant than that the people sharing the house had widely varying tastes.

The pantry held everything from dried beans and nutritional yeast to Pop-Tarts and SpaghettiOs. The cupboards displayed dishes ranging from melamine to fine china, and the drawers had both plastic utensils and sterling silver flatware.

There weren't many places anything could be concealed in the living and dining rooms. Surprisingly for a man whose profession was education, Wally did not find any bookshelves, and the coffee and end tables were completely clear.

Frowning, Wally checked that there were no hidden niches that he had missed, but if there were, he couldn't find them. The room was as sterile and impersonal as if it were a display in a furniture store.

With nowhere else to look, Wally headed toward the guest wing. He'd heard Martinez issue muted commands but nothing to indicate that Arnold had detected anything of interest.

Entering the room Colleen had been occupying, Wally spotted his officer sitting on the edge of the bed flipping through a stack of photographs. It took Martinez a second to realize that Wally was watching her from the door, but when she spotted him, her cheeks reddened and she jumped up. The pictures that had been on her lap spilled onto the floor and scattered at her feet.

"Chief!" Martinez squeaked.

Wally raised a brow. "That's me."

"Uh." Martinez gestured to the strewn snapshots. "These, uh, these were stashed in the false bottom of the nightstand's drawer."

She pointed to the disassembled bedside table and Wally took the camera from his duffel bag and documented the hiding place that Martinez had found. Then he turned to the pictures and took photos of those as well. They were nudes of Colleen Vreesen with several different men—a few snapshots contained more than one guy in the bed with her.

Covering a smile, Wally looked at Martinez and said dryly, "I wasn't aware that the dog could detect porn."

"He can't, sir." Martinez took a breath, regained her composure, and explained, "This was with the photos." She held a small plastic bag holding a few dark specks between her gloved fingers. "It's probably weed."

"Add it to the stuff that you're bringing to Laurel this afternoon." Wally nudged one of the pictures with his toe. "Colleen is going through a custody battle, which makes me think it's odd that she would keep these kinds of pictures of herself around."

"That's true." Martinez raised a dark eyebrow. "Maybe she wasn't the one who put them in the drawer."

"Good point." Wally motioned to the photos. "We'd better have them checked for fingerprints."

"Got it." Martinez gathered the pictures and slipped them into an evidence bag. "There wasn't anything, and I do mean anything, in Tavish's room. It's completely empty. He must have brought everything he owns to my place."

"Speaking of your renter"—Wally gestured for Martinez to follow him as he walked toward the master suite—"how's that arrangement working out for you?"

"Fine." The young officer trailed Wally into the master bedroom. "He's neat, quiet, and pays in cash." She glanced at the dog by her side. "And best of all, his cat and Arnold get along."

"That's all good." Wally stopped and waved for her to go ahead. "But he is a murder suspect, so don't let your defenses down."

"Definitely not, Chief." Martinez made a hand gesture and Arnold began his search.

Wally watched the woman and dog work together. Having a K-9 officer might actually turn out to be the one good thing the mayor ever did for the police department. Arnold seemed to have given Martinez the confidence she'd previously lacked as a rookie.

A few seconds later, the dog alerted, and Wally walked into the master bathroom. Martinez was holding a Kotex box and she opened the lid. One by one, she held out each tampon to Arnold who alerted at six of them. She laid those aside and looked at Wally.

"Are they factory sealed?" Wally asked.

Martinez examined them carefully and said, "They've been opened and glued back shut."

Taking out the camera again, Wally documented the box and its contents, then said, "Change of plans. You're still going to Joliet, but as soon as we're done here, I'll bring this, the pictures, and the baggie we think contains marijuana fragments to Laurel. We need to know what's inside these tampons as soon as possible."

"You're thinking that it might be whatever was making Dr. Wraige sick."

"Yep."

They examined the rest of the suite and the attached garage but didn't find anything else of interest. Then both returned to their vehicles and drove off in opposite directions.

Wally checked in with Thea as he headed toward Laurel. He advised her of his intended destination and asked her to call in Anthony to cover the town's normal patrol duties while he and Martinez were both gone.

She reported that everything was quiet in Scumble River and signed off.

Forty-five minutes later, Wally parked the Hummer behind the crime lab, grabbed the evidence bags from the rear seat, and walked into the squat brick building.

He sketched a quick greeting to the man who buzzed him inside, then marched through the door leading into the rest of the building. One side of the corridor held the crime labs and the other the morgue.

Wally peered through the window of each door until he found an occupied lab. The tech was busy but looked up as Wally entered.

"Chief." The man waved. "I should have the report on your crime scene ready in an hour or so."

"Great." Wally held up the evidence bags he was carrying. "I was hoping you could put a rush on these. I need the pictures fingerprinted and the materials in the other two identified."

"Sure." The guy accepted the evidence and logged it in. "Unless it's something exotic, I should be able to add it to the report and have it to you by the end of the day."

"Thanks." Wally clapped the man in his shoulder. "I appreciate it."

As he was walking out of the lab, Wally heard someone call his name. He turned and saw Doris Ann beckoning to him.

She waved him into the morgue and said, "I was just about to call you. We've figured out the suspicious substance in your vic's stomach contents."

"Excellent." Wally tilted his head toward the lab. "I just turned in a couple of items for analysis. If one of them matches, we might have found the origin of the substance."

"Impressive." Doris Ann waved toward the doorway she was blocking. "Come with me and I'll show you what we've discovered so far."

She led him past a large refrigeration-cooling unit and a smaller freezer, then through the steel door that separated them from the autopsy area.

Wally and Doris Ann passed X-ray equipment, an electric body lift, and an industrial scale. He was thankful to see that the autopsy table was unoccupied, as he had no desire to see anyone's internal organs.

Finally, she escorted him into a small office and sat behind a cluttered desk. Wally took the chair next to it and Doris Ann pulled a folder from the stack in front of her.

Opening the file, she said, "The fragments we found were tobacco."

"He ate a cigarette?" Wally leaned forward to see the line she indicated.

"Doubtful." Doris Ann continued, "From the other matter in his stomach, my best guess would be that the tobacco was concealed in a muffin. The lab is testing the paper muffin cups found at the scene right now for traces of nicotine to confirm my suspicions."

"Wouldn't he notice the tobacco?" Wally asked, making a face.

"It was probably"—she used her fingers to make air quotes—"a 'healthy muffin' with flaxseed meal, oat fiber, and lots of spices to mask the flavor. Or he was told the odd taste was some secret nutritious ingredient."

"Would ingesting tobacco cause the symptoms that Skye noticed?"

"Definitely." Doris Ann pursed her lips. "But the interesting thing is that in the doses that were possible to give him via muffin, the nicotine wouldn't have killed him. It would just have made him miserable."

Wally nodded thoughtfully. "Our K-9 officer alerted to a box of tampons and one of the things he's trained to detect is nicotine. The tampons are one of the items I dropped off at the lab."

"Where did you find it?" Doris Ann asked.

"In Mrs. Wraige's bathroom cabinet."

"Well, you know what they say." Doris Ann grinned. "The murderer is always the wife."

CHAPTER 24

Too Many People

SKYE WAS CHOPPING THE LAST OF THE VEGETABLES FOR THE sauce she was making when she heard Wally's Hummer drive up. It had been a quiet Friday at school. Her only somewhat difficult encounter had been telling Karl that his time as a foreign exchange student in the United States was being cut short.

The boy had been sad to leave all his new friends; however, he'd brightened when Skye had reminded him that he would be seeing his family soon. Karl had admitted to being a little homesick and happy that he'd be back in Germany in time for his mom's birthday. He'd bought her a present that he couldn't wait to give her—a box of Frango Mints and a tin of Garrett Popcorn.

After meeting with Karl, Skye's day had gone as scheduled and she'd been able to leave on time. Okay, she'd slipped away a little early. But to make it up, she'd worked through lunch and completed her sixtieth report of the year.

She'd been determined to get home by three thirty to relieve Dorothy from her nanny duties, and thanks to her five-mile commute and no traffic, she'd made it with seconds to spare. There was only one thing that could have cost her extra time, a red light on the traffic signal at Basin and Kinsman, but she'd gotten lucky and it blinked to green as she approached the intersection.

Dorothy had an appointment to get her hair cut, colored, and permed for the big Valentine's Day dance. She wouldn't tell Skye the identity of her date, but she did say that Skye would approve.

Skye was happy for the widowed housekeeper. Her husband had been gone for nearly a decade and it was easy to see that she was lonely. Skye only hoped that whoever she was seeing was a nice guy.

Adding the diced zucchini and squash to the pan containing the caramelized onions and browned hamburger, Skye thought about the eligible Scumble River men in Dorothy's age range. There really weren't that many she could picture the housekeeper dating.

Before she came up with a guess as to the man's identity, Wally strolled into the kitchen and asked, "What smells so good in here?"

"Probably the pasta sauce that I've been working on for the past hour. I should have read the recipe more carefully. I think my wrist is sprained with all the chopping, slicing, and cubing." Skye gave Wally a quick hug, then shooed him away and turned back to the stovetop to give the mixture a quick stir. She had four minutes, then she'd add the sliced mushrooms. "Why don't you go change? I need to get the garlic butter made for the Italian bread and toss the salad."

Before heading to the master bedroom, Wally stepped over to kiss the twins, who were in their Jumperoos. Carson had gotten Eva the woodland friends version and CJ the rainforest-themed edition. Both babies adored the lights, sounds, and toys attached to the devices and had been happily bouncing away while Skye cooked.

When Wally returned, clad in jogging pants and a navy University of Illinois sweatshirt, Skye had already added the broccoli florets and crushed tomatoes, as well as the Italian herbs. She'd also finished the bread and salad.

Now the sauce could simmer as she and Wally fed the babies.

Meeting him with two warmed bottles, she said, "Grab a twin."

Wally picked up Eva, straightening the yellow bow on her headband and smoothing the gray T-shirt's little yellow ruffle. Skye lifted CJ into her arms, pulling down his matching, minus the ruffle, T-shirt. They both checked the twins' yellow pants and found dry diapers.

Toting the babies and their bottles, Skye and Wally retired to the great room. Getting her little boy into position, Skye could swear he was heavier than yesterday. He and his sister were both developing at an amazingly fast rate. They were already approaching double their birth weight and had grown over six inches.

After her cousin had made a crack about the twins being fat, Skye had consulted their pediatrician. The doctor had assured Skye that their length-to-weight ratio was perfect.

While Wally and Skye fed the babies, Skye told Wally about her day. She had a little boy for counseling that had cracked her up. He'd told her he wanted a kitten, but his mother was allergic, so instead of giving up on getting a pet, he'd built his mom a house out of a refrigerator box and then told his mother that she could live in the backyard. That way his kitty could stay with him in his room without making her sneeze.

Skye and Wally were still snickering as they changed the twins and put them into their cribs. Bingo had followed them and taken up his position on the rocker to perform his duties as guard cat.

Patting Bingo on the head, Skye walked into the kitchen and immediately turned up the flame under the pot of water she had simmering on the stove. She was placing the garlic bread in the oven when Wally joined her. He didn't think she knew, but he always gave their big black cat a treat for protecting the twins while they slept.

Smiling at her softhearted husband, Skye said, "Once the water starts boiling, I'll drop the pasta in and we can eat our salads while it cooks."

"Sounds good." Wally kissed her and started to set the table.

He was just opening the cupboard door when his phone rang. He fished it out of his pocket, put it on the counter, and swiped the speaker icon, then reached for the plates.

May's voice blared from the rectangular device. "You'll never guess what someone just found stuck on the ice in the river by the dam." She took a breath then urged, "Go ahead. Guess!"

"For heaven's sake. Just tell me." Wally glanced at Skye, who had stopped what she was doing to listen.

"Spoilsport," May groused. Wally remained silent as he took silverware from the drawer and she huffed, "Fine. It was Dr. Wraige's stolen car. Some kids who decided to go ice skating found it."

"Son of a bacon bit." Wally swore, then exhaled sharply and said, "Tell Quirk to get the car out of there and have it hauled over to Laurel. He'll need to call the heavy-duty towing company in Kankakee. They own a winch that should be able to remove it from the ice. Then, have him call the crime techs to go over the vehicle and the area around where it went into the river."

"You're not coming in?" May asked, her tone conveying her surprise.

Wally walked to the fridge, grabbed a Sam Adams and a bottle of wine. "I have every confidence that the sergeant can handle this without me." He opened the beer and poured a glass of the zinfandel for Skye. "Quirk knows to call me if he has any questions."

When Wally disconnected, he sat down, took a swig of beer, and as if he hadn't just been informed that a murder victim's car had been found, he commented, "This salad looks great."

"Thanks." While Skye had listened to the exchange, she'd placed the pasta in the boiling water and put the bowl on the table. "It's spring greens, red onion, cherry tomatoes, and Italian dressing with some freshly grated parmesan cheese and some sliced pepperoncini peppers on top to give it a little bite."

Wally helped himself, then forked some into his mouth, chewed, and swallowed. "It's terrific."

She waited for Wally to say something about the phone call, and when he didn't, she said, "I'm glad you didn't have to go to the scene."

"I was tempted, and I'll check it out tomorrow morning, but let's face it, there won't be any useable evidence. And if by some miracle there is, the crime techs will find it before I would."

"True." Skye thought about the situation while she ate her salad. "I appreciate you keeping the promise you made to limit your work hours, but I don't want to stand in the way of your duty."

"Darlin'." Wally's warm brown eyes met hers. "You and the babies are my duty." He took her hand. "If there were a body in the car or if one of my less experienced people were on shift, I'd go. But the car was stolen the day before the homicide and Quirk's a seasoned officer."

"You're right." Skye got up, drained the pasta, and mixed

it into the veggie-laden sauce. This was a more nutritious, but she hoped just as enjoyable, version of spaghetti. "How about so I don't feel guilty, we go over the evidence you do have for Dr. Wraige's murder?"

"That's a good idea." Wally rose to his feet. "I'll get the file and a couple of legal pads and pens while you put the food on the table."

By the time he returned, Skye had their plates full of pasta and a basket of garlic bread between them. While she was waiting, she'd tried a bite of the entrée and was pleased with the results of the new recipe. She was willing to eat healthier, but it had to taste as good as the original dish. An added plus, there was more than enough for a second meal. She'd tell Frannie and Justin to help themselves tomorrow night while they were babysitting.

Wally resumed his seat and told her what he and Zelda had found at the Wraige house, then read her the results of Doris Ann's autopsy.

"Nicotine," Skye muttered. "I would never have guessed that in a million years. Is there any chance he ingested the tobacco by accident?"

"That's extremely doubtful." Wally forked pasta into his mouth and chewed. Then after swallowing, he explained, "The lab found traces of nicotine in the crumbs on the paper muffin cups, so it's a good bet that was how the vic was ingesting the stuff. They also found only Nanette's fingerprints on the tampons."

"So if we agree that Nanette was deliberately feeding her husband the tobacco from the stash you found in her tampon box, how did she make sure no one else ate those muffins?" While she mulled over the scenario, Skye took a sip of her wine, then *thunked* the glass down on the table and said, "Unless they were all in on it."

"That's certainly a possibility." Wally pursed his lips, then shook his head. "But Doris Ann informed me that the nicotine would have made him feel ill, but it wouldn't have killed him."

"Interesting." Skye tilted her head, then asked, "Have you received anything else from the forensics at the scene?"

"I got the lab report a few minutes before I left the station." Wally flipped through pages. "It contained the info on the muffin wrapper and also that the fingerprints on the coffee cups in the master suite sitting room were the vic's, Nanette's, and Colleen's."

"That's strange." Skye took another sip of wine. "Considering that the bus driver told you he overheard a shouting match between Nanette and Dr. Wraige about him coming on to her friend."

"Exactly." Wally continued, "The only fingerprints on the sex photos of Colleen and the baggie with the marijuana dregs were the vic's."

"That's even stranger." Skye ate a few bites of her meal. "It could mean that Colleen never even knew they were in the nightstand's false bottom." Skye chewed thoughtfully. "But why would Dr. Wraige have them, and why would he put them in her room?"

"Another good point." Wally smiled. "Although from everything that I've learned about him, he was a manipulative son of a bull snot. So the question might be what would he gain by planting those in her room?"

"Not to mention"—Skye narrowed her eyes—"how did they get in his possession?"

Wally shrugged. "My best guest would be a private investigator."

"Or…" Skye straightened. "Maybe he had his son do it as sort of a preemployment test." Before Wally could comment, she continued, "And maybe Dr. Wraige put them in the guest room, so Nanette wouldn't find them. Also, if Colleen was aware of the pictures and searching for them, her own room would be the last place she'd look."

Wally continued to eat, then said, "We need to figure out when the snapshots were taken and how long Tavish has been out of the service."

Skye nodded, then said, "Let's put that aside for now and discuss the spate of break-ins at the Wraiges' house. I'm convinced that the burglaries somehow have to be a part of the whole scenario."

"Why is that?" Wally took a long pull from his bottle of beer.

"First, only Dr. Wraige's stuff was stolen." Skye waited for Wally's nod, then continued, "Second, he seemed to be the only one getting the tobacco muffins. And third, he's the one who ended up dead."

"Okay," Wally said slowly. "We also should take into consideration that everything that was stolen was discarded, even the car, and the only fingerprints found on any of the items were the vic's and his son's."

"What were Tavish's prints on?" Skye asked.

Wally flipped through a few sheets of paper in the file. "The jewelry box and its contents, minus the pocket watch, which were left on the steps of the pawnshop, were wiped clean."

"Okay." Skye tapped her nails on the tabletop. "But that's not what I asked."

Wally continued, evidently unperturbed by her impatience. "However, the watch that was found either tossed away or dropped by trees near the cemetery had Tavish's thumbprint inside the back lid."

"Back lid?"

"Yes," Wally explained. "You might not have noticed, but not only did the front open up to reveal the watch face, the back also was hinged to expose the mechanical movements."

"Interesting that Tavish's print was on it," Skye mused.

"The ties were never found," Wally continued. "But if I had to guess, whoever took those just burned them or threw them in the trash. The coin collection abandoned at that dealer in Joliet was also wiped clean."

"Hmm." Skye bit her lip. "And the car could have easily been sold to a chop shop for a pretty penny, but instead it was driven into the river, where it was probably supposed to sink out of sight and be gone forever."

Wally ran his hands through his hair. "The thief never tried to sell any of it. So why would someone go to the trouble of staging a break-in and stealing stuff, and then just get rid of it?"

"The same reason someone would poison a person with a nonlethal substance." Skye tapped her chin. "To make the victim miserable."

"The way Wraige died suggests that whoever murdered him might not have intended to kill him." Wally spread out his hands. "The vic and the murderer got into a tussle and the murderer pushed him. Then, in his weakened state from the nicotine poisoning, Wraige stumbled back and was pierced by cupid's arrow."

"The murder never seemed premediated to me." Skye pushed away her empty plate. "If we take into consideration that all the stolen items were basically thrown away, and you told me that the security cameras were always disabled or obscured, I just can't see the thief being an outsider."

"I agree." Wally got up and began to clear away the dirty dishes.

"Which means that the killer and the burglar has to be

one of the three people living in his house." Skye joined Wally at the sink. "But which one?"

Wally turned around, leaned back against the counter, and crossed his arms. "I have no idea. I'm as confused as a chameleon in a bag of M&Ms."

"Well, even if we knew who it was, we'd still have to prove it." Skye turned on the water and started rinsing the plates as she said to Wally, "You might as well make some coffee because I have a feeling this is going to be a long night."

CHAPTER 25

Silly Love Songs

THE NEXT MORNING, SKYE CHECKED TO SEE IF THE TWINS were still sleeping, thankfully they were, then walked into the kitchen and headed straight to the Keurig. She and Wally had discussed the various scenarios on and off all evening. When they'd finally given up and went to bed, they still hadn't come up with a definitive answer as to who murdered the superintendent.

"We have to figure out which of the three suspects have the most motive to want Wraige dead," Wally said as Skye popped a K-Cup into place, positioned her mug on the tray, and pushed the button.

Staring at the machine, Skye pushed her hair out of her face and asked, "But if it was an accident, then what does motive have to do with it?"

She was attempting to follow the conversation Wally had started as soon as she opened her eyes. Unlike her annoying rise-and-shine husband who leaped out of bed running on all cylinders, she needed a little jump start before she could think straight.

"It may have been an accident." Wally poured cereal into

his bowl and doused it with milk. "But Doris Ann said that if whoever pushed him had called an ambulance, he might have been saved."

Skye frowned. "So either they left him to die or watched him bleed out."

The Keurig gave one last gurgle and Skye snatched up her cup. After adding her favorite French vanilla creamer and two packets of sugar substitute, she took a healthy sip and tried to get her brain to work.

"Yep." Wally ate his Cap'n Crunch, then said, "Who can we get to watch the twins? I'll need you at the station for the interviews."

One thing they had decided last night was that they needed to get all three suspects down to the station and inter-rogate them until one of them confessed. But Dorothy was off on the weekends and one of Skye's biggest no-nos was asking the housekeeper to work on Saturday or Sunday.

"Everyone's busy. Mom and Trixie are getting gussied up for the big dance." Skye toasted an English muffin and joined Wally at the table. "They booked a spa day over in Laurel."

"How about Judy?" Wally asked. "She's watched the twins a few times."

"She's going to Naperville to have the final fitting on her bridal gown." Skye scrunched up her face in thought. "That leaves your dad, but we asked him to sit for the kids once already this week."

"Dad's got a business meeting in Chicago." Wally fin-ished his cereal and drank the remaining milk.

"Frannie and Justin have appointments with florists and DJs. While they're home, they want to get a lot of details finalized for their wedding." Skye spread marmalade on her muffin and licked her fingers. "They're coming over at four." Before Wally could speak, Skye pointed her finger at him and said, "Don't even think about it, mister. I need every second of those two hours to get ready before we leave for the dance."

"You really don't." Wally leaned across the table and gave her a sweet kiss. "You're beautiful without all that makeup and hairspray." Skye narrowed her eyes and he hurriedly added, "But if that makes you happy, we should get the interviews going as soon as possible so you won't feel rushed and you'll have time to relax."

"Then I guess the kids are coming with us." Skye got up and walked over to the sink. "How about Dr. Wraige's car? Did they get it towed last night?"

"They did, and the crime tech I spoke to said there was no evidence on shore or in the car." Wally rubbed his chin. "The interior was wiped clean."

"Shoot!" Skye rinsed her cup and plate and put them in the dishwasher, then returned to the table with a damp cloth to wipe up the crumbs.

"I'm going to start calling our suspects and getting them lined up to come into the police station." Wally took his cell phone from the case hanging off his utility belt.

Wally was already wearing his uniform. Another difference between her husband and Skye was that if she wasn't leaving the house, she'd be happy to stay in her jammies all day. He, on the other hand, immediately showered and put on clothes.

Wally opened the file he had sitting near his coffee mug, but Skye held out a finger to stop him, then said, "What would you think about interviewing the three of them together?" She narrowed her eyes. "It might be interesting to see how they respond to each other's answers, and one might throw the others under the bus."

"I like your idea, but let's talk to them each individually first, then bring them together." Wally flipped through the folder's contents and muttered, "Where in the heck did I put their phone numbers? Ah. There they are."

Before he could start dialing, she asked, "How can you be sure they'll come into the station this morning?" She wasn't getting dressed until she knew they were really going into work.

"Generally, innocent people want to help catch the bad guys." Wally grinned. "And the one who did it is usually worried that if they fail to cooperate with the police, he or she will look guilty."

Skye watched as her gorgeous husband tapped the numbers into his phone. She was still awed at how wonderful everything had turned out for her after her mortifying return to Scumble River. Coming back to her hometown broke and broken, she would have never believed that she could be this happy. And she was always secretly a tiny bit terrified that it might all disappear before her very eyes.

She and Wally had been through so much to be with each other, and one of her strongest wishes was that they would be able to grow old together. She never forgot for a single solitary moment how blessed she was to have him and the babies in her life.

While she'd been lost in thought, evidently Wally's call had been answered because she heard him identify himself and say, "Mrs. Wraige, I'd like to bring you up to speed on your husband's murder investigation. Would you be able to meet me at the Scumble River Police Department?" He paused for her answer, then said, "Say in about an hour?" Another pause. "Okay, two hours is fine. See you then."

After Wally disconnected, Skye beamed. "It was clever that you framed the interview as a way to inform her of the case's progress."

He smirked. "I always use that for family members who are suspects."

"It didn't seem as if she was reluctant to talk to you," Skye commented.

"Nope. In fact, she sounded eager." He shook his head. "And it also sounds as if Colleen will be accompanying her. I could hear her friend in the background insisting that Nanette not come in alone."

"Well played." Skye applauded. "You reeled in two fish with one worm." She poked his arm. "Now you just need to get Tav on the hook."

"I'll take care of that now."

"Okay. I'll throw on some clothes and comb my hair. Once I'm dressed, we better get the twins ready."

"Sounds good." Wally turned his attention back to his phone, and Skye hurried toward the master suite.

When she returned wearing navy slacks and a matching twin set, Wally had already fed and gotten the twins into matching outfits. While he put on their coats and got them into their car seats, Skye packed their diaper bag.

Five minutes later, they were pulling into the police station lot. Skye parked the Mercedes and Wally jumped out. He retrieved the twin stroller frame from the SUV's rear compartment, brought it to the back seat, detached CJ's car seat, and clicked it into place, then did the same with Eva. Skye slung the diaper bag over her shoulders and followed Wally as he pushed the stroller toward the front entrance.

While they walked, Skye remembered she hadn't asked about Dr. Wraige's stepson and touched Wally's arm. "Did Tavish agree to come in this morning?"

"Yep. Once he heard that I intended to speak to his stepmother"—Wally turned and gave Skye a wolfish grin—"wild horses couldn't keep him away. In fact, he insisted on talking to us before she arrived."

"Fantastic." Skye beamed at Wally, then greeted Betty

Houmas, the weekend dispatcher who was standing behind the counter.

Betty buzzed open the door leading to the back of the building, then met Skye and Wally as they stepped into the hallway and said, "Would you like me to keep an eye on those cuties while you two interview the folks you've got coming into the station?"

Wally stiffened. "How do you know we're here to talk to people about the case?"

"You told Roy, and he asked me to get the break room cleaned up."

"In that case"—Wally relaxed—"we'd be much obliged if you'd watch them."

While Wally wheeled the twins into the dispatcher officer and put down their diaper bags, Skye wrote her cell number on a slip of paper, gave it to Betty, and said, "Just text me if you need me."

"Will do." Betty smiled. "Although I have a dozen grandkids, so I doubt that there's anything that these adorable little angels can do that I can't handle." She patted Skye on the shoulder. "But I can understand why a mother would want to make sure her babies were safe."

Skye thanked her, then accompanied Wally down the hallway to the interrogation, a.k.a. break, room. As they walked inside and Wally flipped on the lights, she thought about what Betty had said. There was something about it that tickled her subconscious. What was it?

Frustrated that she couldn't put her finger on it, Skye took a seat. Seconds later, the wall phone buzzed and Wally pressed the intercom button.

"Tavish Wraige is here." Betty's voice echoed from the speaker. "Shall I send him back?"

"No. I'll be right up to get him," Wally answered, then looked at Skye and asked, "Are you ready for this?"

She nodded and he hurried away.

While she waited, she walked to the cupboard over the sink and took down the old-fashioned tape recorder. Six months ago, the city attorney had decreed that the police had to make an audio record of all official interviews. And since the interrogation room wasn't set up with any kind of modern equipment and there was no money in the budget to correct that issue, the police had to make do with what they had lying around.

When Wally returned with Tavish, he seated the man next to Skye, then took the chair opposite him. This was their normal position for when Wally wanted Skye to take the sympathetic role in the interview.

"How are you doing this morning?" Skye asked, turning to face Tavish.

"Good," he answered. "But I'm anxious to hear what's been found out about my father's death."

Turning on the tape recorder, Wally announced the date and time and instructed, "Please state your full name and current address." After Tavish complied, Wally Mirandized him, then when the younger man started to protest, he said, "It's just routine, but if you're uncomfortable and want to call an attorney we can wait."

"No." Tavish crossed his arms. "I don't have anything to hide."

"Great." Skye smiled at him. "We do have a little bit of good news." She watched him carefully. "With the exception of the neckties, all of the stolen items have been recovered."

"Oh?" Tavish's expression was cautious. "Did you arrest the burglar?"

"Sadly, no." Skye patted his arm. "But your father's car was found."

Tavish's shoulders stiffened. It was a slight movement,

but Skye noticed, and when she shot a glance at Wally, he nodded that he'd seen it too.

"It was stuck in some ice on the river near the dam," Wally explained.

"Wow!" Tavish seemed to recover from the surprise and shook his head. "How lucky is it that it didn't sink?"

"I believe that's what the thief hoped it would do," Skye said. "It was discarded just like the rest of your father's stolen possessions."

As she said that and watched Tavish's reaction, she remembered Homer saying that Dr. Wraige and his son had been on the outs for years. He told her that they hadn't spoken since Dr. Wraige divorced Tavish's mother.

"The burglar must have decided the stuff was too hot to fence." Tavish gazed straight ahead, not looking at Skye.

Since Wally hadn't jumped in, Skye assumed it was okay for her to take the lead and said, "Or the items weren't taken because of their monetary value, but because they had a sentimental value to Dr. Wraige."

"What kind of a robber would do that?" Tavish uncrossed his arms and gripped the table edge.

"One who wanted his father to feel as hurt as he felt by his dad." Skye kept her voice soft and understanding.

"Are you accusing me?" Tavish yelped. "What kind of proof do you have?"

"We found your fingerprints," Wally answered.

"But I wiped…" Tavish trailed off. "I mean, of course you did. I lived in the house."

"You did," Wally agreed. "But we know you and your father had a strained relationship, so it's extremely doubtful that you handled his personal items." When Tavish remained silent, Wally added, "And as you started to say, you wiped off almost everything you stole."

"Not that I'm admitting that I took any of those things"—Tavish straightened—"but if I did, it was because he deserved to lose the possessions that he loved. He forced my mother to sign a prenup, which left her nearly penniless when he divorced her. She had to sell everything that was precious to her to support us."

"That's awful." Skye had never been fond of the superintendent, but the more she learned about him, the more she disliked him. "How did he avoid paying child support?"

"Even his sleazy lawyers couldn't get him out of that." Tavish rolled his eyes. "But the agreement was set up so that Mom had to prove every cent was spent on me and not our mutual living expenses or the money was deducted from the next check."

Wally tapped his pen on the table. "Be that as it may, that doesn't excuse—"

Tavish interrupted. "It's my understanding that prosecuting me would be problematic because shared living spaces make it difficult to prove intent to steal. The items could have been borrowed and misplaced."

"Perhaps," Wally conceded. "However, murder is another matter."

"What! No!" Tavish suddenly seemed a lot less sure of himself. "I didn't kill my father. I wasn't even home when it happened."

"But you don't have an alibi," Wally countered. "No one can vouch for where you were."

"Actually." Tavish's cheeks reddened. "I do."

"You said no one saw you in your office," Skye reminded him.

"I…uh…didn't want to get her in trouble," Tavish mumbled. "She's married."

"We'll be discreet," Wally assured him. "Who was with you that morning?"

"Sueann Archmould." Tavish glanced at Skye. "She was with me from eight thirty to nine forty-five. She stopped by to welcome me to the staff and then she said she'd never done it with a soldier and started undressing and—"

Not wanting to hear the sordid details, Skye cut him off and asked, "How did she leave her kids for first and second periods?"

"Sueann has a student teacher," Tavish explained, then added, "And when she left to go back to her classroom, I walked up to the main office to get some info from the secretary."

"We'll have to confirm that." Wally looked at Skye and said, "Would you be okay calling this woman to check on his alibi?"

"I guess." Skye wasn't thrilled at having to admit to a colleague that she was aware of her infidelity, but it was within the scope of her job as the police's psych consultant.

"Use my office."

Skye nodded and headed upstairs. It was an uncomfortable phone call, but once Sueann was assured confidentiality, she admitted to being with Tavish during the time of the murder.

Before returning to the interrogation room, Skye looked in on the twins. Betty had Eva on her lap and CJ was snoozing in his stroller.

Turning to leave, Skye saw Nanette and Colleen enter the station. Unsure of how Wally wanted to proceed with the women, she hurried away before they spotted her.

Wally met her in the hallway and she informed him that Sueann had corroborated Tavish's alibi. She also told him that their next two suspects were waiting for them in the lobby.

"Why don't you let Wraige know he's in the clear for his father's murder and I'll go get the women?" Wally suggested, then added, "But advise him we may still charge him with the thefts. I want to keep him unsettled until we have the killer, but truthfully, I can't see making that charge stick."

"Got it." Skye walked inside the interrogation room, approached Tavish, and said, "Sueann backed up your story so you can leave."

He quickly rose to his feet, but before he got to the door, she added Wally's warning.

"You know," Tavish said, his hand on the doorknob, "I may or may not have taken the jewelry box, ties, and car, but I definitely didn't take the coin collection."

Having imparted that last confusing piece of information, he hurried away.

CHAPTER 26

Stupid Cupid

SKYE AND WALLY STOOD OUTSIDE THE INTERROGATION room window watching Nanette and Colleen through a gap in the blinds. After escorting the women in there and showing them to their seats, Wally had motioned Skye to follow him into the hallway.

Shutting the door behind him, Wally leaned a shoulder against the wall and said, "I had planned to interview these two separately, but now that we know Tavish has an alibi, I reconsidered your earlier suggestion to have the suspects together to see if one would implicate the other, and I think it's a good idea with these two. Is that still your professional opinion?"

"It is." Skye studied the pair of women. "We're ninety-nine percent certain either Colleen or Nanette is the killer. Surely, if the innocent party feels that they might be arrested, they'll give up whatever information about the other they've been holding back."

He narrowed his eyes. "I'd like you to take the empty chair between them. Concentrate your attention on Nanette as much as possible because I have a feeling Colleen won't fall for your sympathetic counselor schtick."

"It's not a schtick." Skye smacked Wally's biceps. "I am empathic."

"Sorry. I do know that." Wally patted her shoulder, then said, "I Mirandized them before bringing them back here. Nanette got a little huffy, but I told her it was just standard operating procedure for anyone talking to the authorities at a police station."

"Did she buy that?"

"Of course." Wally winked. "Women find me very charming and sincere."

Skye made a face. "Don't I know it."

Wally chuckled and opened the interrogation room door, motioning for her to go in before him. She nodded her thanks, then walked over and took the seat that he'd indicated.

There was one chair left and it was on the other side of the table, conveniently arranged to be across from Skye's. He turned on the tape recorder, announced the date and time, and as he had with Tavish, he instructed, "Please state your full names and current addresses." After they obeyed, Wally said, "We have a few questions regarding Dr. Wraige's murder. In order to make you both more comfortable, we are allowing you to remain together during this conversation."

"Questions?" Nanette blinked. "I thought you were going to bring us up-to-date on the investigation."

"We are." Skye turned and smiled reassuringly at the woman. "We just want to clear up a few things first since neither of you have alibis."

"Are we suspects?" Colleen fluttered her eyelashes at Wally. "Do you think we should have a lawyer?"

"You're free to call an attorney," Wally said smoothly. "But we would have to adjourn and wait for him or her to show up." He stared at Nanette. "Didn't you say you had clients scheduled this afternoon?"

Nanette nodded and checked her watch. "I only have an

hour free and since we have nothing to hide, and we want to do everything we can to help the police find Shamus's killer, we'll just go ahead without legal representation, right?" She gave Colleen a firm look until her friend nodded. Once she had Colleen's agreement, Nanette turned her gaze to Skye and asked, "What do you want to know?"

"I understand that your husband wasn't feeling well before he died." Skye started with something that Nanette wouldn't be expecting.

"That's correct." Nanette's tone was cautious. "Shamus had been sick on and off for the past month or so. Why does that matter?"

Colleen brightened. "Did he trip and fall into the statue? Was it an accident after all?"

Skye sent Wally a quick glance. As far as she knew, the details about the way Dr. Wraige had been killed had never been released. Of course, there could have been a leak. Lena, the crime lab's administrative assistant, had a big mouth.

Wally shrugged. He, too, was well aware of the probability that Lena had blabbed about the unusual circumstances surrounding the superintendent's death.

Skye turned back to Nanette and said, "We found muffin wrappers at the scene and remnants of that muffin in Dr. Wraige's stomach contents. Was he the only one that ate those particular breakfast items?"

"Yes. The rest of us didn't need them." Nanette twisted the handle of her purse. "They were a special recipe to improve his cholesterol. It was high during his last checkup so I was preparing healthier options for his meals."

"I wasn't aware that tobacco was considered nutritious," Skye's tone was mild, but Nanette stiffened. Skye kept her voice neutral as she said, "We found the tobacco hidden in your tampons."

Nanette's cheeks reddened and she stuttered, "I...uh... don't know what you're talking about. If you found something like that, then Tavish probably put it there."

"No." Skye shook her head. "Only your fingerprints were on the box and the wrappers."

"Uh..." Nanette gazed frantically around the room as if she expected to find a good excuse for herself on the wall. "I just wanted him to feel a little sick so he'd stop going after other women."

"That was never going to happen," Colleen needled. "He couldn't keep it in his pants if his fly was sewn shut with steel thread."

"He was doing so good until I let you move in!" Nanette cried. "I should have known better. You're such a slut."

"I am not." Colleen tittered, seemingly unscathed by the insult. "I'm just sexually extroverted."

"That's for sure," Nanette huffed. "After what happened between you and my college boyfriend, I was stupid to take you in. Heck, your own parents were willing to see you homeless before they'd let you stay with them."

Skye and Wally exchanged glances, but before either could speak, Colleen leaned around Skye so she could see her friend and whined, "It's not as if I led him on. You know what he did when I told him I wasn't interested."

"That's why I started slipping him the tobacco," Nanette sobbed. "You told me it would decrease his sex drive and would only make him feel sick but not do any permanent harm."

Skye patted the distraught woman's arm as she wept, then after a few seconds of silence, Wally said, "Tell me what happened the morning Dr. Wraige died. Did he find out about the tobacco and attack you? Is that why you killed him?"

"No!" Nanette yelped. "He and I had coffee in our sitting room. I made sure he ate a muffin, then I left for work."

"We found a muffin wrapper in the kitchen as well as in the sitting room." Wally tapped the table. "Were you aware he ate two of them?"

"Absolutely not!" Nanette shouted. "I always told him to only eat one, but he was such a self-indulgent pig, I should have known better." She shook her head. "I wanted him sick, not dead. I needed him to get me pregnant."

"Because you signed a prenup, just like his first wife," Skye murmured, figuring it out as Nanette and Colleen revealed pieces of the puzzle.

"Yes," Nanette admitted. "If he died and we didn't have any kids together, I'd get nothing. All the money in the trust goes to his children. If anyone killed him, it was Tavish."

"Your stepson has an alibi." Wally crossed his arms and said, "Try again."

When Nanette remained silent, Skye said, "Colleen had coffee with both of you up there, too, right? We found her prints on a third cup."

"No." Nanette frowned. "She'd already left before that. There should have only been two cups."

"How do you explain that, Colleen?" Wally asked abruptly, staring at the woman in question.

"Your lab made a mistake." Colleen thrust out her bottom lip, pouting like a two-year-old.

"No. It didn't." Wally continued to focus on her. "They checked twice."

"Oh." Colleen stared at ceiling as if looking for an explanation, then shrugged and, seemingly unaware of how much trouble she was in, giggled. "Oopsie."

Nanette put her hand on her chest and stared at her friend. "But you'd already left for Chicago. How did a cup with your prints get up there?"

Colleen sighed. "I was nearly to Joliet when I realized that

I forgot one of the documents I needed for the meeting with my lawyer. Since I had time, I turned around and came back. The front door was locked and I couldn't find my key, but I remembered that the French doors in the kitchen were usually open." She rolled her eyes. "Of course, because things never work out for me, this time they weren't. It was getting late, so I dumped out my purse, found my key, used it to get in the front door, and went to my room."

"Ah." Wally nodded. "You were the one Dr. Wraige heard trying to gain entrance to the house."

"Probably." Colleen twitched her shoulders.

"If you went to your room to get the paperwork you needed, what were you doing having coffee in the master suite with my husband?" Nanette clearly wasn't buying her friend's explanation.

Skye and Wally exchanged meaningful looks and Wally said, "I'd like to hear your answer to that question too."

"It's none of your business," Colleen snapped, evidently no longer finding Wally as attractive as she had previously.

"But it *is* my business." Nanette's voice broke. "We've been friends for nearly two decades. You promised me after that incident in college that you'd never steal another man from me again. How could you?"

"When I came out of my room with the papers, Shamus spotted me in the hallway. He insisted he had to talk to me, and I couldn't say no." Colleen's voice cracked.

"Why not?" Nanette glared. "You told me you weren't at all attracted to him."

"I wasn't!" Colleen screamed. "But he didn't leave me any choice."

"What are talking about?" Nanette frowned. "Are you saying he raped you?"

"No." Colleen's lips thinned. "Worse."

No one spoke for a few beats and something flickered at the edge of Skye's subconscious. Betty's words about a mother wanting to keep her children safe echoed in Skye's head.

Could it be?

"You know," Skye said casually, "when the police searched the house, the tobacco wasn't the only interesting thing that we found."

"What else was there?" Nanette tilted her head. "I mean Shamus's toys wouldn't exactly be a surprise to any of us."

Skye shook her head. "That's not what I meant. We found sexually explicit pictures of Colleen hidden in the false bottom of the guest room nightstand."

"Where are they now?" Colleen gasped.

Wally flipped open the file and slid copies of the photos toward her. "The only prints on these were Dr. Wraige's."

While Colleen tried to grab the pictures, Nanette reared back from the disturbing images as if they were going to attack her. She swallowed loudly and put her hand over her mouth as if she might vomit.

After taking several deep breaths, Nanette looked at her friend and roared, "Are you crazy? Why would you give those to my husband?"

"You moron," Colleen snapped. "I didn't give them to him. When I turned your precious Shamus down, he hired a private investigator who took these of me during that weekend I went into the city to play."

"Oh." Nanette wavered, her gaze flickering back and forth from Skye to Colleen. "Why did you keep them?"

"She didn't," Skye said slowly as she figured it out. "After Dr. Wraige showed them to her and threatened to give them to her husband's divorce lawyer if she didn't sleep with him, he hid them. It must have amused his sadistic personality to hide them in the room that she was staying in."

"So you *were* sleeping with my husband." Nanette glared.

"No. He was disgusting," Colleen sneered. "But I couldn't hold out much longer. That's why I encouraged you to slip him the tobacco. I hoped it would make him sick enough to leave me alone."

"However"—Skye continued to unravel the puzzle—"when you came back to the house to get that document and the two of you were alone, Dr. Wraige saw his chance and demanded you have sex with him."

Wally leaned forward and asked, "Is that when you decided to murder him?"

Colleen glowered for several seconds, then said, "This isn't how it looks."

"Oh?" Skye glanced at Wally. Where had they heard that before?

"I didn't mean to kill him." Colleen straightened. "I started to go along with his demand for sex, but when he put his clammy hands on me and pulled my face into his crotch, I couldn't stand it so I pushed him away. He was standing on a throw rug and the shove that I gave him rammed him into that ugly cupid statue."

"Did you know he wasn't dead?" Wally asked conversationally. "If you'd have called 911, they might have been able to save him."

"I...I..." Colleen wrinkled her brow, then must have decided to tough it out. "He looked dead to me."

"If it was an accident, why didn't you report it?" Wally leaned back. "And why did you take the coin collection?"

"I...I wanted it to look like a burglary gone bad," Colleen pleaded. "You have to understand. My husband would get my child if it came out that I was involved in something like this."

"Maybe." Skye shrugged. "But all you did was make things worse by trying to hide it. That elaborate hoax about your accident and the Good Samaritan just makes you look more guilty."

Colleen whispered, "That really happened. But on my second drive to the city, not the first."

"Nevertheless"—Wally got to his feet and grabbed his handcuffs—"you're under arrest."

"It was an accident! I was defending myself against being raped!" Colleen screeched. "You can't do this to me." She looked at Nanette. "Do something."

Nanette shook her head, stood, and walked to the door. "You ruined everything. Tavish gets all the money in the trust and I have to start over. You're on your own."

"I...I..." Colleen scrubbed her eyes with her fists. "Maybe I do need an attorney."

"Definitely." Wally handed her his cell phone. "Make your one call."

Several hours later, after Colleen's lawyer had arrived and her case had been turned over to the city attorney, Skye and Wally were finally able to return home. It was nearly four o'clock when they parked in their garage and Frannie and Justin arrived a few second later.

The two couples chatted while Skye and Wally grabbed a bite to eat. Skye was thrilled to see both of her young friends glowing with happiness, and she would have liked to have longer to talk to them, but she really needed to get ready for the dance.

Pushing back from the table, Skye cleaned up from their late lunch and then showed Frannie and Justin around. She introduced them to the twins and told them how to take care of the babies.

Once she was sure they didn't have any questions, Skye hurried into the master suite. She had already stripped down to her underwear when Wally entered the room.

As he sat on the bench to untie his shoes, he said, "I thought Colleen would be a tougher nut to crack."

"Once she realized she was going to lose the custody battle to her ex, she just didn't care anymore." Skye's expression was grim. "From what she said about the guy, I sure hope Collen's daughter gets to stay with her grandparents and isn't forced to live with her father."

"Me too." Wally pulled on a pair of sweatpants and a T-shirt. "Wraige really was an awful excuse for a man. Colleen almost had zero options."

"As I've said before, I'm sick to death of people saying they didn't have a choice." Skye shook her head. "She had options; she just picked the wrong one."

"You're right." Wally kissed Skye's temple.

Skye frowned. She'd been trying to be tougher and less of a pushover, but she couldn't stop a tiny trace of sympathy breaking through her resolve.

Clearing her throat, she asked, "What do you think will happen to Colleen?"

"Because she allowed Wraige to bleed out rather than call for help, the city attorney is charging her with involuntary manslaughter." Wally pursed his lips. "Sentences run from two to five years, but considering the circumstances and the vic's actions, her lawyer will argue self-defense." Wally shrugged. "She'll probably get the minimum."

"Sounds fair." Skye nodded, then grinned. "Now get out of here so I can make myself beautiful for you. We are going to forget all this and have an awesome time tonight."

"We certainly are." Wally walked into the closet and grabbed the hanger holding his dress uniform and the suitcase they'd packed for their hotel stay. "I'll use the guest room to get ready."

"You're the best." Skye smiled at him.

He winked at her as he wheeled the suitcase out of the room. "I have a few surprises in here for you."

"I'll be ready." Skye blew him a kiss and disappeared into the bathroom.

EPILOGUE

My Forever Valentine

A s Skye and Wally entered the Stanley County Country Club ballroom, she found it hard to believe that only a few hours earlier they had been interrogating a murderer. All the while Skye was getting ready for the dance and their overnight stay at the hotel, she'd been thinking about Dr. Wraige's legacy.

His son hated him. And although the statute of limitations had long since expired on his unhappy childhood, Skye could understand how tough it was to get over what Tavish had experienced.

Then there was the superintendent's much younger wife, who after years of his infidelities, had only hung on to their marriage for the money she'd inherit. She would have been so much better off if she'd just realized that there was a difference between giving up and knowing when it was time to cut her losses and leave.

And last, but definitely worst, was Dr. Wraige's sexual blackmail of Colleen. That slimy move had cost him his life.

Skye's musings were interrupted by Wally's warm breath in her ear as he whispered, "Have I told you how beautiful you look tonight?"

"You have." Skye shook off her dark thoughts and kissed him. "But I love hearing it as many times as you feel like saying it."

She smoothed the burgundy velvet skirt over her hips and adjusted the off-the-shoulder sweetheart neckline. Glancing around the beautifully decorated ballroom, she smiled at the red and white balloons floating near the ceiling. The trailing ribbons were just low enough that she could reach up and trail her fingers through them.

"Shall we find our table?" Wally brushed his lips over the back of her neck and she was glad she'd worn her hair up to give him easy access. "Or should we just blow this popsicle stand and head to the inn?"

Skye giggled. "Mom's already spotted us, so that could be awkward."

She pointed to a large table near the rear of the room occupied by May and Jed, Carson and Doris Ann, Loretta and Vince, Trixie and Owen, and Charlie. There were three empty places and Skye's mother was waving them over.

"You have a point." Wally cupped Skye's elbow and guided her through the crowded space.

Skye admired the twinkle lights twisted in scarlet netting to form a heart on the wall above their destination. The whole room was gorgeous.

The extra chair worried Skye. Although she liked Bunny, she sure hoped she wasn't Charlie's date. The feisty redhead tended to hold a grudge, and seeing Carson with another woman would certainly trigger some bitterness, if not an all-out brawl.

Wally and Skye slid into the unoccupied pair of seats between Trixie and Loretta. They exchanged greetings with everyone, and the conversations their appearance had interrupted resumed.

Skye was asking her brother, Vince, if he'd enjoyed the

continuing education class that he'd taken in Chicago on the latest hair-coloring techniques when May leaned around her son and asked, "Did you and Wally get everything straightened out at the station?"

Nine pairs of eyes, including May's, stared at them until Wally cleared his throat and said, "Yes. Dr. Wraige's murderer is in custody." He held up his hand. "But we can't disclose any details until the lawyers have had a chance to work on negotiating a deal."

Loretta's dark topaz eyes sparkled as she drawled, "Well, I know it wasn't his wife because Nanette would have called me to represent her."

As Skye had predicted, her sister-in-law outshone every other woman in the room. It had barely been two months since Loretta had had her second baby, and she already was back to her pre-pregnancy lean, muscled figure.

From her impeccably coifed coal-black braids to her radiant brown complexion, she appeared ready to walk a fashion runway. And her peach T-back beaded bodice gown was certainly worthy of any red-carpet event.

Skye was still admiring her stunning sister-in-law when Trixie piped up. "It looks as if we can also eliminate Dr. Wraige's son as the murderer."

"Why's that?" Skye wondered how her friend had figured out the killer wasn't Tavish.

"Look behind you." Trixie jerked her chin to the left.

While they'd been chatting, the band had started to play "My Funny Valentine" and couples were heading onto the dance floor. Skye discretely turned her head and saw that Tavish and Zelda were gliding to the music.

"Is that Martinez with Wraige?" Wally half rose from his seat, frowning. "Doesn't she know his reputation?"

"Yep." Skye patted her husband's arm and leaned to

whisper in his ear, "It'll be fine, dear. Zelda isn't someone he can play." When he continued to scowl, she added, "But I'll have a chat with her soon to make sure."

"Good." Wally nodded, then as a server approached the table, Wally asked, "What would you like to drink?"

Contemplating her choices, Skye tilted her head, then said, "A strawberry daiquiri, please."

Wally placed her order and requested a beer for himself, then turned to Carson and asked him about his business trip.

While the men were talking, Doris Ann leaned forward and caught Skye's gaze. "So it wasn't the wife or the son who killed the superintendent." She pinched her lip between her fingers and murmured, "Who does that leave?"

Skye kept her expression neutral. "I really can't comment." Then she winked and offered, "But I'm sure the ME can figure it out."

Doris Ann got up, stepped over to where Skye sat, and whispered in her ear, "The best friend?"

Skye nodded but held her fingers to her lips.

"I won't say a word." Doris Ann made a locking motion in front of her mouth.

Then she returned to her seat and asked Jed how the doghouse he was building was coming. Soon she and Jed were engrossed in a conversation about the pros and cons of an A-frame in comparison to ranch-style structures.

Wally finished talking to his father and said to Skye, "Would you like to dance?"

"Sure." Skye rose to her feet and, taking his arm, walked with him over to the dance floor.

Once Skye was in Wally's arms, they were silent as they danced. Skye enjoyed the feeling of being held by her handsome husband and the little kisses he pressed to her head and cheek as they moved around the floor.

When the music ended, they found themselves next to Tavish and Zelda. The two couples smiled and nodded at each other.

Just before they parted, Wally touched Zelda's arm and asked, "Did you get a chance to patrol over by the Dooziers' place?"

"Yes, sir." Zelda straightened. "I saw your memo and made a point to drive by several times. You'll never believe whose kisses Earl's selling."

Skye frowned. "Not one of the kids?" Wally had mentioned his concern and she shared it.

"Nope." Zelda grinned. "He's pimping out his hound dog, not his kids."

"Thank goodness." Wally shook his head. "I wonder if he had any takers."

"None that I saw." Zelda shrugged.

Just then, the band leader announced that dinner was being served and asked everyone to take their seats. Wally and Skye were still chucking about Earl's smooching hound as they returned to their table.

As they approached it, Skye noticed that the chair next to her godfather was now occupied, but all she could see was the woman's back.

"What?" Wally asked, evidently noticing that Skye had slowed.

"Who's that woman with Uncle Charlie?"

Wally squinted, then smiled. "You know how you were trying to figure out who Dorothy was dating? Look closer."

"Oh my gosh." Skye now recognized the set of the woman's shoulders and the dress she was wearing. "Why do you think she didn't want to tell me?"

"Maybe because he's twenty years older than her," Wally suggested.

"Come on." Skye swatted his bicep. "I'm the last one to cause a fuss over dating an older man."

"Hey." Wally pretended to be wounded. "I'm not that much older." He slipped his arm around her. "And I'll prove it to you later tonight."

★★★

The dinner dance at the country club was still going strong when Wally and Skye said their goodbyes. The food had been fabulous and the music romantic, but by eleven, they were both ready to leave.

They talked about the party during the twenty-minute drive to the Laurel Inn, but grew quiet as they registered at the hotel's front desk. Then once they were in their suite, both disappeared into separate bathrooms to change out of their formal attire.

When Skye entered the little sitting room, Wally was already there and he handed her a crystal flute of champagne, then said, "You look amazing."

Skye had put on the lacy nightgown she'd bought at Kohl's and taken down her hair from its elaborate updo. She'd brushed it out over her shoulders and spritzed her curls with a defining spray to make them shiny.

"Thank you." She took a sip from the glass. "You look pretty hot yourself."

Wally was wearing a pair of black satin sleep pants and nothing else. The muscles of his chest and abdomen were bronzed and the sprinkling of dark hair arrowed a sexy trail that disappeared into the elastic waist of his pajamas.

He clinked his flute against Skye's. "To my lovely wife."

She raised her glass. "To the man that I always dreamed of marrying."

"To the woman I always wanted." He slipped his arm around her.

Skye snuggled back against him. "We really didn't need a suite for just one night. A regular room would have been fine."

"True." Wally led her from the parlor into the bedroom. "But a regular room wouldn't have this." He swung open the door and revealed a huge canopy bed draped in gauzy white netting.

She'd wondered why he'd steered her into the smaller powder room and taken the master bath for himself. Now she knew that he'd wanted to surprise her.

A heart made of red rose petals was formed in the center of white satin spread. And facing the bed was a roaring fireplace.

"Oh my!" She could feel her chest tighten with how much she loved him. "I don't even have words. It's…it's perfect."

"Just like you." Wally murmured as he nuzzled her ear. "I know we said we weren't going to exchange gifts, but I couldn't resist."

He took a small oblong box from the pocket of his sleep pants and handed it to her. Skye slid off the ribbon and opened the lid.

Inside was a long silver chain with three charms. She looked closer and blinked back tears. Two were tiny duplicates of hers and Wally's wedding rings, and the other was a disc with two sapphires—the twins' birthstone.

Skye flung her arms around his neck. They'd caught the killer and given Dr. Wraige the justice every living person deserved. Now was their time.

As she kissed Wally's face, she said, "Are you ready to mess up some rose petals?"

"Anytime. Anyplace." Wally swept the comforter from the bed. The petals fluttered to the floor like crimson rain drops. "All you have to do is ask."

Read on for an excerpt from

DEAD IN THE WATER

the first book in the Welcome Back to
Scumble River series by Denise Swanson!

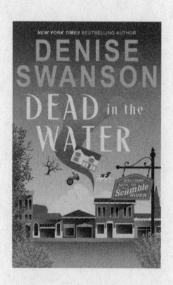

CHAPTER 1

"There's a cyclone coming, Em."

—Uncle Henry

SCHOOL PSYCHOLOGIST SKYE DENISON-BOYD WOKE WITH A start. She jerked upright, nearly falling out of the brown leather recliner, and her black cat, Bingo, hissed his displeasure. With a glare in her direction, the fuming feline settled back on what little lap Skye still had at nearly thirty-four weeks pregnant.

Rain hammered against the glass of the sunroom windows and when lightning ripped open the darkness outside, the table lamp flickered. Skye had been reading the first book in a new mystery series set in a nearby college town, Bloomington-Normal, when she'd dozed off and awakened to a dark and stormy night. The cliché didn't escape her notice.

Skye shivered when the air conditioner suddenly kicked on and goose bumps popped up on her bare arms. Although it had been hot and muggy all day, the television meteorologists had promised that a cold front was headed their way. However, Scumble River was seventy-five miles south of the city and the Chicago weather forecasts were rarely accurate for her tiny corner of Illinois, so Skye wasn't convinced that relief from the heat was on its way.

When her stomach growled, she wrapped her arms around her huge baby belly and whispered, "Patience, sweet pea. Daddy's not here yet."

Skye had been waiting for her husband, Wally, to get home so they could have supper together. Since their marriage eight months ago, she'd gotten used to eating later. But the more advanced her pregnancy, the harder it was to delay a meal. And now she was ravenous.

Wally had called around four to say he would be late because the officer scheduled for the afternoon shift had, at the last minute, called in sick. As the chief of police, Wally needed to find a replacement for the guy before he could leave the station. The town's population might be only a little over three thousand, but someone still had to be on duty at all times.

What time was it? Skye glanced at her wrist, frowning when she discovered her trusty Timex was missing.

Shoot! After her first day back at work after summer vacation, she'd been so warm and sticky that she'd stripped and showered as soon as she got home. The high school's AC had been on the fritz and Skye's office had felt like a sauna.

Because her job included working with students at all three schools in the district, she could have moved over to one of the other buildings. But it was highly unlikely any of them would have been much better. Before she'd claimed the space, her offices at the elementary and junior high had both been storage closets. Even in the best of circumstances, those rooms were usually hot as heck or colder than Antarctica.

Instead of seeking a cooler place to work, Skye had ignored her discomfort and spent the majority of her time getting her calendar set up for the rest of the year. She'd had her testing and counseling schedule mostly in place before she'd left for summer break, but there were always transfer students to accommodate.

She had wasted a good half hour trying to figure out how to pronounce the name of one of the new girls. It was listed as Le-a, and initially, Skye had assumed it was pronounced Leah, but she hated to call the teen by the wrong name. It could be Lee-a, or Lay-a, or even Lei.

Finally, Skye had just telephoned the student's mom to ask, and she was really glad she'd made the call. The girl's mother had explained that her daughter's name was Leedasha. Evidently, the dash in Le-a wasn't silent.

Paying attention to details such as correctly pronouncing names was one of many tidbits Skye intended to pass on to her new intern, Piper Townsend. In fact, she'd hoped to use today, before the students started school, to familiarize the woman with her duties, but Piper had had car trouble and wouldn't arrive until tomorrow.

The woman really should have been better prepared and moved to town over the weekend. Her lack of planning made Skye wonder if she'd hired the right applicant. Of course, there hadn't been that many candidates to choose from. A ridiculously low stipend and the promise of a heavy caseload hadn't exactly been enticing to the new grads.

Plus, there was the fact that Skye would have six weeks at the most to help Piper get settled before going out on maternity leave. In theory, during Skye's absence, a school psychologist from the Stanley County Special Education Cooperative would supervise the woman. In practice, Skye feared that even if it meant she had to guide the intern via telephone while cradling her newborn, she would end up with the brunt of the responsibility.

At that disquieting thought, Skye bit her lip. She really

hoped there wouldn't be any crises until after she got used to being a mother. Coping with—

Oomph! Everything below Skye's waist tightened as if a giant fist had closed around her uterus. She dug her nails into the smooth leather armrest while she tried to breathe through the pain. The first time she'd felt the squeezing sensation, she'd panicked and called her ob-gyn, convinced she was going into labor.

Dr. Johnson had reassured Skye that the baby wasn't about to make an early appearance. Instead, she was experiencing Braxton-Hicks contractions. And although uncomfortable, unless the contractions grew consistently longer, stronger, and closer together, everything was fine.

Now, as she panted through the contraction, Skye gripped the wooden lever on the side of the recliner and pushed until the footrest lowered. Then, risking the wrath of Bingo, she picked up the cat, put him on the floor, and struggled out of the chair.

She shoved her swollen feet into a pair of flip-flops and began to pace. Walking usually provided some relief from the Braxton-Hicks throbbing, but as Skye marched the length of the sunroom, the pain continued. Her doctor had warned her that dehydration could worsen the discomfort and she'd been sweating all day. Maybe water would help.

Heading into the kitchen, Skye snagged a bottle of Dasani from the refrigerator and chugged it. As she drank, she checked the microwave clock. It was five thirty. She'd been asleep for more than an hour. Where was Wally?

When the contractions eased, Skye glanced at the telephone hanging on the wall near the stove. The tiny light on the base glowed a steady red, indicating there was no voicemail. Pulling her cell out of her pocket, she saw she'd missed a text. Wally had sent a message at 4:55, saying he was having trouble finding someone to work.

While Skye contemplated calling him for an update, she hurried to the hall bathroom. Along with all the other joys of her pregnancy, it seemed that the baby was nearly constantly kung fu fighting on Skye's bladder and she always had to pee.

She had just lowered herself onto the toilet when she heard tires crunching over the gravel of the driveway. She assumed it was Wally, but a few seconds later, the sound of two car doors slamming instead of one convinced her she was wrong.

Darn! Why was it that the only time she ever got company was when she was in the bathroom? Of course, since she had been expecting, she had been spending a lot of time in there.

Skye hastily finished her business, straightened her clothes, washed her hands, and hurried into the foyer. She reached for the dead bolt but jerked her hand back. Granted, they lived in a rural area near a small town, but Wally had drummed into her head the need for caution enough times to make Skye peer out the side window rather than fling open the door.

She squinted through the pouring rain. Trudging toward the house were two people huddled under a neon-yellow umbrella. The halogen lamp attached to the garage didn't illuminate the sidewalk and it was too dark to make out their faces.

Flipping on the porch light, Skye frowned when she saw her visitors were Frannie Ryan and Justin Boward. What in the world were those two doing slogging up her sidewalk?

Skye had become extremely close to the pair during their high school years, and after their graduation, that professional relationship had grown into a personal one. Normally, she would have been happy to see her friends, but the young couple should be at college, not on her front porch.

Frannie and Justin both attended the University of Illinois, and the fall term had started last Monday. Before they'd left to drive down to Champaign, Skye had had breakfast with them. And as far as she knew, there was no good reason they'd be back in Scumble River so quickly. Something bad must have happened.

Her pulse racing, Skye threw open the door and demanded, "Why are you here?"

She winced as the words left her mouth. She sounded like her mother. It was a good thing Frannie and Justin were no longer her students, because that wasn't a very empathetic greeting. But between the weather, her advanced pregnancy, and Wally's absence, Skye was spooked.

"Can we come in?" Justin asked, closing the umbrella and leaning it against the outside wall.

"Sure." Skye stepped aside. "Sorry. I'm just surprised to see you."

Justin allowed Frannie to enter first, then followed her into the foyer. At twenty years old, Justin seemed to have finally reached his full height of six feet two. And although he'd probably always have a slender build, his weight was finally catching up with his last growth spurt.

Justin pushed his damp brown hair off his forehead and reached into his pocket for a handkerchief to wipe off his glasses. As he cleaned the lenses, his long-lashed brown eyes blinked, adjusting to the brightness inside the house.

Skye smiled. Justin hadn't been an attractive or socially comfortable teenager. But he was turning into a nice-looking young man who appeared finally to be comfortable in his own skin.

"Let's sit in the kitchen." Skye started down the hallway, forcing herself to be patient. Frannie and Justin would tell her what was up in their own good time. "How about a soda or some tea?"

"A Diet Coke would be great." Frannie caught up to Skye and gave her a one-armed hug.

Frannie was tall and solidly built. Skye had spent most of Frannie's high school years trying to raise the young woman's self-esteem. She'd attempted to help Frannie navigate a world dominated by media that insisted anything above a size four was huge. Unfortunately, much of that work had been undone during Frannie's first semester at a Chicago university.

After a couple of months of feeling like an outcast and missing home, Frannie had returned to Scumble River, completed her freshman and sophomore years at a local community college, and then transferred to U of I. Unlike her previous university experience, U of I's journalism program was more concerned with a student's abilities than her appearance or clothes. It had been just what Frannie needed and she'd thrived.

Justin had also lived at home while getting his associate degree at the same local community college as his girlfriend. Being nine months younger than Frannie, this was his first year joining Frannie in Champaign.

"Any chance of some chips with the pop?" Justin asked, dropping into a chair as if exhausted. "We haven't had dinner yet."

"Sorry," Skye said. "Not much in the way of snack food around here since the doctor gave me heck for gaining fifteen pounds almost overnight. Her exact words were: 'Thou shalt not be bigger than thy refrigerator.'" She patted her gigantic belly and made a face. "I've got salsa chicken in the Crock-Pot for dinner and there's plenty if you'd like some."

"That would be awesome." Justin straightened and reached for the bowl of fruit in the middle of the table. "I'm starving."

Skye took two cans of Diet Coke from the fridge and handed them to Frannie, then reached back into the refrigerator and grabbed the Tupperware container with the Mexican rice. After spooning half into a covered Pyrex bowl, she popped it into the microwave and pressed the reheat button.

Waiting for the side dish to get hot, Skye put plates, silverware, and napkins on the table. Although Justin had already devoured a pear and was gnawing at the core of an apple, Frannie was only chewing on her thumbnail and staring into space.

When the microwave dinged, Frannie jumped, then shot a worried glance at Justin. Something was definitely up. Skye just hoped whatever the problem was, it was fixable.

Justin dug into the chicken as if he were a squirrel and his plate of food was the last acorn on earth. Frannie never lifted her fork to her lips.

Having decided she was too hungry to wait to eat with Wally, Skye helped herself to a serving of the casserole. After pouring herself a glass of milk, she took a seat across from Justin and Frannie.

She waited to see if either of them would start the conversation, but when they both remained silent, Skye said, "Now tell me why you're here and not at college."

"My parents weren't answering their phone and I got worried," Justin mumbled through a mouthful of chicken.

Justin's father was in constant pain due to degenerative arthritis of the spine and his mother suffered from a debilitating depression. Neither was able to hold down a job or handle the minutia of everyday life. Until Justin had left for school last week, he'd been the one to take care of those details.

"Are they all right?" Skye asked, then took a bite of rice.

"As good as they ever are." Justin pushed away his empty dish. "They only have the one cell phone, no landline, and Mom forgot it was in her pocket and tossed it into the hamper." He shrugged. "They don't get many calls, so they didn't miss it until we showed up."

"Luckily it was on and the battery wasn't dead." Frannie rolled her eyes. "We found it by calling the number and zeroing in on the ringing."

"That was clever," Skye murmured. It didn't explain why Justin and Frannie had come to her house, but at least it hadn't been a true emergency. She tilted her head and asked, "So, Justin, your parents were otherwise fine?"

"Yeah." He paused and drained the can of Diet Coke. "But the thing is, I've been wondering for a while if I can leave them on their own."

"I see how that would be a concern." Skye nodded. She hated that Justin might feel he needed to give up college to take care of his parents, but she understood his feelings.

"You can't just stay here and take care of them," Frannie snapped. "You're too good a writer to drop out of school and take a job at a factory."

"It would only be until Mom and Dad were able to get their act together." Justin didn't lift his eyes from the tabletop.

"Which will be never." Frannie's brown eyes flashed. "They need to step up to the plate and be the adults for once. Yes, they both have issues. But they certainly should be able to handle their own lives and allow you to be able to follow your dreams."

Justin scowled and said, "I know that's what you think, Frannie." His lips thinned. Clearly, this was an argument they'd had before. "And yeah. I wish had a father like yours. Someone who cared enough about me to deal with his problems. But my parents aren't ever going to be like him."

"Sorry, sweetie." Frannie scooted her chair over, laid her cheek on her boyfriend's shoulder, looked at Skye, and said, "Isn't there some kind of assistance available to help people like Mr. and Mrs. Boward?"

"Your parents receive social security disability benefits, don't they?" Skye asked.

Justin nodded. "Uh-huh."

"Tomorrow, I'll call the co-op's social worker and see if she can refer me to an agency that is able to provide a caregiver to check on them a few times a week."

Skye got up and made a note on the pad by the phone, then walked into the foyer, grabbed her appointment book from the tote sitting on the coatrack bench, and stuck the slip of paper inside it.

When she got back to the kitchen, the table had been cleared, and Justin was lining up the fruit bowl, napkin holder, and salt and pepper shakers as if there were going to be an inspection.

Frannie poked him and giggled. "You are so OCD."

"I'm not obsessively compulsive." Justin grabbed her finger and kissed it. "I'm just super meticulous."

Justin turned to Skye and said, "It's nearly seven, so we'd better hit the road. We both have early classes tomorrow."

Skye recoiled as a flash of lightning illuminated the kitchen window, immediately followed by an explosion of thunder. "The storm seems to be getting worse."

"I'm sure we'll be fine." Justin put his arm around Frannie.

"Let me call Wally and see how the roads are." Skye snatched the receiver from the base, then repeatedly poked the on button.

"Something wrong?" Frannie wrinkled her brow.

"There's no dial tone." Skye replaced the handset in the holder.

"Try your cell," Justin suggested.

Skye took it from her pocket and blew out a frustrated breath. "No bars."

Frannie and Justin checked their cell phones with no better luck.

"Shoot!" Now Skye really didn't want them to leave. If the phones were all out, the rural roads between Scumble River and Champaign might be flooded.

As she stared at her cell, there was another blinding bolt of lightning, then the distinctive smell of smoke and the crunch of metal being smashed.

Justin, Frannie, and Skye rushed to the front door and peered outside. One of the enormous oak trees that lined the driveway was split down the middle, with the largest part lying across Frannie's car.

"Guess we're not leaving after all." Justin sighed, then shrugged and asked, "Do you have anything for dessert?"

CHAPTER 2

"That is because you have no brains."

—Dorothy

SON OF A BITCH!" CHIEF OF POLICE WALLY BOYD SLAMMED down the telephone. It looked like he was working a double.

Zelda Martinez had been his last hope, and his call had gone directly to her voicemail. Zelda, as Scumble River's youngest and only female officer, was usually eager to work a double shift, not only for the money but also for the experience.

When Tolman had called in sick at the last minute, Wally had known it was going to be tough to find coverage for him, but he hadn't counted on the storm's interference. The Scumble River Police Department had only six full-time officers, including Wally, so it just took one case of the flu or someone on vacation to create a staffing problem.

With two guys stuck on the wrong side of a flooded underpass, two others not answering their phones, and the part-timers, who were supposed to fill in the gaps, unavailable due to their other jobs, Wally was out of options. And as usual, to solve the problem of being short-staffed, he would have to sacrifice time with Skye. He had to figure out a way to employ additional officers before the baby came, because he wasn't going to be an absentee father.

Wally walked over to the dartboard on the back of his door and flipped it over, then returned to his desk, opened a drawer, and took out a handful of darts. Taking careful aim, he released the projectile and watched in satisfaction as it landed smack-dab in the middle of the mayor's forehead.

The police department needed more personnel, but the city council had frozen hiring for all local government services. Although Wally had been begging for an exemption for the PD, with Mayor Dante Leofanti behind the moratorium, he knew he didn't have a chance at getting the council to allow him to take on another couple of officers.

Hizzoner was throwing a tantrum because his plot to outsource the town's law-enforcement services to the county sheriff's department had been thwarted. He had wanted to use the money saved on police salaries to finance building a mega incinerator on the edge of town so he could charge other communities to burn their trash and funnel the money into his mayoral salary. But once his plans became public, Scumble Riverites had protested, and Dante had been forced to give up his scheme. Which meant the police department would be the last city service the mayor would excuse from the freeze.

Although Dante was Skye's uncle, her mother's brother, their relationship hadn't ever been particularly cordial. It had deteriorated even further when Skye and Wally had exposed the mayor's incinerator plans. And because Hizzoner held on to his grudges like a tick stuck to a hound dog, there would be no more money for the PD until he was booted from office.

However, in order for that to happen, someone needed to run against him. Currently, he was running unopposed in the November election, leaving only a little over two months for a write-in candidate to appear.

Hell! Wally threw another dart. This one landed on the mayor's beaky nose. The police department hadn't even been allowed to replace the idiot who had been fired for dealing drugs. Hizzoner had brushed off Wally's reasoning that replacing an officer wasn't the same as a new hire, all the while insisting that the budget didn't have room for another salary.

Wally had hoped the city council members would override the mayor, but they were all either in his back pocket or afraid of his wrath. Even Zeke Lyons, the newest council member and the only one who wasn't one of Dante's old cronies, was too much of a milquetoast to speak up.

When Zeke had been appointed to fill in the vacancy created after Ratty Milind had a stroke while he was screwing his little side dish in the Dollar or Three store's parking lot, Wally had hoped Zeke would change the way the council did business. From what everyone had said about Zeke, he had seemed like a stand-up guy who would put the town's interest before his own. But so far, Zeke hadn't even opened his mouth at any of the council meetings.

Which just proved what Wally's father, Carson, always said—politicians and babies have one thing in common: they both need to be changed regularly and for the same reason. Of course, Carson Boyd was *sarcastic*—so sarcastic that his targets weren't sure if he was joking or a whack job.

Blowing out an exasperated breath, Wally threw the remaining darts, then removed them from the board and flipped it back over. It wouldn't do for the mayor to come visit and see his own face, impaled by the sharp projectiles, staring back at him.

Checking that he had his portable radio and flashlight, Wally turned off the lights in his office, stepped into the hallway, and locked the door behind him. If he couldn't find